Elsie at Nantucket

The Original Elsie Classics

Elsie Dinsmore
Elsie's Holidays at Roselands
Elsie's Girlhood
Elsie's Womanhood
Elsie's Motherhood
Elsie's Children
Elsie's Widowhood
Grandmother Elsie
Elsie's New Relations
Elsie at Nantucket
The Two Elsies
Elsie's Kith and Kin
Elsie's Friends at Woodburn
Christmas with Grandma Elsie
Elsie and the Raymonds
Elsie Yachting with the Raymonds
Elsie's Vacation
Elsie at Viamede
Elsie at Ion
Elsie at the World's Fair
Elsie's Journey on Inland Waters
Elsie at Home
Elsie on the Hudson
Elsie in the South
Elsie's Young Folks
Elsie's Winter Trip
Elsie and Her Loved Ones
Elsie and Her Namesakes

Elsie at Nantucket

Book Ten of
The Original Elsie Classics

Martha Finley

CUMBERLAND HOUSE
NASHVILLE, TENNESSEE

ELSIE AT NANTUCKET BY MARTHA FINLEY
PUBLISHED BY CUMBERLAND HOUSE PUBLISHING, INC.
431 Harding Industrial Drive
Nashville, Tennessee 37211

Cover design by Gore Studio, Inc., Nashville, Tennessee
Photography by Dean Dixon Photography
Hair and Makeup by Calene Radar
Text design by Heather Armstrong

Printed in Canada
3 4 5 6 7 8 9 10 TR 08 07 06 05

PREFACE

THREE YEARS AGO I spent some six weeks on Nantucket Island, making the town of the same name my headquarters but visiting other points of interest to which I take the characters of my story. So, in describing the pleasures of a sojourn there during our heated term, I write from experience; though, in addition to my own notes, I have made use of A. Judd Northrop's *Sconset Cottage Life* to refresh my memory and assist me in giving a correct idea of life led by summer visitors who take up their abode for the season in one of those odd little dwellings which form the "original 'Sconset."

Should my account of the delights of Nantucket as a summer resort lead any of my readers to try it for themselves, I trust they will not meet with disappointment or find my picture overdrawn.

—M.F.

CHAPTER FIRST

How happy they,
Who from the toil and tumult of their lives
Steal to look down where naught but ocean strives.

—BYRON

"WELL, CAPTAIN, FOR HOW long have you Uncle Sam's permission to stay on shore this time?" asked Mr. Dinsmore, as the family at Ion sat about the breakfast table on the morning after Captain Raymond's arrival.

"Just one month certain, sir, with the possibility that the leave of absence may be extended," was the reply in a cheery tone. "And as I want to make the most of it, I propose that our plans for a summer outing be at once discussed, decided upon, and speedily carried out."

"I second the motion," said Mr. Dinsmore. "Are all the grown people agreed? The consent of the younger ones may safely be taken for granted," he added with a smiling glance from one to another.

"I am agreed and ready for suggestions," replied his wife.

"And I," said his daughter.

"Vi is, of course, since the proposition comes from her husband," Edward remarked with a sportive look at her. Then, glancing at his own little wife, he said, "And as I approve, I'm certain Zoe will be equally ready with her consent."

"Have you any suggestions to offer, captain?" asked Mr. Dinsmore.

"I have, sir, and it is that we make the island of Nantucket our summer resort for this year, dividing the time, if you like, between Nantucket Town and the quaint little fishing village Siasconset — 'Sconset, as they call it for short. There is an odd box of a cottage there belonging to a friend of mine, a Captain Coffin, which I have partially engaged until the first of September. It wouldn't hold nearly all of us, but we may be able to rent another for the season. Or we can pitch a tent or two, and those who prefer it can take rooms, with or without board, at the hotels or boarding houses. What do you all say?" he inquired glancing from his mother-in-law to his wife.

"It sounds very pleasant, captain," Elsie said. "But tell us more about it. I'm afraid I must acknowledge shameful ignorance of that portion of my native land."

"A very small corner of the same, yet a decidedly interesting one," returned the captain. He then went on to give a slight sketch of its geography and history.

"It is about fifteen miles long and averages four in width. Nantucket Town is a beautiful, quaint, old place. It has some fine, wide streets and handsome residences; a great many narrow lanes running in all directions; and many very odd-looking old houses. Some of them are inhabited, but not a few are empty — for of the ten thousand former residents only about three thousand now remain."

"How did that happen, Levis?" asked Violet, as he paused for a moment.

"It used to be a great seat of the whale fishery," he answered. "Indeed, that was the occupation of the vast majority of the men of the island. But, as I presume you know, the whale fishery has, for a number of years, been declining. This is partly owing to the scarcity of whales, partly to the discovery of coal oil, which has been largely substituted for whale oil or gas as an illuminant. Substitutes are being found or invented for whale bone, also.

"So the Nantucketers lost their principal form of employment and wandered off to different parts of the country or the world in search of another. The wharves that once presented a scene full of life and bustle are now lonely and deserted. Property there was wonderfully depreciated for a time but is rising in value now with the influx of summer visitors. It is becoming quite a popular resort—not sea-side exactly for there you are right out in the sea."

"Let us go there," said Mrs. Dinsmore. "I think it would be a pleasant variety to get fairly out into the sea for once, instead of merely alongside of it."

"Oh, yes, do let us go!"

"I'm in favor of it!"

"And I!"

"And I," cried one and another. Mr. Dinsmore replied laughingly to his wife, "Provided you don't find the waves actually rolling over you, I suppose, my dear. Well, the captain's description is very appealing so far, but let us hear what more he has to say on the subject."

"Haven't I said enough, sir?" returned the captain with a good humored smile. "You will doubtless want to find some things out for yourselves when you get there."

"Are there any mountains, papa?" asked little Gracie. "I'd like to see some."

"So you shall, daughter," he said. "But we will have to go elsewhere than to Nantucket Island to find them."

"No hills either?" she asked.

"Yes, several ranges of smaller hills—Saul's Hills are the highest. Then there are bluffs south of 'Sconset known as Sunset Heights. Indeed, the village itself stands on a bluff high above the sandy beach where the great waves come rolling in. And there is "Tom Never's Head." Nantucket Town is on high ground sloping gradually up from the harbor. And just out of the town to the northwest are the Cliffs, where you go to find surf bathing—in the town itself you must be satisfied with still bathing. An excellent place, by the way, to teach the children how to swim."

"Then you can teach me, Edward," said Zoe. "I'd like to learn."

"I shall be delighted," he returned gallantly.

"Papa," asked Max, "are there any woods and streams where one may hunt and fish?"

"Hardly anything to be called woods," the captain answered. "Trees of any size are few on the island. Except the shade trees in the town, I think some ragged, stunted pines are all you will find. But there are streams and ponds to fish in, to say nothing of the great ocean. There is some hunting, too, for there are plovers on the island."

"Well, shall we go and see for ourselves, as the captain advises?" asked Mr. Dinsmore, addressing the company in general.

Every voice answered in the affirmative, though Elsie, looking doubtfully at Violet, remarked that she feared Violet was hardly strong enough for so long a journey.

"Ah, that brings me to my second proposition, mother," said Captain Raymond. "That—seeing what a very large company we shall make, especially if we can persuade our friends from Fairview, the Oaks, and the Laurels to accompany us—we charter a yacht and go by sea."

"Oh, captain, what a nice idea!" cried Zoe. "I love the sea—love to be either beside it or on it."

"I think it would be ever so nice!" Rosie exclaimed. "Oh, grandpa and mamma, do say yes!"

"I shall not oppose it, my dear," Elsie said. "Indeed, I think it may perhaps be our best plan. How does it strike you, father?"

"Favorably," he replied. "If we can get the yacht. Do you know of one that might be hired, captain?"

"I do, sir, a very fine one. I have done with it as with the cottage—partially engaged it—feeling fairly certain you would all fall in with my idea."

"Captain," cried Zoe, "you're just a splendid man! I know of only one that's more so." She wore a laughing look as she gazed at her husband.

The captain bowed his acknowledgements. "As high praise as I could possibly ask, my dear sister. I certainly trust that one may always stand first in your esteem."

"He always will," said Zoe. "But," with another arch glance into Edward's eyes, "don't tell him, lest he should grow conceited and vain."

"Don't tell him because it would be no news," laughed Edward, gazing with fondness into the blooming face of the loved flatterer.

The talk went on about the yacht, and before they left the table the captain was empowered to engage her for their use as well as the 'Sconset cottage he had spoken of and one or two more, if they were to be had.

"You will command the vessel, of course, captain?" several voices said inquiringly, all speaking at once.

"If chosen commander by a unanimous vote," came his reply.

"Of course, of course; we'll be only too glad to secure your services," said Mr. Dinsmore, everybody else adding a word of glad assent.

"How soon do we sail, captain?" asked Zoe. "Must we wait for an answer from Nantucket?"

"No, I shall send word by this morning's mail to Captain Coffin that we will take his cottage and two others, if he can engage them for us. But there is no time to wait for a reply."

"Can't we telegraph?" asked Violet.

"No, because there is no telegraph from the mainland to the island.

"Now, ladies all, please make your preparations as rapidly as possible. We ought to be off by the first of next week. I can telegraph for the yacht, and she will be ready for us, lying at anchor in our very own harbor.

"But, little wife," turning to Violet with a tenderly affectionate air, "you are not to exert yourself in the least with shopping, sewing, or packing. I positively forbid it," he added with playful authority.

"That is right, captain," Elsie said with a pleased smile. "She is not strong enough yet for any such exertion, nor has she any need to make it."

"Ah, mamma," said Violet, "are you not forgetting the lessons you used to give us, your children, on the sin of indolence and self-indulgence?"

"No, daughter, nor those on the duty of doing all in our power for the preservation of health as one of God's good gifts to be used in His service."

They had all moved upon the veranda now in the cool shade of the trees and vines for the weather had grown extremely warm.

"I wish we were ready to sail today," said Zoe. "How delicious the sea breeze would be!"

A servant woman stepped from the doorway with a little bundle in her arms, which she carried to Violet.

The captain, standing beside his wife, bent over her and the babe with a face full of love and delight.

"Isn't she a darling?" whispered Violet, gazing down upon the tiny creature with all a young mother's unspeakable love and pride, then up into her husband's face.

"That she is!" he responded. "I never saw a fairer, sweeter babe. I should fear to risk her little life and health in a journey to Nantucket by land. But going by sea will, I think, be more likely to do her good than harm."

"It's all her, she, when you talk about that baby," laughed Rosie. "Why don't you two call her by her name?"

"So we will, little Aunt Rosie, if you will be so kind as to inform us what it is," returned the captain good humoredly.

"I, sir!" exclaimed Rosie. "We have all been told again and again that you were to decide upon her name on your arrival. And you've been here—how many hours? And it seems the poor little dear is nameless yet."

"Apparently not greatly afflicted by it, either," said the captain, adopting Rosie's sportive tone. "My love, what do you intend to call your daughter?"

"Whatever her father appoints as her name," returned Vi laughingly.

"No, no," he said. "You are to name her yourself. You have undoubtedly the best right."

"Thank you. Then, if you like, she shall be mamma's namesake. Her first granddaughter should be, I think, as the first grandson was papa's."

"I highly approve of your choice," he said with a glance of affectionate admiration directed toward his mother-in-law. "And, I pray a strong resemblance in both looks and character descend to her with the name."

"We will all say amen to that, captain," said Edward decidedly.

"Yes, indeed," added Zoe heartily.

"Thank you both," Elsie said with a gratified look. "I appreciate the compliment, but if I had the naming of my little granddaughter, she should be another Violet. There is already another Elsie in the family besides myself, you know, and it makes a little confusion to have too many of the same name."

"Then, mamma, we can make a variety by calling this one 'Else' for short," returned Violet merrily. She held up the babe to receive a caress from her grandmother who had drawn near, evidently with the purpose of bestowing it.

"What a pretty babe she is!" Elsie said, taking her in her arms and gazing delightedly into the tiny face. "Don't you think so, captain?"

"Of course I do, mother," he said with a happy laugh. Then, examining her features critically, "I really fancy I see a slight resemblance to you now, which I trust is destined to increase with increasing years. But, excuse me, ladies, I must go and write that all-important letter at once, or it will be too late for the mail."

He hurried away to the library and entered it hastily but without much noise, for he wore his slippers. He found Lulu there, leaning moodily out of a window.

She had stolen away from the veranda a moment before, saying to herself in jealous displeasure, "Such a fuss over that little bit of a thing! I do believe papa is going to care more for her than for any of us—his own children that he had long before he ever saw Mamma Vi. It's just too bad."

Knowing Lulu as he did, her father instantly perceived what was passing in her mind. It grieved and angered him, yet strong affection was mingled with his displeasure. He silently asked help of God to deal wisely with this child of his love.

He remembered that Lulu was more easily ruled through her affections than in any other way. As she turned toward him with a flushed and shame-faced countenance, he went to her, took her in his arms, held her close to his heart, and kissed her tenderly several times.

"My dear, little daughter," he said. "How often, when far away on the sea, I have longed to do this—to hold my dear Lulu in my arms and feel hers about my neck and her sweet kisses on my lips."

Her arms were instantly thrown round his neck while she returned his kisses.

"Papa," she said, "I do love you so, so dearly, but I 'most wonder that you don't quit loving such a hateful girl as I am."

"Perhaps I might not love an ill-tempered, jealous child belonging to somebody else," he said, as if half in jest, half in earnest. "But you are my very own," he replied, drawing her closer and repeating his caresses. "My very own, and so I have to love you in spite of everything. But, my little girl," and his tone grew very grave as he said, "if you do not fight determinedly against these wrong feelings you will never know rest or happiness in this world or the next.

"Lulu, we won't talk any more about it now. I have no time, as I ought to be writing my letter. Run along and make yourself happy, collecting together such toys and books as you would like to carry with you to Nantucket. Grandma Elsie and Mamma Vi will decide what you and the rest will need in the way of clothing."

"I will, papa. Oh, but I think you are too good to me!" she said, giving him a final hug and kiss. "You're a great deal better than I deserve, but I will try to be good."

"Do, my child," he said. "Not in your own strength. God will help you if you ask Him."

For the moment, thoroughly ashamed of her jealousy of the baby, she ran back to the veranda where the others still were and bent over her as she lay in her mother's arms, kissing her several times.

Violet's face flushed with pleasure. "My dear Lulu, I hope you and little Else are going to be very fond of each other," she said.

"I hope so, Mamma Vi," Lulu answered. Then, in a sudden fit of penitence, added, "But I'm afraid she'll never learn any good from the example of her oldest sister."

"My dear child, resolve that she shall," said Grandma Elsie, standing by. "You cannot avoid having a good deal of influence over her as she grows older, and do not forget that you will have to give an account for the use you make of it."

"I suppose that's so," Lulu answered with a little impatient shrug of her shoulders. "But I wish it wasn't." She turned abruptly away. "Max and Gracie," she called to her brother and sister. "Papa says we may go and gather up any books and toys we want to take with us."

The three ran off together in high glee. The ladies stayed a little longer, deep in consultation about necessary arrangements that must fall to their share. Then, they dispersed to their several apartments with the exception of Violet, who, forbidden to exert herself, remained where she was till joined by her husband. He had finished and dispatched his letter, and it was great happiness to them to be together after their long separation.

Mr. Dinsmore and Edward had walked out along the avenue and were seated under a tree in quite earnest conversation.

"I suppose they are talking tiresome business," remarked Zoe in a petulant tone, glancing toward them as she spoke and apparently addressing Violet, as she was the only other person on the veranda at the moment.

"Yes, no doubt, but we must have patience with them, dear, because it is very necessary," Violet answered with a smile. "Probably they are discussing the question of how the plantation is to be attended to in their absence. You know it won't take care of itself, and the men must have a head to direct their labors."

"Oh, yes, of course, and for that reason Ned is kept very busy while we are here. I do think it will be very delightful to get away to the seashore with him, where there will be nothing to do but enjoy ourselves."

Zoe skipped away with the last word, ran up to her room, and began turning over the contents of bureau drawers and taking garments from wardrobes and closets—selecting such as she might deem it desirable to carry with her on the contemplated trip.

She was humming softly a snatch of lively song, feeling very happy and light hearted, when, coming across a gray traveling dress a little worse for the wear, her song suddenly ceased. Tears gathered in her eyes then began to fall drop by drop as she stood gazing down upon this relic of former days.

"Just one year ago," she murmured. "Papa, papa! I never thought I could live a whole year without you and be happy, too! Ah, that seems ungrateful, when you were so, so good to me! But, no, I am sure you would rather have me happy; and it would be ungrateful to my dear husband if I were not."

She put the dress aside, wiped away her tears, and took down another. It was a dark woolen dress. She had traveled home in it the previous fall and had worn it once since on a very memorable occasion. Her cheek crimsoned at the recollection as she glanced from it to her husband, who entered the room at that instant. Then, her eyes fell.

"What is it, love?" he asked, coming quickly toward her.

"Nothing, only—you remember the last time you saw me in this dress? Oh, Ned, what a fool I was! And how good you were to me!"

He had her in his arms by this time, and she was hiding her blushing face on his shoulder. "Never mind, my dear," he said soothing her with caresses. "It is a secret between ourselves, and always shall be, unless you choose to tell it."

"I? No, indeed!" she said, drawing a long breath. "I think I should almost die of mortification if anyone else should find it out. But I am glad you know it, because if you didn't my conscience wouldn't give me a bit of peace till I confessed to you."

"Ah! And would that be very difficult?"

"Yes, I don't know how I could ever find courage to make the attempt."

"Are you really so much afraid of me?" he asked in a slightly aggrieved tone.

"Yes, for I love you so dearly that your displeasure is perfectly unendurable," she replied, lifting her head to gaze fondly into his eyes.

"Ah, is that it, my darling?" he said in a glow of delight. "I deem myself a happy man in possessing such a treasure as you and your dear love. I can hardly reconcile myself to the thought of a separation for even a few weeks."

"Separation!" she cried with a start and in a tone of mingled pain and incredulity. "What can you mean? But I won't be separated from you. I'm your wife, and I claim the right to cling to you always, always, Edward!"

"And I would have you do so, Zoe, if it could be without a sacrifice of both your comfort and your enjoyment, but—"

"Comfort and enjoyment!" she interrupted. "It is here in your arms or by your side that I find both—nowhere else. But why do you talk so? Is there anything wrong?"

"Nothing except that it seems impossible for me to leave the plantation for weeks to come, unless I can get a better substitute than I know of at present."

"Oh, Ned, I am so sorry!" she cried, tears of great disappointment springing to her eyes.

"Don't feel too badly about it, little wife," he said in a cheery tone. "It is just possible the right man may turn up before the yacht sails, and in that case I can go with the rest of you. Otherwise, I shall hope to join you before your stay at Nantucket is quite over."

"Not my stay! I won't go one step of the way without you, unless you order me!" she added sportively and with a vivid blush. "And I'm not sure that I'll do it even in that case."

"Oh, yes you will," he said laughingly. "You know you promised to be always good and obedient on condition that I would love you and keep you. And I'm doing both to the very best of my ability."

"But you won't be if you send me away from you. No, no, I have the right to stay with you, and I shall claim it always," she returned, clinging to him as if she feared an immediate separation.

"Foolish child!" he said with a happy laugh, holding her close. "Think what you would lose—the sea voyage in the pleasantest of company—"

"No, the pleasantest company would be left behind if you were," she interrupted.

"Well, very delightful company," he resumed. "Then I don't know how many weeks of the oppressive heat here you would have to endure, instead of enjoying cool, refreshing breezes sweeping over Nantucket. Surely, you cannot give it all up without a sigh?"

"I can't give up the thought of enjoying it all with you without sighing and crying, too, maybe," she answered smiling through tears. "But I'd sigh and cry ten times as much if I had to go and leave you behind. No, Mr. Travilla, you needn't indulge the hope of getting rid of me for even a week. I'm quite determined to stay where you stay, and go only where you go."

"Dreadful fate!" he exclaimed. "Well, little wife, I shall do my best to avert the threatened disappointment of your hopes of a speedy departure out of this heated atmosphere and a delightful sea voyage to that famous island. Now, I must leave you and begin at once my search for a substitute as manager of the plantation."

"Oh, I hope you will succeed!" she said. "Shall I go on with my packing?"

"Just as you please, my dear. Perhaps it would be best, as otherwise you may be hurried with it if we are able to go with the others."

"Then I shall, and I'm determined not to look for disappointment," she said in a lively, cheery tone as he left the room.

࿇ ࿇ ࿇ ࿇ ࿇

At the conclusion of his conference with Edward, Mr. Dinsmore sought out his daughter in her own apartments. He found her busied much as Zoe was, looking over clothing and selecting what ought to be packed in the trunks a manservant was bringing in.

She had thrown aside the widow's weeds in which she was wont to array herself when about to leave the seclusion of her own rooms and donned a simple white mourning dress that was very becoming, her father thought.

Excuse my wrapper, papa," she said, turning toward him a bright, sweet face as he entered. "I found my black dress more than a bit oppressive this warm morning."

"Yes," he said, "it is a most unwholesome dress, I think. And for that reason and several others, I should be extremely glad if you would give it up entirely now, daughter."

"Would you, my dear father?" she returned, tears springing to her eyes.

"I should indeed, if it would not involve too great a sacrifice of feeling on your part. I have always thought white the most suitable and becoming dress for you in the summer season, Elsie. So did your husband."

"Yes, papa, I remember that he did. But—I—I should be very loath to give the least occasion for any to say or think he was forgotten by her he loved so dearly, or that she had ceased to mourn his loss."

"Loss, daughter dear?" he said, taking her in his arms to wipe away the tears that were now freely coursing down her cheeks and caress her with exceeding tenderness.

"No, papa, not lost, but only gone before," she answered, a lovely smile suddenly illuminating her features. "Nor does he seem far away. I often feel that he is very near me still and speak to him, though I can neither see him nor hear his loved voice," she went on in a dreamy tone. There was a far away look in the soft, hazel eyes as she stood with her head on her father's shoulder, his arm encircling her waist.

Both were silent for some moments. Then Elsie, lifting her eyes to her father's face, asked, "Were you serious in what you said about my laying aside mourning dress, papa?"

"Never more so," he answered. "It is a gloomy, unwholesome dress, and I have grown very weary of seeing you wear it. It would be very gratifying to me to see you exchange it for more cheerful attire."

"But black is considered the most suitable dress for old and elderly ladies, papa. I am a grandmother, you know."

"What of that?" he said a trifle impatiently. "You do not look old. You are, in fact, just in the prime of life. And it is not like you to be concerned about what people may think or say. Usually your only inquiry is 'Is it right?' 'Is it what I ought to do?'"

"I fear that is a deserved reproof, papa," she said with unaffected humility. "And I shall be governed by your wishes in this matter. They have been law—a law I have loved to obey, dear father—to me almost all my life, and I know that if my husband were here he would approve of my decision."

She could not entirely suppress a sigh as she spoke, nor keep the tears from filling her eyes.

Her father saw and appreciated the sacrifice she would make for him.

"Thank you, my darling," he said. "It seems selfish in me to ask it of you, but though partly for my gratification, it is really still more for your sake. I think the change will be for your health and happiness."

"And I have the highest opinion of my father's wisdom," she said. "I should never, never think of selfishness as connected with him."

Mrs. Dinsmore came in at this moment.

"Ah, my dear," she said, "I was in search of you. What is to be done about Bob and Betty Johnson? You know they will be coming home in a day or two for their summer vacation."

"They can stay at Roselands with their cousins Calhoun and Arthur Conly or at the Oaks if Horace and his family do not wish to join us in the trip to Nantucket."

"Cannot Bob and Betty go with us, papa?" Elsie asked. "I know it would be a very great treat to them."

"Our party promises to be very large," he replied. "But if you two ladies are agreed to invite them I shall raise no objection."

"Shall we not, mamma?" Elsie asked, and Rose gave a hearty assent.

"Now, how much dressmaking has to be done before the family can be ready?" asked Mr. Dinsmore.

"Very little," the ladies told him. Elsie added, "At least, not if you are willing to let me wear black dresses when it is too cool for white, papa. Mamma, he has asked me to lay aside my mourning."

"I knew he intended to," Rose said. "And I think you are a dear, good daughter to do it."

"It is nothing new. She has always been the best of daughters," Mr. Dinsmore remarked with a tenderly affectionate look at Elsie. "And, my dear child, I certainly shall not ask you to stay a day longer than necessary in this hot place, merely to have new dresses made. We must set sail as soon as possible. Now, I must have business chat with you. Don't go, Rose. It is nothing that either of us would care if you heard."

CHAPTER SECOND

Where the broad ocean leans against the land.

— GOLDSMITH

ELSIE FELT SOMEWHAT apprehensive that this early laying aside of her mourning for their father might not meet the approval of her older son and daughters, but it gave them pleasure. One and all were delighted to see her resume the dress of the happy days when he was with them.

Zoe, too, was very much pleased. "Mamma," she said, "you do look so young and lovely in white, and it is nice of you to begin wearing it on the anniversary of our wedding day. Just think, it's a whole year today since Edward and I were married. How fast time flies!"

"Yes," Elsie said, "it seems a very little while since I was as young and light-hearted as you are now, and now I am a grandmother."

"But still happy, are you not, mamma? You always seem to be so to me."

"Yes, child, I have a very peaceful, happy life. I miss my husband, but I know the separation is only for a short time. I know that he is supremely blessed. And with my beloved father and dear children about me, heart and hands are full — delightfully full — leaving no room for sadness and repining." This little talk was on the veranda, as the two stood there for a moment apart from the others. Zoe was looking quite bridelike in a white Indian mull, much trimmed with rich lace, her fair neck and arms adorned with the set of beautiful pearls just presented her by Edward in commemoration of the day.

She called Elsie's attention to them. "See, my dear mamma, what my husband has given me in memory of the day. Are they not magnificent?"

"It is a very fine set," Elsie answered with a smile, glancing admiringly at the jewels and from them to the blooming face of the wearer. "A most suitable gift for his little wife."

"He's so good to me, mamma," Zoe said with warmth. "I love him better every day we live together, and I couldn't think of leaving him behind alone, when you all go off to Nantucket. I do hope he'll be able to find somebody to take his place. But if he isn't, I shall stay here with him."

"That is quite right, dear child. I am very glad you love him so dearly," Elsie said with a very pleased look. "But I hope your affection will not be put to so severe a test. We have heard of a very suitable person, though it is still uncertain whether his services can be secured. We shall probably know by tomorrow."

"Perhaps sooner than that," Mr. Dinsmore said, approaching them just in time to hear his daughter's last sentence. "Edward has gone to have an interview with him and hopes for a definite reply to his proposition. Ah, here he comes now!" as Edward was seen to turn in at the great gates and come up the avenue at a gentle trot. It was too warm for a gallop.

As he drew near he took off his hat and waved it in triumph round his head. "Success, good friends!" he cried, reining in his steed at the veranda steps. Then, as he threw the reins to a servant and sprang to the ground, he cried, "Zoe, my darling, you can go on with your packing. We may confidently expect to be able to sail with the rest."

"Oh, delightful!" she exclaimed, dancing about as gleefully as if she had been a maiden of eight or ten instead of a woman just closing the first year of her married life.

Everybody sympathized in their joy. And everyone was also glad that she and Edward were to be of their party.

All the older ones were very busy for the next few days, no one finding time for rest and quiet chat except the captain and Violet, who keenly enjoyed a monopoly of each other's society during more than a few hours of every day. Mrs. Dinsmore and Elsie had undertaken to attend to all that would naturally have fallen to Violet's share in making ready for the summer's jaunt had she been in robust health. Bob and Betty Johnson, to whom the Oaks had been home for many years, and who had just graduated from school, came home in the midst of the bustle of preparation and were highly delighted by an invitation to join the Nantucket party.

No untoward event occurred to cause either disappointment or delay. All were ready in due season, and the yacht set sail at the appointed time with a full list of passengers, carrying plenty of luggage and with fair winds and sunny skies.

They entered Nantucket harbor on a lovely summer morning with a delicious breeze blowing from the sea. The waves rippled and danced in the sunlight, and the pretty town sat like a queen on the surrounding heights that sloped gently up from the water.

They were all gathered on a deck, eager for a first glimpse of the place.

Most of them spoke admiringly of it, but Zoe said, "It's pretty enough, but too much of a town for me. I'm glad we are not to stay in it. 'Sconset is a smaller place, isn't it, captain?"

"Much smaller," he answered. "Small enough to suit even so great a lover of solitude as you, Mrs. Travilla."

"Oh, you needn't laugh at me," she retorted. "One needn't be a great lover of solitude to care for no more society than is afforded by this crowd. But I want to be close by the bounding sea, and this town is shut off from that by its harbor."

"Where is the harbor, papa?" asked little Gracie.

"All around us, my child. We are in it."

"Are we?" she asked. "I think it looks just like the sea. What's the matter with it, Aunt Zoe?"

"Nothing, only it's too quiet. The great waves don't come rolling in and breaking along the shore. I heard your father say so. It's here they have the still bathing."

"Oh, yes, and papa is going to teach us to swim!" exclaimed Lulu. "I'm so glad, for I like to learn how to do everything."

"That's right," her father said, with an approving smile. "Learn all you can, for 'knowledge is power.'"

They landed with no difficulty, and the gentlemen presently secured a sufficient number of hacks to comfortably accommodate the entire party. After a cursory view of the town during a drive through several of its more important streets, they started on the road to 'Sconset.

They found it, though lonely, by no means an unpleasant drive. There was a road marked out only by rows of parallel ruts across wild moorlands, where the ground was level or slightly rolling. Now and then there was some gentle elevation, a far-off glimpse of harbor or sea, or a lonely farmhouse. The wastes were treeless, save for the presence of a few stunted jack pines. But these gave out a sweet scent, mingling pleasantly with the smell of the salty sea air. And there were wild roses and other flowering shrubs, thistles, tiger lilies, and other wild flowers beautiful enough to tempt our travelers to alight occasionally to gather them.

'Sconset was reached at length, three adjacent cottages found both ready and waiting for their occupancy, and they took possession.

The cottages stood on a high bluff overlooking miles of sea — between which and the foot of the cliff stretched a low, sandy beach a hundred yards or more in width that could be gained by flights of wooden stairs.

The cottages faced inland, and each had a little back yard — grassy and showing a few flowers that reached to within a few yards of the edge of the bluff. The houses were tiny, built low and strong, that they might resist the fierce winds of winter in that exposed position. They were shingled all over to keep out the spray from the waves that would have penetrated any other covering.

Dinner was engaged for the entire party at one of the two hotels, but as it yet was more than an hour before the time set for the meal, all who were not too tired to do so sallied forth to explore the hamlet and its environs.

They found it to consist of about two hundred cottages—similar to those they had engaged for the season, each in a little enclosure. They were built along three narrow streets or lanes running parallel with the edge of the bluff and stood in groups of twos or threes. These were separated by narrow cross-lanes, giving everyone free access to the town pump—the only source of fresh water supply in the place.

The children were particularly interested in the cottage of Captain Baxter with its famous ship's figurehead in the yard.

Back of the original 'Sconset, on the slight ascent toward Nantucket Town, stood a few more pretentious cottages that had been built as summer residences by the rich men of the island, retired sea captains, and merchants. There was one broad street where the larger cottages and the two hotels, the Atlantic House and the Ocean View House, were situated.

Then, on the bluff south of the old village, called Sunset Heights, there were some half dozen cottages. A few were perched on the bluff north of it, also.

The town explored and dinner eaten, the next event was to repair to the beach to watch the rush and tumble of the restless waves. They were fast chasing each other in, and the dash of the spray magnificent as they broke along the shore.

There was little else to see, for the bathing hour was long past—but that was quite enough.

Soon, however, nearly everyone of the party began to feel unaccountably sleepy. Some returned to the cottages for the indulgence of their desire for slumber, and others, spreading cloaks and shawls upon the sand, enjoyed a delicious rest. They were warmed by the sun and fanned by the sea breeze.

For a day or two they did little but sleep and eat, and sleep and eat again. All enjoyed it immensely, too, growing fat and strong.

After those few days' rest, they woke to a new life, made inquiries in regard to all the sights and amusements the island afforded, and began availing themselves of their opportunities.

When it was for a long drive to some notable point, all went together, chartering several vehicles for their conveyance. At other times they frequently broke up into smaller parties, some preferring one sort of sport, some another.

"How many of our party are going to bathe today?" Mr. Dinsmore asked, the second morning after their arrival.

"I for one, if you will bear my company and look out for my safety," said his wife.

"Most assuredly, I will," he answered. "And you too, Elsie?" turning to his daughter.

"Yes, sir," she said. "If you think you can be burdened with the care of two."

"No, mother," spoke up Edward, quickly. "You and Zoe will be my charge, of course."

"Ridiculous, Ned! Of course, Harold and I will take care of mamma!" exclaimed Herbert. "You will have enough to do to look out for your wife's safety." You see, the yacht had touched at Cape May and taken the two college students aboard there.

"I shall be well taken care of," their mother said laughingly with an affectionate glance from one to another of her three tall sons. "But I should like one of you to take charge of Rosie, another of Walter. And, in fact, I don't think I need anything for myself but a strong hold of the rope to insure my safety."

"You shall have more!" exclaimed father and sons in a breath. "The surf is heavy here, and we cannot risk your precious life."

Mr. Dinsmore added, "None of you ladies ought to stay in very long, and we will take you in turn."

"Papa, may I go in?" asked Lulu eagerly.

"Yes, I'll take you in." the captain answered. "But the waves are so boisterous that I doubt if you will care to repeat the experiment. Max, I see, is waiting his chance to ask the same question," he added with a fatherly smile directed to the boy. "My son, you may go in, too, if you will promise to hold on to the rope. I cannot think that otherwise you would be safe in that boiling surf."

"But I can swim, papa," said Max. "And won't you let me go with you out beyond the surf where the water is more quiet?"

"Why yes, you shall," the captain replied with a look of pleasure. "I did not know that you had learned to swim."

"I don't want to go in," said timid little Gracie, as if fearful it might be required of her. "Mamma is not going, and can't I stay with her, papa?"

"Certainly, daughter," was the kind reply. "I suppose you feel afraid of those dashing waves, and I should never think of forcing you in among them against your will."

Betty Johnson now announced her intention to join the bathers. "It's the first chance I've ever had," she remarked. "And I shan't throw it away. I'll hold on to the rope, and if I'm in any danger I suppose Bob or some of the rest of you will come to my assistance?"

"Of course, we will!" all the gentlemen said. Her brother added, "If there's a good chance, I'll take you over to Nantucket Town where there's still bathing and teach you to swim."

"Just what I should like," she said. "I have a great desire to add that to the already large number of my accomplishments."

Miss Betty was a very lively — in fact, quite wild — young lady, whose great desire was for fun and frolic. She liked to have, as she expressed it, "a jolly good time" wherever she went.

The captain drew out his watch. "About time to don our bathing suits," he said. "I understand that eleven o'clock is the proper hour, and it wants but fifteen minutes of it."

Grandma Elsie had kindly seen to it that each little girl that is, Captain Raymond's two and her own Rosie — was provided with a pretty, neatly fitting, and becoming bathing dress.

Violet helped Lulu to put hers on and, surveying her with a smile of gratified motherly pride, told her she looked very well in it, and that she hoped she would enjoy her bath.

"Thank you," said Lulu. "But why don't you go in, too, Mamma Vi?"

"Only because I don't feel strong enough yet to stand up against those heavy waves," Violet answered. "But I am going down to the beach to watch you all and see that you don't drown," she added sportively.

"Oh, Lu, aren't you afraid to go in?" asked little Gracie. She shuddered at the very thought.

"Why no, Gracie, I've bathed in the sea before. I went in a good many times last summer when we were at the shore. Don't you remember?"

"Yes, but the waves there weren't half so big and so strong."

"No, but I'll have a rope and papa, too, to hold to. So why need I be afraid?" laughed Lulu.

"Mamma is afraid, I think," said Gracie, looking doubtfully at her.

"Oh, no, dear," said Violet. "I should not be at all afraid to go in if I were as strong as usual. But, being weak, I know that being buffeted with those great waves would do me more harm than good."

Their cottages being so near the beach, the party all assumed their bathing suits before descending to it. They went down this first time all in one company, forming quite a procession—Mr. and Mrs. Dinsmore heading it and Violet and Gracie, as mere spectators, bringing up the rear.

They, in common with others who had nothing to do but look on, found it an amusing scene. There was a great variety of costume—some neat, well fitting, and modest; some quite immodestly scant; some bright and new; some faded and old. There was, however, little freshness and beauty in any of them when they came out of the water.

Violet and Gracie found a seat under an awning. Max came running up to them.

"Papa is going in with Lulu first," he said. "Then he will bring her out and take me with him for a swim beyond the breakers. I'll just wait here with you till my turn comes."

"See. See. They're in the water!" cried Gracie. "And, oh, what a big, big wave that is coming! There, it would have knocked Lulu down flat if papa hadn't had fast hold of her."

"Yes, it knocked a good many others down," laughed Max. "Just hear how they are screeching and screaming."

"But laughing, too," said Violet. "As if they find it fine sport."

"Who is that man sitting on that bench nearest the water and looking just ready to run and help if anybody needs it?" asked Gracie.

"Oh, that's Captain Gorham," said Max. "To run and help if he's needed is exactly what he's there for. And I presume he always does it for they say no bather has ever drowned here."

Ten or fifteen minutes later a little dripping figure left the water and came running toward them.

"Why, it's Lulu," Gracie said as she drew near, calling out to Max that papa was ready for him as she came.

Max was off like a shot in the direction of the water. Lulu shouted to her sister above the din, "Oh, Gracie, it's such fun! I wish you had gone, too."

Violet hastened to throw a waterproof cloak about Lulu's shoulders and bade her hurry to the house, rub hard with a coarse towel, and put on dry clothing.

"I will go with you, if you wish," she added.

"Oh, no, thank you, Mamma Vi," Lulu answered in a lively, happy tone. "I can do it all quite well myself, and it must be fun for you to sit here and watch the bathers."

"Well, dear, rub till you are in a glow," Violet said as the little girl sped on her way.

"Oh, mamma, see. See!" cried Gracie, more than frightened at the sight. "Papa has gone way, way out, and Maxie is with him. Oh, aren't you afraid they will drown?"

"No, Gracie dear, I think we may safely trust your father's prudence and skill as a swimmer," Violet answered. "Ah, here come Grandma Rose and my mother, but Zoe and Betty seem to be enjoying it too much to leave yet."

"Mamma, let's stay here till our people all come out—papa and Maxie, anyway," Gracie said in a persuasive tone.

"Yes, we will if you wish," said Violet. "I was just thinking I must go in to see how baby is doing, but here comes Dinah bringing her to me."

There was no accident that day, and everybody was enthusiastic in praise of the bathing. Zoe and Betty would have liked to stay in the water much longer than their escorts deemed prudent but yielded to their better judgment.

The next morning there was a division of their forces—the Dinsmores, Mrs. Elsie Travilla, Rosie, Walter, and the Raymonds taking an early start for Nantucket Town, while the others remained behind to enjoy a repetition of the surf bath at 'Sconset.

The Nantucket party drove directly to the bathing house of the town, and the little girls took their first lesson in swimming. They all thought it very nice. Even Gracie soon forgot her timidity in the quiet water with her father to take care of her.

After that they went about the town visiting places of note. They went first to the Atheneum—the oldest house, dating back more than a hundred years. It was no longer habitable but was kept as a relic of olden times—so important that a visit to it is a part of the regular curriculum of the summer sojourner in Nantucket. Then they went to the newsroom, where they wrote their names in the "Visitors' Book." They then traversed the stores to view, among other things, the antique furniture and old crockery on exhibition there and for sale.

Many of these stores, situated on wide, handsome streets, were quite citylike in size and in their display of goods.

Dinner at one of the hotels was next in order, after that a delightful sail on the harbor, around Brant Point, and over the bar out into the sea.

Here the boat flew before the wind, dancing and rocking on the waves to the intense delight of the older children. But Gracie was afraid till her father took her in his arms and held her fast, assuring her they were in no danger.

As she had unbounded confidence in her papa's word and believed he knew all about the sea, this quieted her fears and made the rest of the sail as thoroughly enjoyable to her as it was to the others.

The drive back to 'Sconset, with the full moon shining on moor and sea, was scarcely less delightful to the party. They reached their cottage home full of enthusiasm over the day's experiences—ready to do ample justice to a substantial supper and then enjoy a long and restful night's sleep.

CHAPTER THIRD

And I have loved thee, Ocean!

CAPTAIN RAYMOND, always an early riser, was out on the bluffs before the sun rose, and not five minutes later, Max was by his side.

"Ah, my boy, I thought you were sound asleep and would be for an hour yet," the captain remarked when they had exchanged an affectionate good morning.

"No, sir, I made up my mind last night that I'd be out in time to see the sun rise right out of the sea," Max said. "And there he is just peeping above the waves. There, now he's fairly up! And see, papa, what a golden glory he sheds upon the waters. They are almost too bright to look at. Isn't it a fine sight?"

"Yes, well worth the sacrifice of an extra morning nap—at least once in a while."

"You must have seen it a great many times while out upon the sea, papa."

"Yes, a great many, but it never loses its attraction for me."

"Oh, look. Look, papa!" cried Max. "There's a fisherman going out. He has his dory down on the beach and is just watching for the right wave to launch it. I never can see the difference between waves—why one is better than half a dozen others that he lets pass. Can you, sir?"

"No," acknowledged the captain. "But let us watch now and try to make out his secret."

They did watch closely for ten minutes or more, while wave after wave came rushing in and broke along the beach—the fisherman's eyes all the while intent upon them as he stood motionless beside his boat. Then, suddenly seeming to see the right one—though to the captain and Max it did not look different from many of its neglected predecessors—he gave his dory a vigorous push that sent it out upon the top of that very wave. Then he leapt into the stern, seized his oars, and with a powerful stroke sent the boat out beyond the breakers.

"Bravo!" cried Max, clapping his hands and laughing with delight. "See, papa, how nicely he rides now on the long swells! How I should like to be able to manage a boat like that. May I learn if I have the chance?"

"Yes," said his father. "I should like to have you proficient in all manly accomplishments, but only if you promise not to be foolhardy and run useless risks. I want my son to be brave, but not rash; ready to meet danger with coolness and courage when duty calls, and to have the proper training to enable him to do so intelligently, but not to rush recklessly into it to no good end."

"Yes, papa," Max answered. "I mean to try to be just such a man as my father is. But do you mean that I may take lessons in managing a boat on the sea, if I can find somebody to teach me?"

"I do. I shall inquire about among the fishermen and see who is capable and willing for the task.

Come, let us go down to the beach. We shall have an abundance of time for a stroll before breakfast."

At that moment Lulu joined them with a happy good morning to each. She was in a good mood. "Oh, what a lovely morning! What a delightful place this is!" she cried. "Papa, can't we take a walk along the beach?"

"Yes, Max and I were about to start for one and shall be pleased to have your company."

"I'd like to go out to Tom Never's Head, papa," said Max.

"Oh, so should I!" cried Lulu.

"I believe they say the distance from here to there is about two miles," remarked the captain reflectively. "Such a walk before breakfast in this bracing air, I presume, will not damage children as strong and healthy as these two of mine," he said, regarding them with a fond, fatherly smile. "So come along, and we will try it."

He took Lulu's hand and the three wended their way southward along Sunset Heights, greatly enjoying the sight of the ocean, its waves glittering and dancing in the brilliant sunlight, their booming sound as they broke along the beach, and the exhilarating breeze blowing fresh and pure from them.

"This is a very dangerous coast," the captain remarked solemnly. "It is especially so in winter when it is visited by fierce gales. A great many vessels have been wrecked in the wild surf of the Nantucket coast."

"Yes, papa," said Max, "I heard a story the other day of a ship that was wrecked the night before Christmas eight or ten years ago on this shore. Nobody knew that a ship was near until the next morning when pieces of wreck, floating barrels, and dead bodies were cast up on the beach.

"They found that one man had made it to land alive. They knew it because he was quite a distance from the beach, though entirely dead when they found him. You see, there was just one farmhouse in sight from the scene of the disaster, and they had a light that night because somebody was sick. They suppose the man saw the light and tried to reach it but was too much exhausted by fatigue and the dreadful cold. It seemed his clothes had all been torn off him by the waves. He was stark naked when they found him lying on the ground.

"I think they said the ship was called the *Isaac Newton*. It was loaded with barrels of coal oil and bound for Holland."

"What a terrible death!" Lulu replied with a shudder, clinging more tightly to her father's hand. "Everyone drowned and maybe half frozen for hours before they died. Oh, papa, I wish you didn't belong to the Navy but lived all the time on land! I am so afraid your ship will be wrecked some time," she ended with a sob.

"It is not only upon the water that people die by what we call accident, daughter," the captain answered. "Many horrible deaths occur on land — many to which drowning would, in my opinion, be far preferable.

"But you must remember that we are under God's care and protection everywhere, on land and on sea, and that if we are His children no real evil can befall us. I am very glad you love me, my child, but I would not have you make yourself unhappy with useless fears on my account. Trust the Lord for me and all whom you love, my dear Lulu."

They pressed onward and presently came upon a lovely lakelet near the beach—as clear as crystal and with bushes with dark green foliage growing on all sides but that toward the sea.

They stopped for a moment to gaze upon it with surprise and admiration, but then they pushed on again till they reached the top of the high bluff known as Tom Never's Head.

The trio stood upon its brink and looked off toward the west and north over the heaving, tumbling ocean, as far as the eye could reach to the line where sea and sky seemed to meet. They took in long draughts of the pure, invigorating air and listened to the roar of the breakers below.

"What is that down there?" asked Lulu.

"Part of a wreck, evidently," answered her father. "It must have been there a long while it is so deeply imbedded in the sand."

"I wish I knew its story," said Lulu. "I hope everybody wasn't drowned when it was lost."

"It must have happened years ago, before that life-saving station was built," remarked Max.

"Life-saving station," repeated Lulu, turning to look in the direction of his glance. "What's that?"

"Do you not know what that means?" asked her father. "It is high time you did. Those small houses are built here and there all along our coast by the general government for the purpose of accommodating a band of surfmen in each. They are employed by the government to keep a lookout for vessels in distress and give them all the aid in their power.

"They are provided with lifeboats, buoys, and other necessary equipment to enable them to do so successfully. If it were not too near breakfast time, I should take you over there to see their apparatus.

But we must defer a visit to some other day, which will be quite as well, for then we may bring a larger party with us. Now back home, you two," he added, again taking Lulu's hand. "If your appetites are as keen as mine you will be glad to get there and to the table."

"Two good hours to bathing time," remarked Mr. Dinsmore, consulting his watch as they rose from the breakfast table. "I propose that we utilize them in a visit to Sankaty lighthouse."

All were well satisfied to do so, and presently they set off—some driving, others walking, for the distance was not great. Even feeble folk often found themselves able to take quite long tramps in the bracing sea air.

Max and Lulu preferred to walk when they learned that their father intended to do so, and then Gracie, though extremely fond of driving, begged leave to join their party. The captain finally granted her request, thinking within himself that he would carry her if her strength gave out.

The little face grew radiant with delight. "Oh, you are a nice, good papa!" she cried, giving him a hug and kiss.

"I am glad you think so," he said laughingly as he returned her caress. "Well, as soon as I have helped your mamma into the carriage, we will start."

They set out presently, Gracie holding fast to one of his hands, while Lulu had the other. Tripping merrily along by his side till, passing out of the village, they struck into the narrow path leading to Sankaty. Then the little maid moved along more soberly, looking far away over the rolling billows and watching the progress of some sea-going vessels in the distance.

They could hear the dash of the waves on the beach below but could not see it for the overhanging cliffs. The path ran some yards distant from their brink.

"I want to see where the waves come up," said Lulu. "There's Max looking down over the edge. Can't we go and look, too, papa?"

"Yes, with me along to take care of you," he said, turning from the path and leading them seaward. "But don't venture alone. The ground may crumble under your feet, and you would have a terrible fall, going down many feet right into the sea."

They had reached the brink. Gracie, clinging tightly to her father's hand, took one timid peep, then drew back in terror. "Oh, papa, how far down it is!" she exclaimed. "Oh, let's get away for fear the ground will break and let us fall."

"Pooh! Gracie, don't be such a coward," said Lulu. "I shouldn't be afraid even if papa hadn't hold of our hands."

"I should be afraid for you, Lulu, as venturesome as you are," said the captain, drawing her a little farther back. "Max, my son, be careful."

"Yes, sir, I will. Papa, do you know how high this bluff is?"

"They say the bank is eighty-five feet high where the lighthouse stands, and I presume it is about the same here. Now, children, we will walk on."

Gracie's strength held out wonderfully. She insisted she was not at all tired, even when the end of their walk had been reached.

The other division of the party had arrived some minutes before, and several were already making the ascent to the top of the lighthouse tower. The rest were scattered, waiting their turn in the neat parlor of the keeper's snug little home or wandering over the grassy expanse between it and the sea.

"There are Grandma Elsie and mamma in the house," cried Gracie, catching sight of them through a window.

"Yes," said her father. "We will go in there and wait our turn with them," he continued, leading the way as he spoke. "Do you want to go up into the tower, Gracie?"

"Oh, no, papa!" she cried. "What would be the use? And I am afraid I might fall."

"What, with your big, strong father to hold you fast?" he asked laughingly, sitting down and drawing her to a seat upon his knee as they entered the tiny parlor.

"It might tire you to hold me so hard. I'm getting so big now," she answered naively, looking up into his face with a loving smile and stealing an arm about his neck.

"Ah, no danger of that," he laughed. "Why, I believe I could hold even your mamma or Lulu without being greatly exhausted by the exertion.

"My dear," turning to Violet, "shall I have the pleasure of helping you to the top of the tower?"

"Thank you, I think I shall not try it today," she answered. "They tell me the steps are very steep and hard to climb."

"Ah, so I suppose, and I think you are wise not to attempt it."

"But I may, mayn't I, papa?" Lulu said. "You know I always like to go everywhere."

"I fear it will be a hard climb for a girl your size," he answered doubtfully.

"Oh, but I want to go and I don't care if it is a hard climb," she said coaxingly, coming close to his side and laying her hand on his shoulder. "Please, papa, do say I may."

"Yes, since you are so desirous," he said in an indulgent tone.

Max came hurrying in. "We can go up now, papa," he said. "The others have come down."

Edward and Zoe were just behind the boy. "Oh, you ought all to go up," cried the latter. "The view is just splendid."

"Mother," said Edward, "the view is very fine, but there are sixty steps, each a foot high. A pretty hard climb for a lady, I should think. Will you go up? May I have the pleasure of helping you?"

"Yes," she answered. "I am quite strong and well, and I think the view will probably pay for the exertion."

They took the lead, and the captain followed with Lulu. Max brought up the rear.

Having reached the top and viewed the great light — one of the finest on the coast — from the interior, Elsie stepped outside and, holding fast to Edward's hand, made the entire circuit, enjoying the extended view on all sides.

Stepping in again, she drew a long breath of relief. "I should not like to try that in a strong wind," she said. "Or at all if I were easily made dizzy. No, nor in any case without a strong arm to cling to for safety, for there is plenty of space to fall between the iron railing and the masonry."

"I should tremble to see you try it alone, mother," Edward said.

"It is a trifle dangerous to be about outside," acknowledged the keeper.

"Yet safe enough for any sailor," laughed the captain, stepping out.

"Oh, papa, let me go, too. Please do!" gently pleaded Lulu.

"Why should you care to?" asked her father.

"To see the prospect, papa. Oh, do let me! There can't be any danger with you to hold me tight."

For answer he leaned down and helped her up the step, then led her slowly round, giving her time to take in all the beauties of the scene and taking care of Max, too, who was slowly following.

"I presume you are a little careful whom you allow to make that round?" the captain observed inquiringly to the keeper when again they stood safe inside.

"Yes, and we have never had an accident. But I don't know but there was a narrow escape from it the other day.

"Of course, crowds of people come here almost every day while summer visitors are on the island. We can't always judge what kind they are, and we know it is not an uncommon thing for people standing on the brink of a precipice or any height to feel an uncontrollable inclination to throw themselves down it. Therefore, we are on the watch.

"Well, the other day I let a strange woman out there, but presently, when I saw her looking down over the edge and heard her mutter to herself, 'Shall I know him when I see him? Shall I know him when I see him?' I pulled her inside in a hurry."

"You thought she was deranged and about to commit suicide by precipitating herself to the ground?" Edward said inquiringly.

"Exactly, sir," returned the keeper.

All of their number who wished to do so having visited the top of the tower, the party prepared to leave the light.

"Are you going to walk back, papa? Mayn't I go with you?" pleaded Gracie.

"No, daughter, we must not try your strength too far," he said, lifting her into the carriage where Grandma Elsie and Violet were already seated. "I am going on a mile further to Sachacha Pond, ladies," he remarked. "Will you drive there or directly home?"

"There, if there is time to go and return before the bathing hour," they answered.

"Quite, I think," he replied. The carriage moved on, and he with Max and Lulu and several of the young gentlemen of the company followed on foot.

Sachacha Pond they found to be a pretty sheet of water only slightly salt, a mile long and three quarters of a mile wide, and separated from the ocean by a long, narrow strip of sandy beach. No stream entered it, but it was the reservoir of the rainfall from the low-lying hills sloping down to its shores. Quidnet—a hamlet of perhaps a dozen cottages and houses—stood on its banks.

It was to this pond people went to fish for perch—calling it fresh water fishing—and to "bob" for eels.

The party had not come to fish this time, yet had an errand aside from a desire to see the spot—namely, to make arrangements for going sharking the next day.

Driving and walking on to Quidnet, the party soon found an old, experienced mariner who possessed a suitable boat and was well pleased to undertake the job of carrying their party out to the sharking grounds on the shoals. He would need a crew of two men—easily found among his neighbors, he said. He would also provide the necessary tackle. The bait would be perch, which they could catch here in the pond before setting out for the trip by sea to their destination—about a mile away.

Captain Raymond, Mr. Dinsmore, his three grandsons, and Bob Johnson were all to be of the party. Max was longing to go, too, but hardly thought he would be allowed. He was hesitating whether to make the request when his father, catching his eager, wistful look, suddenly asked, "Would you like to go, Max?"

"Oh, yes, papa. Yes, indeed!" was the eager response. The boy's heart bounded with delight at the answer, which came in a kindly, indulgent tone, "Very well, you may."

Lulu, hearing it, pleadingly cried, "Oh, couldn't I go, too, papa?"

"You? A little girl?" her father said, turning an astonished look upon her. "Absurd! No, of course you can't."

"I think I might," persisted Lulu. "I've heard that ladies go sometimes, and I shouldn't be a bit afraid or get in anybody's way."

"You can't go; so let me hear no more about it," the captain answered decidedly as they turned toward home—the arrangements for the morrow's expedition being completed.

"Wouldn't Lulu like to ride?" Violet asked, speaking from the carriage window. "She has already done a good deal of walking today."

The carriage stopped, and the captain picked Lulu up and put her in it without waiting for her to reply—for he saw that she was sulking over his refusal of her request.

She continued silent during the short drive to the cottage and scarcely spoke while hurriedly dressing for the bath in the surf.

The contemplated sharking expedition was the chief topic of conversation at the dinner table, and it was quite evident that those who were going looked forward to a good deal of sport.

The frown on Lulu's face grew darker and darker as she listened. Why should she not have a share in the fun as well as Max? She was sure she was quite as brave, and not any more likely to be seasick. And papa ought to be as willing to give enjoyment to his daughter as to his son.

She presently slipped away to the beach and sat down alone to brood over it, nursing her ill humor and missing much of the enjoyment that she might have had because this—a very doubtful one at best—was denied her.

Looking round after a while and seeing her father sitting alone on the beach at some little distance, she went to him and asked, "Why can't I go with you tomorrow, papa? I don't see why I can't go as well as Max."

"Max is a boy and you are a girl, which makes a vast difference whether you see it or not," the captain answered. "But I told you to let me hear no more about it. I am astonished at your assurance in approaching me again on the subject."

Lulu was silent for a moment, but she then said complainingly, "And I suppose I'll not be allowed to take my bath either?"

"I don't forbid you," the captain said kindly, putting his arm about her and drawing her in between his knees. "You may go, provided you promise to keep fast hold of the rope all the time you are in. With that and Captain Gorham keeping close watch, you will not be in much danger, I think. But I should be much easier in mind—it would give me great satisfaction—if my little girl would voluntarily relinquish the bath for this one day that I shall not be here to take care of her. For possibly she might be swept away, and it would be a terrible thing to me to lose her."

"I 'most wonder you don't say a good thing, papa, as I'm so often naughty and troublesome," she said, suddenly becoming humble and penitent.

"No, it would not be true. Your naughtiness often pains me deeply, but I must continue to love my own child in spite of it all," he responded, bending down and imprinting a kiss upon her lips.

"And I love you, papa. Indeed, I do," she said with her arm round his neck, her cheek pressed close to his. "And I won't go in tomorrow. I'm glad to promise not to if it will make you feel easier and enjoy your day more."

"Thank you, my dear child," he said. "I have not the least doubt of your affection."

☆ ☆ ☆ ☆ ☆

Edward had spread a rug on the sand just high enough on the beach to be out of the reach of the incoming waves, and Zoe, with a book in her hand, was reclining upon it, resting on her elbow and gazing far out over the water.

"Well, Mrs. Travilla, for once I find you alone. What has become of your other half?" said a lively voice at her side.

"Oh, is it you, Betty?" Zoe exclaimed, quickly turning her head and glancing up at the speaker.

"No one else. I assure you," returned the lively girl, dropping down on the sand and folding her hands in her lap. "Where did you say Ned was?"

"I didn't say, but he has gone to help mamma down with her shawls and so forth."

"He's the best of sons as well as of husbands," remarked Betty. "But I'm glad he's away for a moment just now, as I want a private word with you. Don't you think it is just a trifle mean and selfish for all our gentlemen to be going off on a pleasure excursion without so much as asking if one of us would like to accompany them?"

"I hadn't thought anything about it," replied Zoe.

"Well, think now, if you please. Wouldn't you go if you had an invitation? Don't you want to go?"

"Yes, if it's the proper thing. I do like to go everywhere with my husband. I'll ask him about it. Here he comes, mamma with him."

She waited till the two were comfortably settled by her side, then said with her most pleasing smile, "I'd like to go sharking, Ned. Won't you take me along tomorrow?"

"Why, what an idea, little wife!" he exclaimed in surprise. "I really hate to say no to any request of yours, but I do not think it would be entirely safe for you. We are not going on the comparatively quiet waters of the harbor, but out into the ocean itself and that in a whaleboat. We may have very rough sailing. Besides, it is not at all impossible that a man-eating shark might get into the boat alive and, as I heard an old fisherman say yesterday, 'make ugly work.'"

"Then I don't want to go," Zoe said. "And I'd rather you wouldn't. Just suppose you should get a bite from a shark?"

"Oh, no danger!" laughed Edward. "A man is better able to take care of himself than a woman is of herself."

"Pooh!" exclaimed Betty. "I don't believe any such thing, and I want to go. I want to be able to say I've done and seen everything any other summer visitors do and see on this island."

"That seems a foolish reason, is it not, Betty?" mildly remonstrated her Cousin Elsie. "But, I suppose, you will have to ask my father's consent, as he is your guardian."

"No use whatever," remarked Bob, who had joined them a moment before. "I know uncle well enough to be able to tell you that beforehand. Aren't you equally sure of the result of such a request, Ned?"

"Yes."

"Besides," pursued Bob teasingly, "there wouldn't be room in the boat for a fine lady like my sister, Betty, with her flounces and frills. Also, you'd likely get awfully sick with the rolling and pitching of the boat and, leaning over the side for the purpose of depositing your breakfast in the sea, tumble in among the sharks and give them one instead."

"Oh, you horrid fellow!" she exclaimed, angrily. "I shouldn't do anything of the kind. I should wear no frills, be no more likely to an attack of seasickness than yourself, and could get out of the way of a shark quite as nimbly as any one else."

"Well, go and ask uncle, then," he laughed.

Betty made no move to go. She knew as well as he how Mr. Dinsmore would treat such a request.

The weather the next morning was all that could be desired for sharking, and the gentlemen set off in due time—all in fine spirits.

They were absent all day, returning early in the evening quite elated with their success.

Max had a wonderful tale to tell Lulu and Gracie of papa's skills, the number of sand sharks, and the tremendous "blue dog," or man-eater, their father had caught.

"I thought all sharks were man-eaters," said Lulu.

"No, the sand sharks are not."

"Did everybody catch a man-eater?"

"No. Nobody but papa took a full grown one. Grandpa Dinsmore and Uncle Edward each caught a baby one, and all of them took big fellows of the other kind. I suppose they are the most common, and it's a good thing, because, of course, they are not nearly so dangerous."

"How many did you catch, Maxie?" asked Gracie.

"I? Oh, I helped catch the perch for bait, but I didn't try for sharks. Of course, a boy wouldn't be strong enough to haul such big fellows in. I tell you even the men had a hard tug, especially with the blue dog.

"The sand sharks they killed when they'd got 'em close up to the gunwale by pounding them on the nose with a club—a good many hard whacks it took, too. But the blue dog had to be stabbed with a lance. And I should think it took considerable courage and skill to do it—he was such a big, strong, wicked-looking fellow. You just ought to have seen how he rolled over and over in the water and lashed it into a foam with his tail, how angry his eyes looked, and how he showed his sharp, white teeth. I thought once he'd be right in among us the next minute, but he didn't. They got the lance down his throat just in time to put a stop to that."

"Oh, I'm glad he didn't!" Gracie said, drawing a long breath. "Do people eat the sharks, Maxie?"

"No, indeed. Who'd want to eat a fish that may have grown fat on human flesh?"

"What do they kill them for, then?"

"Oh, to rid the seas of them, I suppose, and because there is a valuable oil in their livers. We saw our fellows towed ashore, cut open, and their livers taken out."

CHAPTER FOURTH

There is none other name under heaven given among men whereby we must be saved.

—*Acts 4:12*

THEY WERE ALL DOWN on the beach when Max had been telling his story. The evening was beautiful—warm enough to make the breeze from the sea extremely enjoyable. The whole family party was gathered there, sitting upon the benches or camp chairs, while others rested on rugs and shawls spread upon the sand.

Max seemed to have finished what he had to say about the day's exploits, and Gracie rose and went to her father's side.

He drew her to his knee with a slight caress. "What has my little girl been doing all day?"

"Playing in the sand most of the time, papa. I'm so glad those horrid sharks didn't get a chance to bite you or anybody today. Such big, dreadful looking creatures Maxie says they were."

"Not half so large as some I have seen in other parts of the world."

"Oh, papa, will you tell us about them? Shall I call Max and Lulu to hear it?"

"Yes, if they wish to come, they may."

There was scarcely anything the children liked better than to hear the captain tell of his experiences at sea, and in another moment his own three, Rosie, Walter, and several of the older people were gathered about him, expecting quite a treat.

"Quite an audience," he remarked. "And I'm afraid I shall disappoint you all, for I have no yarn to spin. I have only a few items of information to give in regard to other varieties of sharks than are found on this coast.

"The white shark, found in the Mediterranean and the seas of the warmer parts of the world, is the largest and most feared of any of the monsters of the deep. One that was caught was thirty-seven feet long. It has a hard skin and is grayish-brown above and whitish on the underside. It has a large head and a big, wide mouth armed with a terrible apparatus of teeth—six rows in the upper jaw and four in the lower."

"Did you ever see one, papa?" asked Gracie, visibly shaken.

"Yes, many a one. They will follow a ship to feed on any animal matter that may be thrown or fall overboard. They have frequently followed mine to the great disturbance of the sailors who have a superstitious belief that it augurs a death on board during the voyage."

"Do you believe that tale, captain?" softly queried little Walter.

"No, my boy. Certainly not. How should a fish know what is about to happen? Do you think God would give them a knowledge of the future that He conceals from men? No, it is a very foolish idea that only an ignorant, superstitious person could for a moment entertain. Sharks follow the ships simply because of what is occasionally thrown into the water. They are voracious creatures and sometimes swallow articles which even their stomachs cannot digest. A lady's workbox was found in one and the papers of a slave ship in another."

"Why, how could he get them?" asked Walter.

"Only because they had been thrown overboard," said the captain.

"Do those big sharks bite people, captain?" pursued the child.

"Yes, indeed. They will not only bite off an arm or leg when an opportunity offers, but they have also been known to swallow a man whole."

"A worse fate than that of the prophet Jonah," remarked Betty. "Do the sailors ever attempt to catch them, captain?"

Sometimes, using a piece of meat as bait and putting it on a very large hook attached to a chain — for a shark's teeth find no difficulty in going through a rope. When they have hooked him and hauled him on board, they have need to be very careful to keep out of the reach of both his teeth and his tail. They usually rid themselves of danger from the latter by a sailor springing forward and cutting it above the fin with a hatchet.

"In the South Sea Islands they have a curious way of catching sharks by setting a log of wood afloat with a rope attached — a noose at the end. The sharks gather round the log, apparently out of curiosity, and one or another is apt soon to get his head into the noose and is finally wearied out by the log."

"I think that's a good plan," said Gracie. "Because it doesn't put anybody in danger of being bitten."

No one spoke again for a moment or two. The silence was broken by the sweet voice of Mrs. Elsie

Travilla, "Tomorrow is Sunday. Does anyone know if there is any service that will be held anywhere near here?"

"Yes," replied Mr. Dinsmore. "There will be preaching in the parlors of one of the hotels and I move that we attend in a body."

The motion was seconded and carried, and when the time came nearly everyone went. The service occupied an hour. After that almost everybody sought the beach, but though some went in the surf — doubtless looking upon it as a hygienic measure, therefore lawful even on the Lord's day — there was not the usual boisterous fun and frolic.

Harold, by some maneuvering, got his mother to himself for a time, making a comfortable seat for her in the sand and shading her from the sun with an umbrella.

"Mamma," he said, "I want a good talk with you. There are some questions, quite suitable for Sunday, that I want to ask. And see," holding them up to view. "I have brought my Bible and a small concordance with me, for I know you always refer to the law and to the testimony in deciding matters of faith and practice."

"Yes," she said, "God's Word is the only infallible rule of faith and practice. 'All scripture is given by inspiration of God, and is profitable for doctrine, for reproof, for correction, for instruction in righteousness!'"

"Yes, mamma, I have the reference here — 2 Timothy, third chapter, and sixteenth verse. And should not the next verse, 'That the man of God may be perfect, thoroughly furnished unto all good works,' stir us up to much careful study of the Bible?"

"Certainly, my dear boy. And, oh, what cause for gratitude that we have an infallible instructor and guide! But what did you want to ask me?"

"A question that was put to me by one of our fellows at college, and which I was not prepared to answer. The substance of it was this: 'If one who has lived for years in the service of God should be suddenly cut off while committing some sin, would he not be saved because of his former good works?'"

"Is any son or daughter of Adam saved by good works?" she asked with a look and tone of surprise.

"No, mother, certainly not. How strange that I did not think of answering him with that query. But he maintained that God was too just to overlook—make no account of—years of holy living because of perhaps a momentary fall into sin."

"We have nothing to hope from God's justice," she replied. "It wholly condemns us. 'There is none righteous, no, not one . . . Therefore by the deeds of the law there shall no flesh be justified in His sight.'

"But your friend's question is very plainly answered by the prophet Ezekiel," opening her Bible as she spoke. "Here it is in the eighteenth chapter, twenty-fourth verse.

"'But when the righteous turneth away from his righteousness and committeth iniquity, and doeth according to all the abominations that the wicked man doeth, shall he live? All his righteousness that he hath done shall not be mentioned: in his trespass that he hath trespassed, and in his sin that he hath sinned, in them shall he die.'"

"Nothing could be plainer," Harold said. "I shall refer my friend to that passage for his answer, and also remind him that no one can be saved by works.

"Now, mamma, there is something else. I have become acquainted with a young Jew who interests me greatly. He is gentlemanly, refined, educated, very intelligent, and devout—studying the Hebrew Scriptures constantly and looking for a Savior yet to come.

"I have felt so sorry for him that I could not refrain from talking to him of Jesus of Nazareth and trying to convince him that He was and is the true and promised Messiah."

Elsie looked deeply interested. "And what was the result of your efforts?" she asked.

"I have not succeeded in convincing him yet, mamma, but I think I have raised doubts in his mind. I have called his attention to the prophecies in his own Hebrew Scriptures in regard to both the character of the Messiah and the time of His appearing, and shown him how exactly they were all fulfilled in our Savior. I think he cannot help seeing that it is so, yet tried hard to shut his eyes to the truth.

"He tells me he believes Jesus was a good man and a great prophet, but not the Messiah—only a human creature. To that I answer, 'He claimed to be God, saying, "I and My Father are One." "Verily, verily, I say unto you, before Abraham was I am," and allowed himself to be worshipped as God. Therefore either He was God or He was a wretched imposter, not even a good man.'

"But, mamma, I have been asked by another, a professed Christian, 'Why do you trouble yourself about the belief of a devout Jew? He is not seeking salvation by works, but by faith. Then he is safe, even though he looks for a Savior yet to come?' How should you answer that question, mamma?"

"With the eleventh and twelfth verses of the fourth chapter of Acts. 'This is the stone which was set at naught of you builders, which is become the head of the corner. Neither is there salvation in any other, for there is none other name under heaven given among men, whereby we must be saved.'

"That name is the name of Jesus of Nazareth, the crucified One. He is the only Savior. We speak — the Bible speaks — of being saved by faith, but faith is only the hand with which we lay hold on Christ.

"'A Savior yet to come?' There is none. And will faith in a myth save the soul? No, nor in any other than Him who is the Door, the Way, the Truth, the Life.

"'He is mighty to save,' and He alone; He Himself said, 'No man cometh unto the Father, but by Me.'

"And is it not for the very same sin of rejecting the true Messiah, killing Him and imprecating His blood upon them and their children, that they have been scattered among the nations and have become a hissing and a byword to all people?"

"True, mamma, and yet are they not still God's own chosen people? Are there not promises of their future restoration?"

"Yes, my son, there are many, in both the Old Testament and the New. Zechariah tells us, 'They shall look upon Me whom they have pierced, and they shall mourn for Him as one mourneth for his only son, and shall be in bitterness for him, as one that is in bitterness for his firstborn.' And Paul speaks of a time when the veil that is upon their hearts shall be taken away, and it shall turn to the Lord.

"Harold, let me read the first five verses of the sixty-second chapter of Isaiah — they are so beautiful.

"'For Zion's sake will I not hold My peace, and for Jerusalem's sake I will not rest, until the righteousness thereof go forth as brightness, and the salvation thereof as a lamp that burneth.'

"'And the Gentiles shall see thy righteousness, and all kings thy glory; and thou shalt be called by a new name which the mouth of the Lord shall name.'

"'Thou shalt be a crown of glory in the hand of the Lord, and a royal diadem in the hand of thy God.'

"'Thou shalt no more be termed Forsaken; neither shall thy land any more be termed Desolate: but thou shalt be called Hephzi-bah, and thy land Beulah: for the Lord delighted in thee, and thy land shall be married.'

"'For as a young man marrieth a virgin, so shall thy sons marry thee: and as the bridegroom rejoiceth over the bride, so shall thy God rejoice over thee.'"

※ ※ ※ ※ ※

Mr. and Mrs. Dinsmore sat together not many paces distant, each with a book. However, Rose's was half closed while she gazed out over the sea.

"I am charmed with the quiet of this place," she remarked presently. "Never a scream of a locomotive to break it, no pavements to echo to the footsteps of the passerby, no sound of factory or mill, or rumble of wheels—scarcely anything to be heard, even on weekdays, but the thunder of the surf and occasionally a human voice."

"Except the blast of Captain Baxter's tin horn announcing his arrival with the mail or warning you that he will be off for Nantucket in precisely five minutes, so that if you have letters or errands for him you must make all haste to hand them over," Mr. Dinsmore said with a smile.

"Ah, yes," she assented, "but with all that, is it not the quietest place you ever were in?"

"I think it is. There is delightful Sunday stillness today. I cannot say that I should desire to pass my life here, but a sojourn of some weeks is a very pleasant and restful variety."

"I find it so," said his wife. "I feel a very strong inclination to be down here, close by the waves, almost all the time. If agreeable to the rest of our party, let us pass the evening here by the sea while singing hymns."

"A very good suggestion," he responded. Elsie and the others being of the same opinion, it was duly carried out.

CHAPTER FIFTH

Sudden they see from midst of all the main
The surging waters like a mountain rise,
And the great sea, puff'd up with proud disdain
To swell above the measure of his guise,
As threat'ning to devour all that his power despise.

— *S*PENSER

WHAT WITH BATHING, driving, and wandering about on foot over the lovely moors, time flew fast to the 'Sconseters.

It was their purpose to visit every point of interest on the island and to try all its typical amusements. They made frequent visits to Nantucket Town, particularly that the children might take their swimming lessons in the quiet water of its harbor. They also repeated such drives and rambles as they found exceptionally enjoyable.

Max wanted to try camping out for a few weeks in company with Harold and Herbert Travilla and Bob Johnson, but preferred to wait until his father should leave them—not feeling willing to miss the rare pleasure of his society. And the other lads, quite fond of the captain themselves, did not object to waiting.

In the meantime, they went blue fishing and tried it by both accepted modes—the "heave and haul" from a rowboat or at anchor and trolling from a yacht under full sail. They went plover hunting, eel bobbing, and perch fishing.

The ladies sometimes went with them on their fishing excursions—Zoe and Betty more often than any of the others. Lulu went, too, whenever she was permitted, which was usually when her father made one of the party.

"We haven't been on a 'squantum' yet," remarked Betty one evening, addressing the company in general. "Suppose we try that tomorrow."

"Suppose you first tell us what a 'squantum' is," said Mrs. Dinsmore.

"Oh, Aunt Rose, don't you know that that is the Nantucket name for a picnic?"

"I acknowledge my ignorance," laughed the older lady. "I did not know it till this moment."

"Well, auntie, it's one of those typical things that every conscientious summer visitor here feels called upon to do as a regular part of the Nantucket curriculum. How many of us are agreed to go?" glancing from one to another.

Not a dissenting voice was raised and Betty proceeded to unfold her plans. Vehicles sufficient for transportation of the whole party were to be provided, baskets of provisions also. They would take an early start, drive to some pleasant spot near the beach or one of the ponds, and make a day of it—sailing, or rather rowing, about the pond, fishing in it, cooking and eating what they caught (fish were said to be delicious just out of the water and cooked over the coals in the open air), and lounging on the grass, drinking in at the same time the sweet, pure air and the beauties of nature as seen upon the Nantucket moors and hills, and in glimpses of the surrounding sea.

"Really, Betty, you grow quite eloquent," laughed her brother. "Nantucket has inspired you."

"I think it sounds ever so nice," said little Gracie. "Won't you go and take us, papa?"

"Yes, if Mamma Vi will go along," he answered with an affectionate look at his young wife. "We can't go without her, can we, Gracie?"

"Oh, no, indeed! But, of course, you will go, mamma, won't you?"

"If your papa chooses to take me," Violet said in a sprightly tone. "I think it would be very pleasant, but I cannot either go or stay unless he does, for I am quite resolved to spend every one of the few days he will be here close by his side."

"And as all the rest of us desire the pleasure of his company," said her mother, "his decision must guide ours."

"There, now, captain," cried Betty, "you see it all rests with you. So please say yes and let us begin our preparations."

"Yes, Miss Betty, I certainly will not be so ungallant as to refuse such a request from such a quarter, especially when I see that all interested in the decision hope I will not."

That settled the matter. Preparations were at once set on foot—the young men started in search of the necessary conveyances, the ladies ordered the provisions, inquiries were made in regard to different localities, and a spot on the banks of Sachacha Pond, where stood a small deserted old house, was selected as their objective point.

They started directly after breakfast and had a delightful drive over the moors and fenceless fields, around the hills and tiny emerald lakes bordered with beautiful wild shrubbery, bright with golden rod, wild roses, and field lilies. Here and there among the heather grew creeping mealberry vines with bright red fruit-like beads and huckleberry bushes that tempted the pleasure seekers to alight again and again to gather and eat the fruit.

Everybody was in the most amiable mood and the male members of the party indulgently assisted the ladies and lifted the children in and out that they might gather floral treasures for themselves, or alighted to gather for them again and again.

At length they reached their destination, left their conveyances, spread an awning above the green grass that grew luxuriantly about the old house, deposited their baskets of provisions and extra wraps underneath it, put the horses into a barn near at hand, and strolled down to the pond.

A whaleboat, large enough to hold the entire company, was presently hired. As they all embarked, it moved slowly out into the lake. All who cared to fish were supplied with tackle and bait and the sport began.

Elsie, Violet, and Gracie declined to take part in it, but Zoe, Betty, and Lulu were very eager and excited, sending forth shouts of triumph or of merriment as they drew one victim after another from the water. The fish seemed eager to take the bait and were caught in such numbers that soon the word was given that quite enough were now on hand and the boat was headed for the shore.

A fire was made in the sand, and while some broiled the fish and made coffee, others spread a snowy cloth upon the grass and placed on it bread and butter, cold biscuits, sandwiches, pickles, cakes, jellies, canned fruits, and other delicacies.

It was a feast fit for kings and queens and all the more enjoyable that the salty sea air and the pleasant exercise had sharpened the appetites of the fortunate partakers.

Then, the meal disposed of, how restful it was to lounge upon the grass, chatting, singing, or silently musing with the sweet, bracing air all about them. The pretty sheet of water was almost at their feet, while away beyond it and the dividing strip of sand the ocean waves tossed and rolled, showing here and there a white, slowly moving sail.

So thoroughly did they enjoy it all that they lingered till the sun, nearing the western horizon, reminded them that the day was waning.

The drive home was not the least enjoyable part of the day. They took it in leisurely fashion, by a different route from the one they had taken in the morning, and with frequent haltings to gather berries, mosses, lichens, grasses, and strange beautiful flowers, or to gaze with delighted eyes upon the bare brown hills purpling in the light of the setting sun, and the rapidly darkening vales, Sankaty lighthouse with the sea rolling beyond on the one hand and on the other the quieter waters of the harbor, with the white houses and spires of Nantucket Town half encircling it.

They had enjoyed the "squantum," marred by no mishap, no untoward event, so much that it was unanimously agreed to repeat the experiment, merely substituting some other spot for the beautiful one visited that day.

Their next excursion was to Wanwinet, which is situated on a narrow neck of land that, jutting out into the sea, forms the head of the harbor—

Nantucket Town standing at the opposite end, some half dozen miles away.

Summer visitors to the latter place usually went to Wanwinet by boat, up the harbor, taking their choice between a sailboat and a tiny steamer that plies regularly back and forth during the season. But this 'Sconset party drove across the moors, sometimes losing their way among the hills, dales, and ponds. But they rather enjoyed that as a prolongation of the pleasure of the drive. In spite of the detention, they reached their destination in good season to partake of the dinner of all obtainable luxuries of the sea, served up in every possible form, which is usually considered the main object of the trip to Wanwinet.

They found the dinner—served in a large open pavilion, whence they might gaze out over the dancing, glittering waves of the harbor and watch the white sails come and go while eating—quite as good as they had been led to expect.

After dinner they wandered along the beach, picking up shells and any curious things they could find—now on the Atlantic side, now on the shore of the harbor.

Then a boat was chartered for a sail of a couple of hours. That was followed by the drive home to 'Sconset by a different course from that of the morning and varied by the gradually fading light of the setting sun and succeeding twilight casting weird shadows here and there among the hills and vales.

The captain predicted a storm for the following day, and though the others could see no signs of its approach, it was upon them before they rose the next morning, raining heavily, while the wind blew a gale.

There was no getting out for sitting on the beach, bathing, or rambling about, and they were at close quarters in the cottages.

They whiled away the time with books, games, and conversations.

They were speaking of the residents of the small island — their correct speech, intelligence, uprightness, and honesty.

"I wonder if there was ever a crime committed here?" Elsie said, inquiringly. "And if there is a jail on the island?"

"Yes, mother," Edward answered. "There is a jail, but so little use for it that they think it hardly worth while to keep it in decent repair. I heard that a man was once put in for petty theft, and that after being there a few days, he sent word to the authorities that if they didn't repair it so that the sheep couldn't break in on him, he wouldn't stay."

There was a general laugh, then Edward resumed. "There has been one murder on the island, as I have been informed. A mulatto woman was the criminal, a white woman the victim, the motive revenge. The colored woman was in debt to the white one, who kept a little store, and, enraged at repeated duns, went to her house and beat her over the head with some heavy weapon — I think I was told a whale's tooth.

"The victim lingered for some little time, but eventually died of her wounds. The other was tried for murder.

"It is said the sheriff was extremely uneasy lest she should be found guilty of murder in the first degree, and he should have the unpleasant job of hanging her. But the verdict was manslaughter, and the sentence imprisonment for life.

"So she was consigned to jail, but very soon allowed to go out occasionally to do a day's work."

"Oh, Uncle Edward, is she alive now?" Gracie asked with a look of alarm.

"Yes, I am told she is disabled by disease and lives in the poorhouse. But you need not be frightened, little girl. She is not at all likely to come to 'Sconset, and if she does we will take good care that she is not allowed to harm you."

"And I don't suppose she'd want to either, unless we had done something to make her angry, Gracie," said Lulu.

"But we are going to Nantucket Town to stay a while when we leave 'Sconset," remarked Gracie uneasily.

"But that woman will not come near you, daughter. You need not have the least fear of it," the captain said, drawing his little girl to his knee with a tender caress.

"Ah," said Mr. Dinsmore, "I heard the other day of a curiosity at Nantucket which we must try to see while there. I think the story connected with it will particularly interest you ladies and little girls."

"Oh, grandpa, tell it!" cried Rosie. "Please do. A story is just what we want and need this dull day."

The others joined in the request, and Mr. Dinsmore kindly complied, all gathering closely about him, anxious to catch every word.

"The story is this. Nearly a hundred years ago there lived in Nantucket a sea captain named Coffin, who had a little daughter of whom he was very fond."

Gracie glanced up smilingly into her father's face and nestled closer to him.

"Just as I am of mine," said his answering look and smile as he drew her closer still.

But Mr. Dinsmore's story was going on.

"It was Captain Coffin's custom to bring home some very desirable gift to his little girl whenever he returned from a voyage. At one time, when about to sail for the other side of the Atlantic, he said to her that he was determined on this voyage to find and bring home to her something that no other little girl ever had or ever could have."

"Oh, grandpa, what could that be?" exclaimed little Walter.

"Wait a moment and you shall hear," came the mysterious reply.

"What the captain brought on coming back was a wax baby—a very lifelike representation of an infant six months old. He said it was a wax cast of the Dauphin of France, that poor unfortunate son of Louis XVI and Marie Antoinette. He said that he had found it in a convent and paid for it a sum of money so enormous that he would never tell anyone, not even his wife, how large it was."

"But it isn't in existence now, at this late day, surely?" Mrs. Dinsmore remarked inquiringly as her husband paused in his narrative.

"It is claimed that it is by those who have such a thing in possession, and I presume they tell the truth. It has been preserved with extreme care as a great curiosity.

"The little girl to whom it was given by her father lived to grow up but has been dead many years. Shortly before her death she gave it to a friend, and it has been in that family over forty years."

"And is it on exhibition, papa?" asked Elsie.

"Only to such as are fortunate enough to get an introduction to the lady owner through some friends of hers, so I understand. However, photographs have been taken and are for sale in the stores."

"Oh, I hope we will get to see it!" exclaimed Lulu quite eagerly.

"As far as I'm concerned, I'm bound to manage it somehow," said Betty.

"How much I should like to know what was really the true story of that poor unfortunate child," said Elsie reflectively, sighing as she spoke.

"It—like the story of the Man in the Iron Mask—is a mystery that will never be satisfactorily cleared up until the Judgment Day," remarked her father.

"Oh, do tell us about it," the children cried in eager chorus.

"All of you older ones have certainly some knowledge of the French Revolution, in which Louis XVI and his beautiful queen lost their lives?" Mr. Dinsmore said, glancing about upon his grandchildren. "And you have not forgotten that two children survived them—one sometimes called Louis XVII, as his father's lawful successor to the throne, and a daughter older than the boy.

"These children remained in the hands of their cruel foes for some time after the beheading of their royal parents. The girl was finally restored to her mother's relatives, the royal family of Austria. But the boy, who was most inhumanly treated by his jailer, was supposed to have died in consequence of that brutal abuse, having first been reduced by it to a state of extreme bodily and mental weakness.

"The story of the death of the poor little dauphin, not of the cruel treatment to which he was subjected has, however, been contradicted by another story. I suppose it will never be made certain in this world, which was the true account.

"The dauphin was born in 1785, and his parents were beheaded in 1793. That would make him about eight years old at the time of their death.

"In 1795 a French man and woman, having come directly from France, appeared in Albany, New York. They had in their charge a girl and boy — the latter about nine years old and feeble in both body and mind.

"The woman had also a number of articles of dress that she claimed had belonged to Marie Antoinette, who had given them to her on the scaffold.

"That same year two Frenchmen came to Ticonderoga, visited the Indians in that vicinity, and placed with them such a boy as the one seen at Albany — of the same age and condition of mind and body.

"He was adopted by an Iroquois chief named Williams and given the name Eleazer Williams.

"He gradually recovered his health, and at length the shock of a sudden fall into the lake so far restored his memory that he recollected some of the scenes in his early life in the palaces of France. One thing he recalled was being with a richly dressed lady whom he addressed simply as 'mamma.'

"Some time later — I cannot now recall the exact date — a Frenchman named Beranger died in New Orleans. He confessed on his deathbed that he had brought the dauphin to this country and placed him with the Indians of Northern New York. He stated that he had taken an oath of secrecy for the protection of the lad, but he could not die without confessing the truth."

"I'm inclined to think the story of the dauphin's death in France was not true," remarked Betty.

"Didn't Beranger's confession arouse inquiry, grandpa?" asked Zoe. "And did Eleazer Williams hear of it?"

"I think I may say yes to both your queries," Mr. Dinsmore answered. "Eleazer's story was published in the newspapers some years ago, and I remember he was spoken of as a very good Christian man, a missionary among the Indians. It was brought out in book form also under the title *The Lost Prince: A Life of Eleazer Williams.*

"Eleazer himself stated that in 1848 he had an interview on board a steamer from Buffalo, with the Prince de Joinville, who then told him he was the son of Louis XVI and Marie Antoinette. Joinville tried to induce him to sign away his right to the throne of France, but Eleazer refused to do so.

"In his published statement he said he thought the Prince would not deny having made that communication. But the Prince did deny it, though he acknowledged that the interview had taken place."

"Did Eleazer ever try to get the throne, grandpa?" asked Max.

"No, he never urged his claim, and I dare say he was happier as an obscure Indian missionary than he would have been as King of France. He died at the age of seventy."

"Poor Marie Antoinette!" sighed Elsie. "I never could read her story without tears, and the very thought of her sorrows and sufferings makes my heart ache."

"I don't think I ever read it," said Zoe. "Though I have a general idea what it was all about."

"We have Abbott's life of her at Ion," said Rosie. "I'll get it for you when we go home."

Harold stepped to the window. "It is raining very little now, if at all," he said. "The sea must be in a fine rage. Let's go and have a look at it."

"Oh, yes, let's go!" cried Betty, springing up. "But I'm afraid we've missed the finest of it, for the wind isn't blowing half so hard as it was an hour ago."

"Don't be discouraged," said Captain Raymond, sportively. "The waves are often higher than ever after the wind has subsided."

"Oh, papa, may I go, too?" Gracie pleaded.

"Yes, if you put on your waterproof cloak and overshoes it will not hurt you to be out for a short time," answered the indulgent father. "Lulu, don't go out without yours, either."

All were eager for the sight. There was a moment of hasty preparation, and they trooped out and stood upon the edge of the high bank at the back of their cottages gazing upon the sea in its, to most of them, new and terrible aspect. From shore to horizon it was one mass of seething, boiling waters. Far out in the distance the huge waves reared their great foam-crested fronts and rushed furiously toward the shore. They rapidly chased each other in till with a tremendous crash and roar they broke upon the beach, sending showers of spray, and depositing great flakes of foam which the wind sent scudding over the sand. Each, as it retreated, was instantly followed by another and another in unbroken, endless succession.

Half a mile or more south of 'Sconset there was a shoal that the locals called "the rips" where wind and tide occasionally, coming in opposition, caused a fierce battle of the waves—a sight well worth a good deal of exertion to behold.

"Wind and tide are having it out on the rips," the captain presently remarked. "Let us go down to the beach and get the best view we can of the conflict."

"Papa, may we go, too?" asked Lulu, as the older people hastily made a move toward the stairway that led to the beach. "Oh, do please let us!"

Gracie did not speak, but her eyes lifted to his, pleading as earnestly as Lulu's tongue. He hesitated for an instant, then stooped, took Gracie in his arms, and said to Lulu, "Yes, come along. It is too grand a sight for me to let you miss it," he answered as they hurried after the others.

Violet had not come out with the rest. Her babe had taken her attention just at that time, and Captain Raymond promised that he would give her the sight afterward on taking the children in.

On they went over the wet sands—Mr. Dinsmore and his wife, Edward and his, Betty holding on to Harold's arm, Rosie and Walter helped along by Herbert and Bob.

To Max Raymond's great content and a little to the discomfiture of her sons, who so delighted in waiting upon and in every way caring for her, Elsie had chosen him for her companion and escort. With Lulu they hastened after the others and were just ahead of the captain and Gracie, who brought up the rear.

The thunder of the surf prevented any attempt at conversation. But now and then there was a little scream, ending with a shout of laughter from one or another of the feminine part of the procession as they were overtaken by the edge of a wave and their shoes filled with the foam or their skirts wet by it. It was not a very serious matter as all had learned ere this that salt water does not cause one to take cold.

Arrived at the spot from where the very best view of the conflict could be had, they stood long gazing upon it, awestruck and fascinated by the terrific grandeur of the scene. It could best be described in the words of another more gifted author who wrote: "Yonder comes shoreward a great wave, towering above all its brethren. Onward it comes, swift as a racehorse, graceful as a great ship, bearing right down upon us. It strikes 'The Rips,' and is there itself struck by a wave approaching from another direction. The two converge in their advance, and are dashed together—embrace each other like two angry giants, each striving to mount upon the shoulders of the other and crush its antagonist with its ponderous bulk. Swift as though they mount higher and higher, in fierce, mad struggle, until their force is expended; their tops quiver, tremble, and burst into one great mass of white, gleaming foam; and the whole body of the united wave, with a mighty bound, hurls itself upon the shore and is broken into a flood of seething waters—crushed to death in its own fury.

"All over the shoal the waves leap up in pinnacles, in volcanic points, sharp as stalagmites, and in this form run hither and yon in all possible directions, colliding with and crashing against others of equal fury and greatness—a very carnival of wild and drunken waves; the waters hurled upward in huge masses of white. Sometimes they unite more gently, and together sweep grandly and gracefully along parallel with the shore; and the cavernous hollows stretch out from the shore so that you look into the trough of the sea and realize what a terrible depth it is. The roar, meanwhile, is horrible. You are stunned by it as by the roar of a great waterfall. You see a wave of unusual magnitude rolling in from far beyond the wild revelry of waters on 'The Rips.' It leaps into the arena as if fresh and eager for the fray, clutches another Bacchanal like itself, and the two towering floods rush swiftly toward the shore. Instinctively you run backward to escape what seems an impending destruction. Very likely a sheet of foam is dashed around you, shoe-deep, but you are safe — only the foam hisses away in impotent rage. The sea has its bounds; 'hitherto shalt thou come, but no further.'"

CHAPTER SIXTH

She is peevish, sullen, froward,
Proud, disobedient, stubborn, lacking duty;
Neither regarding that she is my child,
Nor fearing me as if I were her father.

— SHAKESPEARE

A DAY OR TWO OF bright, breezy weather had succeeded the storm, and another "squantum" had been arranged for. It was to be a more pretentious affair from the former one, other summer visitors uniting with their party and a different spot selected for it.

By Violet's direction the maid had laid out, the night before, the dresses the two little girls were to wear to the picnic, and they appeared at the breakfast table already attired in them—for the start was to be made shortly after the conclusion of the meal.

The material of the dresses was fine. They were neatly fitting and prettily trimmed, but rather dark in color with high necks and long sleeves—altogether suitable for the occasion and far from unbecoming. Indeed, as the captain glanced at the two neat, little figures, seated one on each side of him, he felt the risings of fatherly pride in their attractiveness of appearance.

And even exacting, discontent Lulu was well enough pleased with her mamma's choice for her till, upon leaving the table and running out for a moment into the street to see if the carriages were in sight, she came upon a girl about her own age, who was to be of the company, very brightly appareled in thin white tarlatan and pink ribbons.

"Good morning, Sadie," said Lulu. "What a nice day for the 'squantum,' isn't it?"

"Yes, and it's most time to start. You're not dressed yet, are you?" glancing a trifle scornfully from her own gay plumage to Lulu's plainer attire.

The latter flushed hotly but made no reply. "I don't see anything of the carriages yet," was all she said. Then, darting into the cottage occupied by their family, she rushed to her trunk and throwing it open, hastily took from it a white muslin, coral ribbons and sash, and with headlong speed tore off her plain-colored dress and arrayed herself in them.

She would not have had time but for an unexpected delay in the arrival of the carriage that was to convey her parents, brother, sister, and herself to the "squantum" ground.

As it was, she came rushing out at almost the last moment, just as the captain was handing his wife into the vehicle.

Max met her before she had reached the outer door. "Lu, Mamma Vi says you will need a wrap before we get back—probably even going, and you're to bring one along."

"I shan't need any such thing! And I'm not going to be bothered with it!" cried Lulu, in a tone of angry impatience, hurrying on toward the entrance as she spoke.

"Whew! What have you been doing to yourself?" exclaimed Max, suddenly noting the change in attire. While Gracie, standing in the doorway, turned toward them with a simultaneous exclamation, "Why, Lulu—" then broke off, lost in totally quiet astonishment at her sister's audacity.

"Hush, both of you! Can't you keep quiet?" snapped Lulu, turning from one to the other. Then, as her father's tall form darkened the doorway, and a glance up into his face showed her that it was very grave and stern, she shrank back abashed, frightened by the sudden conviction that he had heard her impertinent reply to her mamma's message, and perhaps noticed the change in her dress.

He regarded her for a moment in silence, while she hung her head in shame and fright. Then he spoke in tones of grave displeasure, "You will stay at home today, Lulu. We have no room for either disrespectful or disobedient children—"

"Papa," she interrupted, pleadingly and angrily, "I haven't been disobedient or disrespectful to you."

"It is quite the same," he said. "I require you to be obedient and respectful to your Mamma Vi. Impertinence to her is something I will by no means allow or fail to punish whenever I know of it. Sorry as I am to deprive you of an anticipated pleasure, I repeat that you must stay at home and go immediately to your room and resume the dress she directed you to wear today."

So saying, he took Gracie's hand and led her to the carriage, while Max followed after one regretful look at Lulu's sorely disappointed face.

Gracie, clinging about her father's neck as he lifted her up, pleaded for her sister. "Oh, papa, do please let her go. She hasn't been naughty for a long while, and I'm sure she's sorry and will be good."

"Hush, hush, darling!" he said, wiping the tears from her eyes. He then placing her by Violet's side.

"What is wrong?" inquired the latter with some concern. "Is Gracie not feeling well?"

"Never mind, my love," the captain answered, assuming a cheerful tone. "There is nothing wrong except that Lulu has displeased me, and I have told her she cannot go with us today."

"Oh, I am sorry!" Violet said, looking very pained. "We shall all miss her. I should be glad, Levis, if you could forgive her, for—"

"No, do not ask it," he said hastily, adding with a smile of ardent affection into the azure eyes gazing so pleadingly into his. "I can scarcely bear to say no to you, dearest, but I have passed sentence upon the offender and cannot revoke it."

The carriage drove off. The others had already gone, and Lulu was left alone in the house, the one maidservant who had stayed behind having already wandered off to the beach.

"There!" cried Lulu, stamping her foot with great passion, then dropping into a chair. "I say it's just too bad! She isn't old enough to be my mother, and I won't have her for one. I shan't mind her! Papa had no business to marry her. He hardly cares for anybody else now, and he ought to love me better than he does her. She isn't a bit of relation to him, while I am his own child.

"And I shan't wear dowdy, old-womanish dresses to please her, along with other girls of my size that are dressed up in their best. I'd rather stay at home than be mortified that way, and I just wish I had told him so."

She was in so rebellious a mood that instead of at once changing her dress in obedience to her father's command, she presently rose from her chair, walked out at the front door, and paraded through the village streets in her finery, saying to herself, "I'll let people see that I do have some decent clothes to wear."

Returning after a little, she was much surprised to find Betty Johnson stretched full length on a lounge with a paper-covered novel in her hand. She seemed to be devouring it with great avidity.

"Why, Betty!" she exclaimed. "Are you here? I thought you went with the rest to the 'squantum.'"

"Just what I thought in regard to your highness," returned Betty, glancing up from her book with a laugh. "I stayed at home to enjoy my book and the bath. What kept you?"

"Papa," answered Lulu with a frown. "He wouldn't let me go."

"Because you put on that dress, I presume," laughed Betty. "Well, it's not very suitable, that's a fact. But I had no idea that the captain was such a connoisseur in matters of that sort."

"He isn't! He wouldn't know or care if it wasn't for Mamma Vi," burst out Lulu vehemently. "And she's no business to dictate about my dress either. I'm old enough to judge and decide for myself."

"Really, it is a great pity that one so wise should be compelled to submit to dictation," observed Betty with exasperating irony.

Lulu, returning a furious look that her tormentor feigned not to see, marched into the adjoining room and gave tardy obedience to her father's order about the dress.

"Are you going in this morning?" asked Betty, when Lulu had returned to the little parlor.

"I don't know. Papa didn't say whether I may or not."

"Then I should take the benefit of the doubt and follow my own inclination in the matter. It's ten o'clock now. The bathing hour is eleven. I shall be finished my book by that time, and we'll go in together if you like."

"I'll see about it," Lulu said, walking away.

She went down to the beach and easily whiled away an hour watching the waves and the people and digging in the sand. When she saw the others going to the bathhouses she hastened back to her temporary home.

As she entered Betty was tossing aside her book. "So here you are!" she cried, yawning and stretching herself. "Are you going in?"

"Yes. If papa is angry I'll tell him he should have forbidden me if he didn't want me to do it."

They donned their bathing suits and went in with the crowd. Though no mishap befell them, and they came out safely again, Lulu found that for some reason her bath was not half so enjoyable as usual.

She and Betty dined at the hotel where the family had frequently taken their meals, then they strolled down to the beach and seated themselves on a bench under an awning.

After a while, Betty proposed taking a walk.

"Where to?" asked Lulu.

"To Sankaty Lighthouse."

"Well, I'm agreed. It's a nice walk. You can look out over the sea all the way," said Lulu, getting up. But a sudden thought seemed to strike her. She paused and hesitated.

"Well, what's the matter?" queried Betty.

"Nothing, only papa told me I was to stay at home today."

"Oh, nonsense! What a little goose!" exclaimed Betty. "Of course that only meant you were not to go to the 'squantum,' so come along."

Lulu was by no means sure that that was really all her father meant, but she wanted the walk. So, she suffered herself to be persuaded, and they went.

Betty had been a wild, ungovernable girl at school, glorying in contempt for rules and daring "larks." She had not improved in that respect, and so far from being properly ashamed of her wild pranks and sometimes really disgraceful frolics, liked to describe them. She was charmed to find in Lulu a deeply interested listener.

It was thus they amused themselves as they strolled slowly along the bluff toward Sankaty.

When they reached there a number of carriages were standing about the entrance of the light, several visitors were in the tower, and others were waiting their turn.

"Let us go up the tower, too," Betty said to her little companion. "The view must be finer today than it was when we were here before, for the atmosphere is clearer."

"I'm afraid papa wouldn't like me to," objected Lulu. "He seemed to think the other time that I needed him to take care of me," she added with a laugh, as if it were quite absurd that one so old and wise as herself should be supposed to need any such protection.

"Pooh!" said Betty. "Don't be a baby. I can take care of myself and you, too. Come, I'm going up and round outside, too, and I dare you to do the same."

Poor, proud Lulu was one of the silly people who are not brave enough to refuse to do a wrong or unwise thing if anybody dares them to do it.

"I'm not a bit afraid, Miss Johnson. You need not think that," she said, bridling. "And I can take care of myself. I'll go."

"Come on, then. We'll follow close behind that gentleman, and the keeper won't suppose we are alone," returned Betty, leading the way.

Lulu found the steep stairs very hard to climb without the help of her father's hand and reached the top quite out of breath.

Betty, too, was panting. But they both presently recovered themselves. Betty stepped outside just behind the gentleman who had preceded them up the stairs, and Lulu climbed quickly after her, frightened at the perilous undertaking, yet still determined to prove that she was equal to it.

But she had advanced only a few steps when a sudden rush of wind caught her skirts and nearly took her off her feet.

Both she and Betty uttered a cry of fright, and at the same instant Lulu felt herself seized from behind and dragged forcibly back within the window from which she had just emerged.

It was the face of a stranger that met her gaze as she looked up with frightened eyes.

"Child," he said, "that was a narrow escape. Don't try it again. Where are your parents or guardians, that you were permitted to step out there with no one to take care of you?"

Lulu blushed and hung her head in silence. Betty, who had followed her in as fast as she could, generously took all the blame upon herself.

"Don't scold her, sir," she said. "It was all my doing. I brought her here without the knowledge of her parents and dared her to go out there."

"You did?" the lightkeeper exclaimed, turning a severe look upon the young girl. "Suppose I had not been near enough to catch her and she had been precipitated to the ground from that great height—how would you have felt?"

"I could never have forgiven myself or had another happy moment while I lived," Betty said, in tremulous tones. "I can never thank you enough, sir, for saving her," she added warmly.

"No, nor I," said the keeper. "I should always have felt that I was to blame for letting her go out. But you were close behind, sir, and the other gentleman before, and I took you to be all one party. Of course, I thought that you would take care of the little girl."

"She has had a severe shock," the gentleman remarked, looking at Lulu, who was very pale and trembling like a leaf. "You had better wait and let me help you down the stairs. I shall be ready in a few moments."

Betty thanked him and said they would wait.

While they did so she tried to jest and laugh with Lulu, but the little girl was in no mood for such things. She felt sick and dizzy at the thought of the danger she had escaped but a moment ago. She made no reply to Betty's remarks and indeed seemed scarcely to hear them.

She was quite silent, too, while being helped down the stairs by the kind stranger, but she thanked him prettily as they separated.

"You are heartily welcome," he said. "But if you will take my advice, you will never go needlessly into such danger again."

With that he shook hands with her, bowed to Betty, and moved away.

"Will you go in to the parlor and rest awhile, Lu?" asked Betty.

"No, thank you. I'm not tired, and I'd rather be close by the sea. Tell me another of your stories, won't you? It will help me forget how near I came to falling."

Betty good-naturedly complied, but found Lulu a less interested listener than before.

The "squantum" party was late in returning and when they arrived Betty and Lulu were in bed. However, the door between the room where Lulu lay and the parlor was ajar, and she could hear all that was said there.

"Where is Lulu?" her father asked of the young maidservant who had been left behind.

"Gone to bed, sir," was the answer.

The captain stepped to the chamber door, pushed it wider open, and came to the bedside.

Lulu pretended to be asleep, keeping her eyes tightly shut. All the time she had the feeling that he was standing there and looking down at her.

He sighed slightly, turned away, and went from the room. Then she buried her face in the pillows and cried bitterly but softly so he would not hear.

"He might have kissed me," she said to herself. "He would if he loved me as much as he used to before he got married."

Then his sigh seemed to echo in her heart, and she grew remorseful over the thought that her misconduct had grieved as well as displeased him.

How much more grieved and displeased he would be if he knew how she had disregarded his wishes and commands during his absence that day!

Soon he would be ordered away again, perhaps to the other side of the world — in danger from the treacherous deep and maybe from savages, too. He would be in some of those far away places where his vessel would touch at. And so their separation might be for years or forever in this world. If she continued to be the bad girl she could not help acknowledging to herself she now was, how dared she hope to be with her Christian father in another life? She had no doubt that he was a Christian. It was evident from his daily walk and conversation. And she was equally certain that she herself was not.

And what a kind, affectionate father he had always been to her. She grew more and more remorseful as she thought of it. And if he had been beside her at that moment she would certainly have confessed all the wrongdoing of the day and asked for his forgiveness.

But he was probably in bed now—for all was darkness and silence in the house. So she lay still and presently forgot all vexing thought in sound, refreshing sleep.

When she awoke again the morning sun was shining brightly, and her mood had changed.

The wrongdoings of the previous day were the merest trifles, and it would really be quite ridiculous to go and confess them to her father. She supposed, indeed was quite sure, that he would be better pleased with her if she made some acknowledgment of sorrow for the fault for which he had punished her. But the very thought of doing so was so galling to her pride that she was stubbornly determined not to do anything of the kind.

She was thinking it all over while dressing and trying hard to believe herself a very ill-used, instead of naughty, child. It was a burning shame that she had been scolded and left behind for such a trifling fault. But she would let papa and everybody else see that she didn't care. She wouldn't ask one word about what kind of time they had had. She hoped it hadn't been so very nice, and she would show papa, too, that she could do very well without caresses and endearments from him.

Glancing from the window, she saw him out on the bluff back of the cottage. Though she was now dressed, she did not, as usual, run out to put her hand in his and with a glad good morning hold up her face for his kiss.

She went quickly to the dooryard looking upon the village street and peeped into the window of the room where Gracie was dressing with a little help from Agnes, their mamma's maid.

"Oh, Lu, good morning," cried the little girl. "I was so sorry you weren't with us yesterday at the 'squantum.' We had ever such a nice time—only I missed you very much."

"Your sympathy was wasted, Gracie," returned Lulu with a grand air. "I had a very pleasant time at home, my dear."

"Dar now, you's done finished, Miss Gracie," said Agnes, turning to leave the room. Then, laughing to herself as she went, "Miss Lu she needn't think she don't 'ceive nobody wid dem grand airs ob hers. 'Spect we all knows she been glad nuff to go ef de cap'n didn't tole her she got for to stay behin'."

Gracie ran out and joined her sister at the door. "Oh, Lu, you would have enjoyed it if you had been with us," she said, embracing her. "But we are going to have a drive this morning. We're to start as soon as breakfast is over and only come back in time for the bath. Papa says you can go, too, if you want to and are a good girl. And you—"

"I don't want to," said Lulu with a cold, offended air. "I like to be by myself on the beach. I enjoyed it very much yesterday, and I shall enjoy it today. I don't need anybody's company."

Her conscience gave her a twinge as she spoke, reminding her that she had passed but little of her day alone on the beach.

Gracie gazed at her with wide-open eyes, lost in astonishment at her strange mood. Hearing her father's steps within the house, she turned about and ran to meet him and claim her morning kiss.

"Where is your sister?" he asked when he had given it.

"The little one is asleep, papa," she answered merrily. "The other one is at the door there."

He smiled. "Tell her to come in," he said. "We are going to have prayers."

Lulu obeyed the summons, but she took a seat near the door without so much as glancing toward her father.

When the short service was over, Gracie seated herself upon his knee and Max stood close beside him, both laughing and talking right merrily. But Lulu sat where she was, gazing in moody silence into the street.

At length, in a pause in the talk, the captain said in a kindly tone, "One of my little girls seems to have forgotten to bid me good morning."

"Good morning, papa," muttered Lulu sullenly, her face still averted.

"Good morning, Lucilla," he said. She knew by his tone and use of her full name that he was by no means pleased with her behavior.

At that moment they were all summoned to breakfast by the bell.

Lulu took her place with the others and ate in silence, scarcely lifting her eyes from her plate, while everybody else was full of cheerful chat.

A carriage was at the door when they left the table.

"Make haste, children," the captain said. "I would like to have plenty of time for a long drive before the bathing hour."

Max and Gracie moved promptly to obey, but Lulu stood still.

"I spoke to you, Lulu, as well as to the others," her father said in his usual kindly tone. "You may go with us if you wish."

"I don't care to, papa," she answered, turning moodily away.

"Very well, I shall not compel you. You may do just as you please about it," he returned. "Stay at home if you prefer it. You may go down to the beach, if you choose, but nowhere else."

"Yes, sir," she muttered and walked out of the room, wondering in a frightened way if he knew or suspected where she had been the day before.

In fact, he did neither. He believed Lulu a more obedient child than she was and had no idea that she had not done exactly as he bade her.

This time she was so far obedient that she went nowhere except to the beach. But while wandering about there she was nursing unkind and rebellious thoughts and feelings—trying hard to convince herself that her father loved her less than he did his other children and was more inclined to be severe with her than with them. In her heart of hearts she believed no such thing, but pretending to herself that she did, she continued her unlovely behavior all that day and the next. She sulked alone most of the time—doing whatever she was bidden, but with a sullen air. She seldom spoke unless she was spoken to, never hanging lovingly about her father, as had been her wont, but rather she seemed to avoid being near him whenever she could.

It pained him deeply to see her indulging so evil a temper, but he thought best to appear not to notice it. He did not offer her the caresses she evidently tried to avoid, and he seldom addressed her. When he did speak to her it was in his accustomed, kind, fatherly tones, and it was her own fault if she did not share in every pleasure provided for the other children.

In the afternoon of the second day, they were all gathered upon the beach as usual, when a young girl who seemed to be a newcomer in 'Sconset drew near and accosted Betty as an old acquaintance.

"Why, Anna Eastman, who would have expected to see you here?" cried Betty in accents of pleased surprise, springing up to embrace the stranger.

Then she introduced her to Elsie, Violet, and Captain Raymond, who happened to be sitting near, as an old school friend.

"And you didn't know I was on the island?" remarked Miss Eastman laughingly to Betty, when the introductions were over.

"I hadn't the least idea of it. When did you arrive, Anna?"

"Several days since—last Monday, and this is Friday. By the way, I saw you on Tuesday, though you did not see me."

"How and where?" asked Betty in surprise, not remembering at the moment how she had spent that day.

"At Sankaty Lighthouse. I was in a carriage out on the green in front of the lighthouse and saw you and that little girl yonder"—nodding in Lulu's direction—"come out on the top of the tower. Then, a puff of wind took the child's skirts, and I fairly screamed with fright, expecting her to fall and be crushed to death. But somebody jerked her back within the window just in time to save her. Weren't you terribly frightened, dear?" she asked, addressing Lulu.

"Of course, I was," Lulu answered in a most ungracious tone. She then rose and sauntered away along the beach. "What did she tell it for, hateful thing!" she muttered to herself. "Now papa knows it, and what will he say and do to me?"

She had not ventured to look at him. If she had, she would have seen his face grow suddenly pale, then assume an expression of mingled sternness and pain.

He presently rose and followed her, though she did not know it till he had reached her side and felt him take her hand in his. He sat down, making her sit by his side.

"Is this true what I hear of you, Lulu?" he asked.

"Yes, papa," she answered in a low, unwilling tone, hanging her head as she spoke. She dared not look him in the face.

"I did not think one of my children would be so disobedient," he said in pained accents.

"Papa, you never said I shouldn't go to Sankaty Lighthouse," she muttered.

"I never gave you leave to go, and I have told you positively, more than once, that you must not go to any distance from the house without express permission. Also, I am sure you could not help understanding, from what was said when I took you to the lighthouse, that I would be very far from willing that you should go up into the tower and especially outside, unless I were with you to take care of you. Besides, what were my orders to you just as I was leaving the house that morning?"

"You told me to change my dress immediately and to stay at home."

"Did you obey the first order?"

Lulu was silent for a moment. Then, as her father was evidently waiting for an answer, she muttered, "I changed my dress after a little while."

"That was not obeying—I told you to do so immediately," he said in a tone of severity. "What did you do in the meantime?"

"I don't want to tell you," she muttered.

"You must, and you are not to say you don't want to do what I bid you. What were you doing?"

"Walking round the town."

"Breaking two of your father's commands at once. What next? Give me a full account of every manner in which you spent the day."

"I came in soon and changed my dress, then went to the beach till the bathing hour. Then, Betty and I went in together. Then we had dinner at the hotel and came back to the beach for a little while. Then, we went to Sankaty."

"Filling up the whole day with repeated acts of disobedience," he said.

"Papa, you didn't say I mustn't go in to bathe, or that I shouldn't take a walk."

"I told you to stay at home, and you disobeyed that order again and again. And you have been behaving badly ever since, showing a most unamiable temper. I have overlooked it, hoping to see a change for the better in your conduct without my resorting to punishment. But I think the time has now come when I must try that with you, Lucilla."

He paused for some moments, wondering at her silence. She, at length, ventured a timid look up into his face.

It was so full of pain and distress that her heart smote her, and she was seized with a sudden fury at herself as the guilty cause of his suffering.

"Lulu," he said with a sigh that was almost a groan, "what am I to do with you?"

"Whip me, papa," she burst out. "I deserve it. You've never tried that yet and maybe it would make me a better girl. I almost wish you would, papa," she went on in her vehement way. "I could beat myself for being so bad and hurting you so."

He made no answer to that, but presently said in moved tones, "What if I had come back to find the dear, little daughter I had left a few hours before in full health and strength, lying a crushed and mangled corpse. You might have been killed without a moment's time to repent of your disobedience to her father's known wishes and commands. Could I have hoped to have you restored to me in another world, my child?"

"No, papa," she said, half under her breath. "I know I wasn't fit to go to heaven, and that I'm not fit now. But would you have been really sorry to lose such a bad, troublesome child?"

"Knowing that, as you yourself acknowledge, you were not fit for heaven, it would have been the heaviest blow I have ever had," he said. "My daughter, you are fully capable of understanding the way of salvation. Therefore, you are accountable, and, so long as you neglect it, you are also in danger of eternal death. I shall never be easy about you till I have good reason to believe that you have given your heart to the Lord Jesus and devoted yourself entirely to His blessed service."

He ceased speaking and gave her a few moments for silent reflection. He then set her on her feet, rose, took her hand, and led her back toward the village.

"Are you going to punish me, papa?" she asked presently, in a frightened tone.

"I shall take the matter into consideration," was all he said, and she knew that she was in some real danger of receiving what she felt to be her deserts.

CHAPTER SEVENTH

The rod and reproof give wisdom: but the child left to himself bringeth his mother to shame.

— PROVERBS 29:15

LULU HATED SUSPENSE. It seemed to her worse than the worst certainty. So when they had gone a few steps farther, she said, hesitating and blushing very deeply, "Papa, if you are going to punish me as—as I—said I 'most wished you would, please don't let Mamma Vi or anybody know it, and—"

"Certainly not. It shall be a secret between our two selves," he said as she broke off without finishing her sentence. "If we could manage it," he added a little doubtfully.

"They all go down to the beach every evening, you know, papa," she suggested in a timid, hesitating way, trembling as she spoke.

"Yes, that would give us a chance. But, Lulu, I have not said positively that I intend to punish you in that way."

"No, sir; but—oh, do please say certainly that you will or you won't."

The look he gave her as she raised her eyes half fearfully to his face was very kind and affectionate, though grave and judicial. "I am not angry with you," he said. "The sense of being in a passion or out of patience does not describe me — not in the least. But I feel it to be my duty to do all I possibly can to help you to be a better child. Noticing, as I have said, for the last two or three days what a willful, wicked temper you were indulging, I have been considering very seriously whether I ought not to try the remedy you have yourself suggested. I am afraid I ought, indeed. Do you still think, as you told me a while ago, that this sort of punishment might be a help to you in trying to be good?"

Lulu hesitated a moment, then, as if determined to own the truth though it were to pass sentence upon herself, said impetuously, "Yes, papa, honestly I do, though I don't want you to do it one bit. But," she added, "I shan't love you any less if you whip me ever so hard, because I shall know you don't like to do it, and wouldn't except for the reason you've given."

"No, indeed, I should not," he said. "You are to stay behind tonight when the others go to the beach."

"Yes, papa, I will," she answered submissively and with a perceptible tremble in her voice.

Gracie and Max were coming to meet them, so there was no opportunity to talk any more on the subject. She walked on in silence by her father's side, trying hard to act and look as if nothing was amiss with her and clinging fast to the hand in which he had taken hers, while Gracie took quick possession of the other.

"You ought to have three hands, papa," laughed Max a little ruefully.

"Four," corrected Gracie. "For some day little Elsie will be wanting one."

"I shall have to manage it by taking you in turn," the captain said, looking down upon them with a fatherly smile.

Violet and some of the other members of their party were still seated where they had left them on the benches under the awning just out of reach of the waves, and thither the captain and his children bent their steps.

Sitting down by his wife's side, he drew Gracie to his knee and Lulu close to his other side, keeping an arm round each while chatting pleasantly with his family and friends.

Lulu was very silent, constantly asking herself with no little uneasiness what he really intended to do with her when, according to his direction, she should stay behind with him after tea while the others returned to the beach.

One thing she was determined on—that she would, if possible, obey the order without attracting anyone's notice. Everybody must have seen how badly she had been behaving, but the thought of that was not half so galling to her pride as the danger of suspicion being aroused that punishment had been meted out to her on account of it.

Max watched her rather curiously and took an opportunity on their return to the house to say privately to her, "I'm glad you've turned over a new leaf, Lu, and begun to behave decently to papa. I've wondered over and over again in the last few days that he didn't take you in hand in a way to convince you that he wasn't one to be trifled with. It's my opinion that if you'd been a boy you'd have got a trouncing long before this."

"Indeed!" she cried, with an angry toss of her head. "I'm glad I'm not a boy if I couldn't be one without using such vulgar words."

"Oh, that isn't such a very bad word," returned Max, laughing. "But I can tell you, from sad experience, that the thing is bad enough sometimes. I'd be quaking in my shoes if I thought papa had any reason to consider me deserving of one."

"I don't see what you mean by talking so to me," exclaimed Lulu, passionately. "But I think you are a Pharisee—making yourself out so much better than I am!"

The call to supper interrupted them just there and perhaps saved them from a downright quarrel.

Lulu had no appetite for the meal and it seemed to her that the others would never finish eating. Then, they lingered unusually long about the house before starting for their accustomed evening rendezvous—the beach. She was on thorns all the time.

At last someone made a move, and catching a look from her father that she alone saw or understood, she slipped unobserved into her bedroom and waited there with a fast-beating heart.

She heard him say to Violet, "Don't wait for me, my love. I have a little matter to attend to here and will follow you in the course of half an hour."

"Anything I can help you with?" Violet asked.

"No, thank you," he said. "I need no assistance."

"A business letter to write, I presume," she returned laughingly. "Well, don't make it too long, for I grudge every moment of your time."

With that she followed the others, and all was quiet except for the captain's measured tread, for he was slowly pacing the room to and fro.

Impatient, impetuous Lulu did not know how to endure the suspense. She seemed to herself like a criminal awaiting execution. Softly she opened the door and stepped out in front of her father, stopping him in his walk.

"Papa," she said with pale, trembling lips, looking beseechingly up into his face, "whatever you are going to do to me, won't you please do it at once and let me have it over?"

He took her hand and, sitting down, drew her to his side putting his arm around her.

"My little daughter," he said very gravely, but not unkindly, "my responsibility in regard to your training weighs very heavily on my mind. It is plain to me that you will make either a very good and useful woman or one who will be a curse to herself and others, for you are too energetic and impulsive, too full of strong feeling to be lukewarm and indifferent in anything.

"You are forming your character now for time and eternity, and, as your father, I must do whatever lies in my power to help you form it aright for good and not for evil. You inherit a sinful nature from me and have very strong passions that must be conquered or they will prove to be your ruin. I fear you do not see the great sinfulness of their indulgence and that it may be that I am partly to blame for that in having passed too lightly over such exhibitions of them as have come to my notice. In short, perhaps if I had been more justly severe with your faults you would have been more thoroughly convinced of their heinousness and striven harder and with greater success to conquer them.

"Therefore, after much thought and deliberation and much prayer for guidance and direction, I have fully decided that I ought to punish you severely for the repeated acts of disobedience you have been guilty of in the last few days and this constant exhibition of ill-temper.

"It pains me exceedingly to do it, but I must not consider my own feelings where my dear child's best interests are concerned."

"Is it because I asked you to do it, papa?" she inquired. "I never thought you actually would when I said it."

"No, I have been thinking seriously on the subject ever since you behaved so badly the day of the 'squantum,' and I had very nearly decided the question just as I have fully decided it now. I know you are an honest child, even when the truth is against you. Tell me, do you not yourself think I am right. Lulu?"

"Yes, sir," she answered, low and tremulously, after a moment's struggle with herself. "Oh, please do it at once, so it will be over soon!"

"I will," he said, rising and leading her into the inner room. "You shall not have the dreadful torture of anticipation a moment longer."

Though the punishment was severe beyond Lulu's worst anticipation, she bore it without outcry or entreaty, feeling that she richly deserved it. She determined that no one who might be within hearing should learn from any sound she uttered what was going on. Tears and now and then a half-suppressed sob were the only evidence of suffering that she allowed herself to give.

Her father was astonished at her fortitude, and more than ever convinced that she had in her the elements of a noble character.

When the punishment was over he took her in his arms, laying her head against his chest. Both were silent, her tears falling like rain.

At length, with a heart-broken sob, she said, "You hurt me terribly, papa. I didn't think you would ever want to hurt me so."

"I did not want to," he answered in moved tones. "It was sorely against my inclination. I cannot tell you how gladly I should have borne twice the pain for you if by doing so I could have made you a good girl. I know you have sometimes troubled yourself with foolish fears that you had less than your fair share of my affection, but I have not a child who is nearer or dearer to me than you are, my darling. I love you very much."

"I'm so glad, papa. I 'most wonder you can," she sobbed. "And I love you dearly, dearly. I know I've not been acting like it lately, but I do, and just as much now as before. Oh, papa, you don't know how hard it is for me to be good!"

"I think I do," he said. "I am by nature quite as bad as you are, having a violent temper. It would most certainly have been my ruin had I not been forced to learn to control it. Indeed, I fear it is from me you get your temper.

"I had a good Christian mother," he went on, "who was very faithful in her efforts to train her children aright. My fits of passion gave her great concern and anxiety. I can see now why she used to look so troubled and distressed.

"Usually she would shut me up in a room by myself until I had had time to cool down. Then she would come to me, talk very seriously and kindly of the danger and sinfulness of such indulgence of temper. She would tell me there was no knowing what dreadful deed I might some day be led to commit in my fury, if I did not learn to rule my own spirit. Therefore, for my own sake, she must punish me to teach me self-control. She would then chastise me, often quite severely, and leave me to myself again to reflect upon the matter. Thus, she finally succeeded in so convincing me of the great guilt and danger of giving rein to my fiery temper and the necessity of gaining mastery over it, that I fought hard to do so, and with God's help have, I think, gained the victory.

"It is the remembrance of all this and how thankful I am to my mother now for her faithfulness, that has made me determined to be equally faithful to my own dear, dear little daughter. Unfortunately I lack the daily opportunity for the same constant watchfulness over my children."

"Oh, papa, if you only could be with us all the time!" she sighed. "But I never thought you had a temper. I've seen some people fly at their naughty children in a great passion and beat them hard. I should think if you had such a bad temper as you say, you'd have treated me so many a time."

"Very likely I should if your grandmother had not taught me to control my wicked temper," he said. "You may thank her that you have as good a father as you have."

"I think I have the best in the world," she said, putting her arm round his neck. "And now that it's over, papa, I'm glad you did punish me so hard, for

I don't feel half so mean. It seems as if I have sort of paid for my naughtiness toward you."

"Yes, toward me. The account is settled between us, but remember that you cannot so atone for your sin against God. Nothing but the blood of Christ can avail to blot out that account against you, and you must ask to be forgiven for His sake alone. We will kneel down and ask it now."

Violet glanced again toward the cottages on the bluff, wondering and becoming a trifle impatient at her husband's long delay. But at length, she saw him approaching, leading Lulu by the hand.

There was an unusual gravity, amounting almost to sternness, in his face. Lulu's wore a more subdued expression than she had ever seen upon it, while traces of tears were evident upon her cheeks.

"He has been talking seriously to her in regard to the ill temper she has shown during the past few days," Violet said to herself. "Poor wayward child! I hope she will take the lesson to heart and give him less trouble and anxiety in the future."

He kept Lulu close at his side all the evening. She seemed well content to stay there. Her head was on his shoulder, his arm around her waist, while she listened silently to the talk going on around her or to the booming of the waves upon the beach not many yards away.

When it was time for the children to retire, he took her and Gracie to the house. At the door he bent down and kissed Gracie goodnight, saying, "I shall not wait to see you in your bed, but I shall come in to look in on you before I go to mine."

"May I have a kiss, papa?" Lulu asked in a wishful, tremulous voice, as though she were more than a trifle uncertain whether her request would be granted.

"Yes, my dear little daughter, as many as you wish," he replied, taking her in his arms and bestowing them with hearty good will and affection.

"Papa, I'm sorry—oh, very sorry for all my naughtiness," she whispered in his ear while clinging about his neck.

"It is all forgiven now," he said. "I trust it will never be repeated."

Lulu was very good, submissive, and obedient during the remainder of her father's short stay among them.

She was greatly distressed when, two weeks later, orders came for him to join his ship the following day. She clung to him with devoted, remorseful affection and distress in the prospect of impending separation, while he treated her with even more than his usual kindness. He drew her often caressingly to his knee, and his voice took on a very tender tone whenever he spoke to her.

It was in the evening he left them, for he was to drive over to Nantucket Town and pass the night there in order to take the early boat leaving for the mainland the next morning.

Mr. Dinsmore went with him, intending to go to Boston for a few days, perhaps on to New York also, then return to Siasconset.

Harold, Herbert, Bob, and Max set out that same evening for their camping ground. That left Mr. Edward Travilla the only man of the party to take care of the women and children.

However, they would all have felt safe enough in that very quiet spot, or anywhere on the island, without any such protection.

Lulu went to bed that night full of remorseful regret that through her own willfulness she had lost many hours of her father's prized company, besides grieving and displeasing him.

Oh, if she could but go back and live the last few weeks over, how differently she would behave! She would not give him the least cause to be displeased with or troubled about her.

As often before, she felt a great disgust at herself, and a longing desire to be good and gentle like Gracie, who never seemed to have the slightest inclination to be quick-tempered or rebellious.

"She's so sweet and dear!" murmured Lulu half aloud, and reaching out a hand to softly touch the little sister sleeping quietly by her side. "I think papa would love her ten times better than me. But he says he doesn't, and he always tells the truth. I wish I'd been made like Gracie, but I'm ever so glad he can love me in spite of all my badness. Oh, I am determined to be good the next time he's at home so that he will enjoy his visit more. It was a burning shame in me to spoil this one so. I'd like to beat you for it, Lulu Raymond, and I'm glad he didn't let you escape."

Violet and her mother were passing the night together—lying side by side they talked to each other in loving confidence of such things as lay nearest their hearts. Naturally Vi's thoughts were full of the husband from whom she had just parted—for how long, no one knew—it might be months or years.

"Mamma," she said, "the more I am with him and study his character, the more I honor and trust and love him. It is the one trial of my otherwise exceptionally happy life that we must pass so much of our time apart, and that he has such a child as Lulu to mar his enjoyment of—"

"Oh, dear daughter," interrupted Elsie, "do not allow yourself to feel otherwise than very kindly toward your husband's child. Lulu has some very noble traits, and I trust you will try to think of them rather than of her faults — serious as they may seem to you."

"Yes, mamma. There are some things about her that are very lovable, and I really have a strong affection for her, even aside from the fact that she is his child. Yet, when she behaves in a way that distresses him, I can hardly help wishing that she belonged to someone else.

"You surely must have noticed how badly she behaved for two or three days. He never spoke to me about it or tried not to let me see that it interfered with his enjoyment — for he knew that that would spoil mine. But for all that I knew his heart was often heavy over her misconduct.

"She certainly does love her father. How she clung to him after she had heard that he must leave us so soon — almost with a remorseful affection, it seemed to me."

"Yes, and though she only shed but few tears in parting from him, I could see that she was almost heart-broken. She is a unusual child, but if she takes the right turn, will assuredly make a very noble and useful woman."

"I hope so, mamma. That will, I know, repay him for all his care and anxiety on her account. No father could be fonder of his children or more willing to do or endure anything for their sake. Of course, I do not mean anything wrong. He would not do wrong himself or suffer wrongdoing in them, for his greatest desire is to see them truly good, real Christians. I hope my darling, as she grows older, will be altogether a comfort and a blessing to him."

"As her mother has been to me and always was to her father," Elsie responded in loving tones.

"Thank you, mamma," Violet said with emotion. "Oh, if I had been an undutiful daughter and given pain and anxiety to my best of fathers, how my heart would ache at the remembrance, now that he is gone. And I feel deep pity for Lulu when I think what sorrow she is preparing for herself in case she outlives her father, as in the course of nature she is likely to do."

"Yes, poor child!" sighed Elsie. "Doubtless she is even now enduring the reproaches of conscience aggravated by the fear that she may not see her father very soon again.

"She and Gracie, to say nothing of my own dear Vi, will be feeling lonely tomorrow. Edward, Zoe, and I have planned various little excursions by land and water to give occupation to your thoughts and pleasantly while away the time."

"You are always so kind, dearest mamma," said Violet. "You are always thinking of others and planning for their enjoyment."

ﾊ ﾊ ﾊ ﾊ ﾊ

"Oh, how lonely it does seem without papa, our dear, dear papa!" was Gracie's waking exclamation. "I wish he could live at home all the time like other children's fathers do! When will he come home to us again, Lulu?"

"I don't know, Gracie. I don't believe anybody knows," returned Lulu sorrowfully. "But you have no occasion to feel half so badly about it as I."

"Why not?" cried Gracie, a little indignantly. Even her gentle nature was aroused at the apparent insinuation that he was more to Lulu than to herself. "You don't love him a bit better than I do."

"Maybe not, but Mamma Vi is more to you than she is to me—though that wasn't what I was thinking of. I was only thinking that you had been a good child to him all the time he has been at home, while I was so very, very naughty that—"

Lulu broke off suddenly and went on with her dressing in silence.

"That what?" asked Gracie.

"That I grieved him very much and spoiled half his pleasure," Lulu said in a choking voice. Then turning suddenly toward her sister, her face flushed hotly. Her eyes were full of tears, and she was bitterly ashamed of what she was moved to tell. Yet, with a heart aching so for sympathy that she hardly knew how to keep it back, "Gracie, if I tell you something will you never, never, never, breathe a single word of it to a living soul?"

Gracie, who was seated on the floor putting on her shoes and stockings, looked up at her sister in silent astonishment.

"Come, answer," exclaimed Lulu, impetuously. "Do you promise? I know if you make a promise you'll keep it. But I won't tell you without, for I wouldn't have Mamma Vi, or Max, or anybody else but you know, for all the world."

"Not papa?"

"Oh, Gracie, papa knows. It's a secret between him and me—only—only I have a right to tell all about it if I choose."

"I'm glad he knows, because I couldn't promise not to tell him if he asked me and said I must. Yes, I promise, Lulu. What is it?"

Lulu had finished her dressing, and dropping down on the carpet beside Gracie she began, half averting her face and speaking in low, hurried tones. "You remember that morning we were all going to the 'squantum' I changed my dress and put on a white one, and because of that, and something I said to Max that papa overheard, he said I must stay at home. And he ordered me to take off that dress immediately. Well, I disobeyed him. I walked round the town in that dress before I took it off, and instead of staying at home I went in to bathe, took a walk in the afternoon with Betty Johnson to Sankaty Lighthouse, and went up in the tower and outside, too."

"Oh, Lulu!" cried Gracie. "How could you dare to do so?"

"I did, anyway," said Lulu. "And you know I was very ill-tempered for two days afterward. So, when papa knew it all he thought he ought to punish me, and he did."

"How?"

"Oh, Gracie! Don't you know? Can't you guess? It was when he and I stayed back while all the rest went to the beach — that evening after Betty's friend told of seeing me at Sankaty."

"Oh, Lu," she said pityingly, putting her arms about her sister. "I'm so sorry for you! How could you bear it? Did he hurt you very much?"

"Oh, yes, terribly, but I'm glad he did it — though I wouldn't for anything let anybody know it but you.

I'd feel so mean if I hadn't paid for my badness. Papa was so good and kind to me—he always is—and I had been behaving so hatefully to him.

"And he wasn't in a bit of a passion with me. I believe, as he told me, he did hate to punish me, and only did it to help me to learn to conquer my bad temper."

"And to be obedient, too?"

"Yes, the punishment was for that, too, he said. But now don't you think I have reason to feel worse about his going away just now than you?"

"Yes," admitted Gracie. "I'd feel ever so badly if I'd done anything to make dear papa sad and troubled. And I think I should be frightened to death if he was going to whip me."

"No, you wouldn't," said Lulu. "For you would know papa wouldn't hurt you any more than he thought necessary for your own good. Now let me help you dress, for it must be near breakfast time."

"Oh, thank you. Yes, I'll have to hurry. Do you love papa as well as ever, Lu?"

"Better," returned Lulu, emphatically. "It seems odd, but I do. I shouldn't though if I thought he took pleasure in beating me or punishing me in any way."

"I don't b'lieve he ever likes to punish any of us," said Gracie.

"I know he doesn't," said Lulu. "And it isn't any odder that I should love him in spite of his punishments, than that he should love me in spite of my naughtiness. Yes, I do think, Gracie, we have the best father in the world."

"'Course, we have," responded Gracie. "But then we don't have him half the time. He's 'most always on his ship," she added tearfully.

"Are you ready for breakfast, dears?" asked a sweet voice at the door.

"Yes, Grandma Elsie," they answered, hastening to claim the good morning kiss she was always ready to bestow.

Lulu's heartache had found some relief in her confidence to her sister, and she showed a pleasanter and more cheerful face at the table than Violet expected to see her wear.

It grew brighter still when she learned that they were all to have a long, delightful drive over the hills and moors, starting almost immediately upon the conclusion of the meal.

The weather was charming, everybody in most amiable a mood, and in spite of the pain of the recent parting from him whom they so dearly loved, that would occasionally make itself felt in the hearts of wife and children, the little trip was an enjoyable one to all.

Just as they drew up at the cottage door on their return, a blast of Captain Baxter's tinhorn announced his arrival with the mail. Edward, waiting only to assist the ladies and children to alight, hurried off to learn if they had any interest in the contents of the mailbag.

CHAPTER EIGHTH

Be not too ready to condemn
The wrongs thy brothers may have done;
Ere ye too harshly censure them
For human faults, ask, "Have I none?"

— MISS ELIZA COOK

THE LITTLE GIRLS TOOK up their station at the front door to watch for their Uncle Edward's return with the mail.

Gracie presently cried out joyfully, "Oh, he's coming with a whole handful of letters! I wonder if one is from papa."

"I'm afraid not," said Lulu. "He would hardly write last night, leaving us so late as he did. He would hardly have had time before the leaving of the early boat this morning."

The last word had scarcely left her lips when Edward reached her side and put a letter into her hand—a letter directed to her and unmistakably in her father's handwriting.

"One for you, too, Vi," he said merrily, tossing it into her lap through the open window.

"Excuse the unceremonious delivery, sister mine. Where are grandma and mamma? I have a letter for each of them."

"Here," answered his mother's voice from within the room. Then, as she took the missives from his hand, "Ah, I knew papa would not forget either mamma or me."

"Where's my share, Ned?" asked Zoe, issuing from the inner room, where she had been engaged in taking off her hat and smoothing her fair tresses.

"Your share? Well, really I don't know, unless you'll accept the mail carrier as such," he returned quite sportively.

"Captain Baxter?" she asked in mock astonishment. "I'd rather have a letter instead."

"But you can't have either," he returned laughing. "You can only have the postman who delivered the letters here—nothing more. You have no choice."

Lulu, who received her letter with a smothered exclamation of intense, joyful surprise, ran swiftly away with it to the beach. She never stopped till she had gained a spot beyond and away from the crowd. A spot where no prying eye would watch her movements or note if the perusal of her treasure caused any emotion.

There, seated upon the sand, she broke open the envelope with fingers trembling with eagerness. It contained only a few lines in Captain Raymond's bold handwriting, but they breathed such fatherly love and tenderness as brought the tears in showers from Lulu's eyes—tears of intense joy and filial love. She hastily wiped them away and read the sweet words again and again. Then, kissing the paper over and over, she placed it in her blouse, rose up, and slowly wended her way back toward the house with a lighter, happier heart than she had known for some days.

She had not gone far when Gracie came tripping over the sands to meet her, her face sparkling with delight as she held up a note to view, exclaiming,

"See, Lu! Papa did not forget me. It came inside of mamma's letter."

"Oh, Gracie, I am glad," said Lulu. "But it would be very strange for papa to remember the bad child and not the good one, wouldn't it?" she concluded, between a sigh and a smile.

"I'm not always good," said Gracie. "You know I did something very, very bad last winter one time—something you would never do. I b'lieve you'd speak the truth even if you knew you'd be killed for it."

"You dear little thing!" exclaimed Lulu, throwing her arm round Gracie and giving her a hearty kiss. "It's very good of you to say it, but papa says I'm an honest child and own the truth even when it's against me."

"Yes, you said you told him all about how you had disobeyed him. If it had been I, I wouldn't have ever said a word about it for fear he'd punish me."

"Well, you can't help being timid. If I were as timid as you are, no doubt I'd be afraid to own up, too. And I didn't confess till after that Miss Eastman had told on me," said Lulu. "Now let's sit down on the sand, and if you'll show me your letter, I'll show you mine."

Gracie was more than willing, and they busied themselves with the other's letters, reading and rereading and with loving talk about their absent father till summoned to the supper table.

Lulu was very fond of being on the beach, playing in the sand, wandering hither and thither, or just sitting gazing dreamily out over the waves. Her father had allowed her to go do so, only stipulating that she should not go out of sight or into any place that looked at all dangerous.

"I'm going down to the beach," she said to Gracie, when they had left the table that evening. "Won't you go, too?"

"Not yet," said Gracie. "Baby is awake and looks so sweet that I'd rather stay and play with her for a little while first."

"She does look pretty and sweet," assented Lulu, glancing toward the babe, who was cooing in her nurse's arms. "But we can see enough of her after we get home to Ion, and we haven't the sea any more. I'll go now, and you can come and join me when you are ready."

Leaving the house, Lulu turned southward toward Sunset Heights and strolled slowly on, gazing seaward for the most part and drinking in with delight the delicious breeze as it came sweeping on from no one knows where. It tore at the crests of the waves and scattered the spray hither and yon.

The tide was rising, and it was keen enjoyment to watch the great billows chasing each other in and dashing higher and higher onto the sands below. Then the sun drew near his setting, and the sea, reflecting the gorgeous coloring of the clouds, changed every moment from one lovely hue to another.

Lulu slowly walked on and on down the shore, willfully refusing to think how great might be the distance she was putting between herself and home. At length she sat down, the better to enjoy the lovely panorama of cloud and sea and sun and sky which still continued to enrapture her with its ever-changing beauty.

By and by the colors began to fade and give place to a silvery gray, which gradually deepened and spread till the whole sky was fast growing black with clouds that, even to her inexperienced eye, portended a storm.

She started up and sent a sweeping glance around on every side. Could it be possible that she was so far from the tiny 'Sconset cottage that at present she called home? Here were Tom Never's Head and the life saving station almost close at hand. She had heard papa say those were a good two miles from 'Sconset, so she must be very nearly that distance from home. She was all alone, too, and with night and a storm fast coming on.

"Oh me! I've been disobedient again," she said aloud, as she set off for home at her most rapid pace. "What would papa say? It wasn't exactly intentional this time, but I should not have been so careless."

Alarmed at the prospect of being overtaken by darkness and tempest alone out in the wild, she used her best efforts to move with speed. But she could scarcely see to pick her steps or take a perfectly direct course, and now and again she was startled by the flutter of a frightened night bird across her path as she wandered among the sand dunes, toiling over the yielding soil. The booming of the waves and the melancholy cadences of the wind as it rose and fell filled her ears.

She was a brave child, entirely free from childlike superstitious fears. Having learned that the island harbored no burglars or murderers, and that there was no wild beast upon it, her only fear was of being overtaken by the storm or lost on the moors, unable to find her way till daybreak.

But, gaining the top of a sand-hill, the star-like gleam of Sankaty Light greeted her delighted eyes. She cried out with a joyful exclamation, "Oh, now

I can find the way!" she sprang forward with renewed energy. She soon found the path to the village and pursued it with quickened steps and a light heart, although the rain was now pouring down accompanied with occasional flashes of lightening and peals of thunder. And in few moments pushed open the door of the cottage and stepped into the astonished presence of the ladies of the party.

She had not been missed till the approach of the storm drove them all within doors. Then, perceiving that the little girl was not among them, the question passed from one to another, "Whereever could Lulu be?"

No one could say where. Gracie remembered that she had gone out intending to take a stroll along the beach, but did not mention in which direction.

"And she has never been known to stay out so late, and—and the tide is coming in," cried Violet, sinking pale and trembling into a chair. "Oh, mamma, if she is drowned, how shall I answer to my husband for taking so little care of his child?"

"My dear daughter, don't borrow trouble," Elsie said cheerfully, though her own cheek had grown very pale. "It was in my care he left her, not in yours, dear."

"Don't fret, Vi," Edward said. "I don't believe she's drowned. She has more sense than to go where the tide would reach her, but I'll go at once to look for her and engage others in the search as well."

He started for the door.

"She may be out on the moors, Ned," called Zoe, running after him with his waterproof coat. "Here, put this on."

"No time to wait for that," he said.

"But you must take time," she returned, catching hold of him and throwing it over his shoulders. "Men must obey their wives once in a while. Lu's not drowning. Don't you believe it. She may as well get a wetting as you."

Gracie, hiding her head in Violet's lap, was sobbing bitterly, the latter stroking her hair in a soothing way, but too full of grief and alarm herself to speak any comforting words.

"Don't cry, Gracie. Vi, don't look so distressed," said Betty. "Lulu, like myself, is one of those people that need never be worried about—the bad pennies always turn up again."

"Then she isn't fit for heaven," remarked Rosie in an undertone not meant for her sister's ear. "But I don't believe," she added in a louder key, "that there is anything worse the matter than too long a walk for her to get back in good season."

"That is my opinion, Vi," said Mrs. Dinsmore. And Elsie added, "Mine also."

No one spoke again for a moment or two, and in the silence the heavy boom of the surf on the beach below came distinctly to their ears. Then there was a vivid flash of lightning and a terrific thunder crash, followed instantly by a heavy downpour of rain.

"And she is out in all this!" exclaimed Violet in tones of deep distress. "Dear child, if I only had her here safe in my arms, or if her father were here to look after her!"

"And punish her," added Rosie. "It's my humble opinion that if ever a girl her age needed a good whipping, she does."

"Rosie," said her mother with unusual severity, "I will not allow you to talk in that way. Lulu's faults are different from yours, but perhaps no worse. For while she is passionate and not sufficiently amenable to authority, you are showing yourself both uncharitable and Pharisaical."

"Well, mamma," Rosie answered, blushing deeply at the reproof. "I cannot help feeling angry with her for giving poor Vi so much unnecessary worry and distress of mind. And I am sure her father must have felt troubled and mortified by the way she behaved for two or three days while he was here."

"But he loves her very deeply," said Violet. "He loves her so dearly that to lose her in this way would surely break his heart."

"But I tell you he is not going to lose her in this way," said Betty in a lively tone. "Don't be a bit afraid of it."

But Violet could not share that comfortable assurance. To her it seemed more than likely Lulu had been too venturesome, and that a swiftly incoming wave had carried her off her feet and swept her in its recoil into the boiling sea.

"I shall never see the dear child again!" was her anguished thought. "And oh, what news to write to her father! He will not blame me, I know, but oh, I cannot help blame myself that I did not miss her sooner and send some one to search for her and bring her back."

Elsie read her daughter's distress in her speaking countenance, and sitting down by her side, she tried to cheer her with loving, hopeful words.

"Dear Vi," she said, "I have a strong impression that the child is not lost and will be here presently. But whatever has happened, or may happen, stay your heart, dear one, upon your God. Trust Him for the child, for your husband, and for yourself. You know that troubles do not spring out of the ground, and to His children He gives help and deliverance out of all He sends them.

"'God is our refuge and strength, a very present help in trouble.' 'He shall deliver thee in six troubles: yea in seven there shall no evil touch thee.'"

There was perhaps not more than a half hour of this trying suspense between Edward's departure in search of the missing child and her sudden appearance in their midst—sudden it seemed because the roar of the sea and howling of the storm drowned all other sounds from without, and prevented any echo of approaching footsteps.

"Lulu!" they all cried in varied tones of surprise and relief, as they started up and gathered about her dripping figure.

"Where have you been?"

"How wet you are!"

"Oh, dear child, I am so glad and thankful to see you. I have been terribly frightened about you!" This last was from Violet.

"I—I didn't mean to be out so late or to go so far," stammered Lulu. "And I didn't see the storm coming up in time, and it caught and hindered me. Please, Mamma Vi and Grandma Elsie, don't be angry about it. I won't ever do so again."

"We won't stop to talk about it now," Elsie said, answering for Violet and herself. "Your clothes must be changed instantly, for you are as wet as if you had been in the sea. And that with fresh water, so there is great danger of your taking cold."

"I should think the best plan would be for her to be rubbed with a coarse towel till reaction sets in fully and then directly to bed," said Mrs. Dinsmore.

"If that is done we may hope to find her as well in the morning as if she had not had this exposure to the storm."

Lulu made no objection nor resistance, being only too glad to escape so easily. Still she was not quite sure that some punishment might not be in store for her on the morrow. And she had an uncomfortable impression that were it not for her father's absence it might not be a very light one.

When she was snugly in bed, Grandma Elsie came to her, bringing with her own hands a great tumbler of hot lemonade.

"Drink this, Lulu," she said in her own sweet voice and with a loving look that made the little girl heartily ashamed of having given so much trouble and anxiety. "It will be very good for you, I think, as well as palatable."

"Thank you, ma'am," Lulu said, tasting it. "It is delicious, so strong of both lemon and sugar."

"I am glad you like it. Drink it all if you can," Elsie said.

When Lulu had drained the tumbler it was carried away. Grandma Elsie, still sitting beside the bed, asked, "Are you sleepy, my child? If you are we will defer our talk till tomorrow morning. If not, we will have it now."

"I'm not sleepy," Lulu answered, blushing and averting her face. She added to herself, "I suppose it's got to come, and I'd rather have it over."

"You know, my child, that in the absence of your father and mine you are in my care. I am responsible for you, while you are accountable to me for your good and bad behavior. Such being the case, it is now my duty to ask you to give an account of your whereabouts and doings in the hours that you were absent from us this evening."

Lulu replied by an exact statement of the truth, pleading in excuse for her escapade her father's permission to stroll about the beach, even alone, for her enjoyment of the exercise of walking along the bluff, and her absorbing interest in the changing beauty of sky and sea. These all tended to render her oblivious of time and space, so that on being suddenly reminded of them she found herself much farther from home than she had supposed.

"Was it not merely within certain limits you were given permission to ramble about the beach?" Elsie asked gently.

"Yes, ma'am. Papa said I was not to go far, and I did not intend to. Indeed, indeed, Grandma Elsie, I had not the least intention of disobeying, but I forgot everything in the pleasure of the walk and the beautiful sights."

"Do you think that is sufficient excuse, and ought to be accepted as fully exonerating you from blame in regard to this matter?"

"I don't think people can help forgetting sometimes," Lulu replied, a trifle sullenly.

"I remember that in dealing with me as a child my father would never take forgetfulness of his orders as any excuse for disobedience. And though it seemed hard then, I have since thought he was right, because the forgetfulness is almost always the result of not having deemed the matter of sufficient importance to duly charge the memory with it.

"In the Bible God both warns us against forgetting and bids us always to remember: 'Remember all the commandments of the Lord, and do them.'

"'Remember the Sabbath day, to keep it holy.'

"'Beware lest thou forget the Lord.'

"'The wicked shall be turned into hell, and all the nations that forgot God.'

"You see that God does not accept forgetfulness as a sufficient excuse, or any excuse for sin."

"Then you won't, of course," muttered Lulu, carefully avoiding looking into the kind face bending over her. "How am I to be punished? I don't feel as if anybody has a right to punish me but papa," she added with a flash of indignant anger.

"I heartily wish he were here to attend to it," was the response, in a kindly pitying tone. "But since, unfortunately, he is not, and my father, too, is absent, the unpleasant duty devolves upon me. I have no thought of being very severe with you, and, perhaps, if you knew all the anxiety and sore distress suffered on your account this evening — particularly by your mamma and little sister — you would be sufficiently punished already."

"Did Mamma Vi care?" Lulu asked softly in an incredulous tone.

"My child, she was almost distracted," Elsie said. "She loves you for both your own and your father's sake. Besides, as she repeated again and again, she was sorely distressed on his account, knowing his love for you to be so great that to lose you would well nigh break his heart."

A flash of joy illumined Lulu's face at this new testimony of her father's love for her, but passed away as suddenly as it came.

"I do feel punished in hearing that you were so troubled about me, Grandma Elsie," she said. "And I mean to be very, very careful not to cause such anxiety again. Please tell Mamma Vi I am sorry to have given her pain. But she really shouldn't care anything about such a naughty girl."

"That, my child, she cannot help," Elsie said. "She loves your father far too well not to love you for his sake and for your own."

After a little more kindly admonishing talk, she went away, leaving a tender, motherly kiss upon the little girl's lips.

At the door Gracie met her with a request for a good night kiss, which was promptly granted.

"Good night, dear little one. Pleasant dreams and a happy awakening, if it be God's will," Elsie said, bending down to touch her lips to the rosebud mouth and let the small arms twine themselves around her neck.

"Good night, dear Grandma Elsie," responded the child. "Oh, aren't you ever so glad God brought our Lulu safely home to us?"

"I am indeed, dear. Let us not forget to thank Him for it in our prayers tonight."

Lulu heard, and as Gracie's arm went round her neck the next moment, and the sweet lips, tremulous with emotion, touched her cheek, she asked with feeling, "Were you so distressed about me, Gracie? Did Mamma Vi care so very much that I might be drowned?"

"Yes, indeed, Lu, dear Lu. Oh, what could I do without my dear sister?"

"You have another one now," suggested Lulu.

"That doesn't make any difference," said Gracie. "She's the darling baby sister, and you are the dear, dear big sister."

"Papa calls me his little girl," remarked Lulu, musingly. "Somehow I like to be little to him and big to you. Oh, Gracie, what do you suppose he will say when he hears about tonight—about my being so bad and so soon after he went away, too?"

"Oh, Lu, what made you?"

"Because I was careless—didn't think, and I begin to believe that it was because I didn't choose to take the trouble," she sighed. "I'm really afraid if papa were here I should get just the same sort of punishment he gave me before. Gracie, remember, don't ever tell anybody about that."

"No, Lu, I promised I wouldn't. But I think you'd be punished enough with all of the wetting and the fright. Weren't you 'most scared to death?"

"No, I was frightened, but not nearly so much as that. Not so much as I should be if papa were to walk in just now. Because he'd have to hear all about it, and then he'd look so sorry and troubled and punish me besides."

"Then you wouldn't be glad to see papa if he came back?" Gracie said in a reproachfully inquiring tone.

"Yes, I should," Lulu answered promptly. "The punishment wouldn't last long, you know. He and I would both get over it pretty soon, and then it would be delightful to have him with us again."

Lulu woke the next morning feeling no ill effects whatever from her exposure to the storm.

Before she and Gracie had quite finished dressing, Grandma Elsie was at their door, asking if they were well. She stayed for a little chat with them, and Lulu asked what her punishment was to be.

"Simply a prohibition of lonely rambles," Elsie answered, with a grave but kindly look. "And I trust it will prove sufficient. You are to keep near the rest of us for your own safety."

CHAPTER NINTH

He that spareth his rod hateth his son;
but he that loveth him chasteneth him betimes.

—*P*ROVERBS *13:24*

WHEN THE MORNING boat had touched in at Nantucket pier there were among the throng which poured ashore two fine looking gentlemen—one in the prime of his life, the other growing a little elderly—who sought out at once a conveyance to 'Sconset.

The hackman who had driven them in before recognized them with evident pleasure mingled with surprise.

"Glad to see you back again, cap'n," he remarked, addressing the younger of his two passengers. "But it's kind of unexpected, isn't it? I understood you'd gone to join your ship, expecting to sail directly for foreign parts."

"Yes, that was all correct," returned Captain Raymond, merrily, for it was he in company with Mr. Dinsmore. "But orders are sometimes countermanded, as they were in this instance, to my no small content."

"They'll be dreadful glad to see you at 'Sconset," was the next remark. "Surprised, too. By the way, sir, your folks had a fright last evening."

"A fright?" inquired both gentlemen in a breath, and exchanged a look of concern.

"Yes, sirs, about one of your little girls, Cap'n— the oldest one I understood it was. Seems she wandered off alone to Tom Never's Head or somewhere in the neighborhood. She was caught by the darkness and storm and didn't find her way home till the older folks had begun to think she'd been swept away by the tide, which was coming in to be sure. They thought it might have been the backward flow of a big wave that had rushed up a little too quick for her, taking her off her feet and hurrying her into the surf before she could safely struggle up again."

All the captain's happiness was gone, and his face wore a pained, troubled look.

"But she did reach home in safety at last?" he inquired hesitantly.

"Oh, yes, all right except for the wetting, which probably did her no harm. But now maybe I'm telling tales out of school," he added with a laugh. "I shouldn't like to get the little girl into trouble. So I hope you'll not be too hard on her, Cap'n. I dare say the fright has been punishment enough to keep her from doing the like again."

"I wish it may have been," was all the captain said.

Then he fell into a reverie so deep that he scarcely caught a word of the brisk conversation in regard to some of the points of interest on the island carried on between Mr. Dinsmore and the hackman.

Lulu was having an uncomfortable day. When she met the family at the breakfast table, Grandma Rose seemed to regard her with cold displeasure. "Mamma Vi" spoke gently and kindly, hoping she felt no injury from last night's exposure but looked wretchedly ill. In answer to her mother's inquiries, Violet admitted that she had been awake most of the night by a violent headache, to which Rosie added in an indignant tone and with an angry glance at Lulu, "Brought on by anxiety in regard to a certain young miss who is always misbehaving and causing a world of trouble to her best friends."

"Rosie, Rosie," Elsie said reprovingly. "Let me hear no more such remarks, or I shall send you from the table."

Lulu had appeared in their midst, feeling humble and contrite. She had been conscience-smitten at the sight of her mamma's pale face, but the sneer on Betty's face, the cold, averted looks of Edward and Zoe, and then Rosie's taunt had roused her quick temper to almost a white heat.

She rose, pushing back her chair with some noise, and turned to leave the table at which she had just seated herself.

"What is it, Lulu?" asked Grandma Elsie in a tone of gentle kindness. "Sit still, my child, and ask for what you want."

"Thank you, ma'am," said Lulu. "I do not want anything but to go away. I'd rather do without my breakfast than stay here to be insulted."

"Sit down, child," repeated Elsie as gently and kindly as before. "Rosie will make no more unkind remarks, and we will all try to treat you as we would wish to be treated were we in your place."

No one else spoke. Lulu resumed her seat and ate her breakfast, but with little appetite or enjoyment. Upon leaving the table, she tried to avoid contact with any of those who had caused her offense.

"May I go down to the beach, Grandma Elsie?" she asked in low, constrained tones with her eyes upon the floor.

"If you will go directly there, to the seats under the awning which we usually occupy, and not wander from them farther than they are from the cliff," Elsie answered. "Promise me that you will keep within those bounds, and I shall know I may trust you, for you are an honest child."

The cloud lifted slightly from Lulu's brow at those kindly words. She gave promise and walked slowly away.

As she descended the stairway that led down the face of the cliff, she saw that Edward and Zoe were sitting side by side on one of the benches under the family's awning.

She did not fancy their company just now and knew hers would not be acceptable to them. She thought she would pass them and seat herself in the sand a little farther on.

Edward was speaking as she came up behind them, and she heard him say, "It was the most uncomfortable meal ever eaten in our family—and all because of that ungovernable child."

Lulu flushed hotly and stepping past turned and confronted him with flashing eyes.

"I heard you, Uncle Edward, though I had no intention of listening," she said. "I say it is very unjust to blame me so when it was Rosie's insulting tongue and other people's cold, contemptuous looks that almost drove me wild."

"You are far too easily driven wild," he said. "It is high time you learned to have some control over your temper. If I were your father I'd teach it to you, even if I must try the virtue of a rod again and again. You should also learn proper submission to authority, young lady, if it had to be taught in the same manner."

Lulu was too angry to speak for a moment. She stood silent, trembling with passion. But at length she burst out, "It's none of your business how papa manages me, Mr. Travilla, and I'm very glad he's my father instead of you!"

"You are a very saucy girl, Lulu Raymond," said Zoe, reddening with anger on her husband's account. "And shamefully ungrateful for all Mr. Travilla's kind exertions on your behalf last night."

"Hush, hush, Zoe. Do not remind her of it," Edward said. "'A benefit upbraided forfeits thanks.' I should have done quite the same for anyone in danger and distress."

"What was it?" asked Lulu. "Nobody told me he had done anything."

"He was out for hours in that storm, hunting for you," replied Zoe with a proudly admiring glance at her husband.

"I'm very much obliged," said Lulu, her voice softening. "And sorry to hear that you suffered on my account," she added.

"I did not suffer anything worth mentioning," he responded. "However, your mamma was very sorely distressed—thinking you might be in the sea. In consequence, she had a dreadful headache all night, and since such dire consequences may follow upon your disregard for the rules and lawful authority, Lulu, I insist that you be more amenable to them.

"I believe that you think that when your father and grandpa are both away you can do pretty much as you please. But you shall not while I am about. I won't have my mother's authority set at defiance by you or anyone else."

"Who wants to set it at defiance?" demanded Lulu, wrathfully. "Not I, I am sure. But I won't be ruled by you—for papa never said I should."

"I think I shall take down this conversation and report it to him," Edward said, only half in earnest.

Lulu turned quickly away, greatly disturbed by the threat, but she resolved that her alarm should not be perceived by either him or Zoe. Walking a few yards from them, she sat down upon the sand and amused herself digging in it, but her thoughts were busied with the problem, "What will papa say and do if that conversation is reported to him?"

A very short consideration of the question at hand convinced her that if present her father would say she had been extremely impertinent, punish her for it, and make her apologize.

Presently came a glance toward the cottages on the bluff showed Violet and Gracie descending the stairway. She rose and hurried to meet them.

"Mamma Vi," she said as soon as within hearing, "I am ever so sorry to have frightened you so last night and to have given you a headache. But you oughtn't to care whether such a naughty girl as I am is drowned or not."

"How can you talk so, Lulu dear?" Violet answered, putting her arm round the child's waist and giving her a gentle kiss. "Do you think your Mamma Vi has no real love for you? If so, you are much mistaken. I love you, Lulu, for yourself, and dearly for your father's sake. Oh, I wish you loved him well enough to try harder to be good in order to add to his happiness. It would add to it more than anything else that I know of. Your naughtiness does not deprive you of his fatherly affection, but it does rob him of much enjoyment, which he would otherwise have."

Lulu hung her head in silence, turned, and walked away full of self-accusing and penitent thoughts. She was not crying. Tears did not come so readily to her eyes as to those of many children her age, but her heart was aching with remorseful love for her absent father.

"To think that I spoiled his visit home," she sighed to herself. "Oh, I wish he could come back to have it over again, and I would try to be good and not spoil his enjoyment in the very least!"

"Come back now?" something seemed to reply. "Suppose he should. Wouldn't he punish you for your behavior since he left only two days ago?"

"Yes," she sighed. "I haven't the least doubt that if he were here and knew all, he would punish me severely again. And I suppose he wouldn't be long in the house before he would hear it all; yet for all that I should be—oh, so glad if he could come back to stay a good while."

Last night's storm had spent itself in a few hours and the morning was bright and clear. However, a long drive planned for that day by our friends was unanimously postponed, as several of them had lost sleep and wanted to make it up with a nap.

Violet sought her couch immediately after dinner and slept off the last remains of her headache. About the middle of the afternoon, she was preparing to go down to the beach, where all the others were, except Gracie, who was seldom far from mamma's side, when the outer door opened, and a step and a voice were heard that she had not hoped to hear again for months or years.

The next moment she was in her husband's arms, her head pillowed on his shoulder, while his lips were pressed again and again to brow, cheek, and lips. Gracie's glad shout arose in sweet, silvery tones, "Papa has come back! Papa has come back! My dear, dear papa!"

"Can it be possible, my dear, dear husband?" cried Violet, lifting to his a face radiant with total happiness. "It seems too good to be true."

"Not quite as good as that," he said with a joyous laugh. "But it is quite a satisfaction to find that you are not sorry to see me."

"Of which you were terribly afraid, of course," she returned merrily. "Do tell me at once how long our powers of endurance of such uncongenial society are to be taxed?"

"Ah, that is beyond my ability."

"Then we may hope for weeks or months?" she said rapturously.

"Certainly we are not forbidden to hope," he answered, smiling tenderly upon her.

"Oh, I am so glad!" she said with a happy sigh, leaning her head on his shoulder and gazing fondly up into his face. His right arm was about her waist, while Gracie clung to his other hand, holding it lovingly between her own and pressing her lips to it again and again.

"My darling little girl," he said presently, letting Violet go to take Gracie in his arms. "Are you glad to see papa back again so soon?"

"Oh, yes, indeed. Nothing else could have made me so very, very glad!" she cried, hugging him close and giving and receiving many tender caresses.

"But how did it come to be so, Levis—that you should return so soon?" Violet asked.

"Through some unlooked-for change in the plans and purposes of the higher powers," he answered lightly. "My orders were countermanded with no reason given, and I may remain with my family till further orders. And, as you say, we will hope it may be months before they are received."

"And you were glad to come back to us?" Violet said, inquiringly, with but a shade of doubt in her tender tones.

"Yes, indeed. I was full of joy till I heard that one of my children had been disobeying me, bringing serious consequences upon herself and others."

His countenance had grown very grave and stern. "Violet, where is Lulu?" he asked, glancing about in search of her.

"Down on the beach with the rest of the family," Violet answered.

"Can you give me a true and full account of her behavior since I have been away?" he asked.

"My dear husband," Violet said entreatingly, "please, do not ask me."

"Pardon me, dearest," he returned. "I should not have asked you. Lulu must tell me herself. Thankful I am that many and serious as are her faults, she is yet so honest and truthful that I can put full confidence in her word and feel sure that she will not deceive me, even to save herself from punishment."

"I think that is high praise, and that Lulu is deserving of it," remarked Violet, very glad of an opportunity to speak a word in the child's favor.

Captain Raymond gave her a pleased, grateful look. "You were going to the beach, were you not?" he said. "Then, please go on. I shall follow after I have settled this matter with Lulu. There can be no comfort for her or myself till it is settled.

Gracie, go and tell your older sister to come here to me immediately."

"Do be as lenient as your sense of duty will allow, dear husband," whispered Violet in his ear then hastened on her way.

Gracie was lingering, gazing at him with wistful, tear-filled eyes.

"What is it?" he asked, bending down to smooth her hair caressingly. "You should go at once, little daughter, when papa bids."

"I would, papa, only—only, I wanted to—to ask you not to punish Lulu very hard."

"I am glad my little Gracie loves her sister," he said. "You need never doubt, my darling, that I dearly love both her and you. Go now and give her my message."

All day long Lulu had kept herself as far apart from the others—her sister excepted—as lay in her power. She was sitting now alone in the sand—no one within several yards of her, her hands folded in her lap, while she gazed far out to sea, her eyes following a sail in the distant offing.

"Perhaps that is papa's ship," she was saying to herself. "Oh, how long will it be before we see him again? And oh, how sorry he will be when he hears about last night and this morning!"

At that instant she felt Gracie's arms suddenly thrown round her, while the sweet child voice exclaimed in an ecstasy of delight, "Oh, Lu, he has come! He has, he has!"

"Who?" Lulu asked, with a start and tremble that reminded Gracie of the message she had to deliver and that Lulu's pleasure at their father's unexpected return could not be so unalloyed as her own. She had forgotten all of that for the moment in the rapture and delight she herself felt at his coming.

"Papa, Lulu," she answered, sobering down a good deal. "And I was 'most forgetting that he sent me to tell you to come to him immediately."

"Did he?" Lulu asked, trembling more than before. "Does he know about last night, Gracie? Did Mamma Vi tell him?"

"He knows 'bout it. Somebody told him before he got to 'Sconset," said Gracie. "But mamma didn't tell him at all. He asked her, but she begged him to please not ask her. Mamma doesn't ever tell tales on us, I'm sure."

"No, I don't believe she does. But what did papa say then?"

"That you should tell him all about it yourself. He said you were an honest child, serious as your faults were, and he could trust you to own the truth, even when you were to be punished for it. But, Lulu, you have to go right up to the house. Papa said 'immediately.'"

"Yes," Lulu replied, getting upon her feet very slowly and looking a good deal frightened. "Did papa seem very angry?"

"I think he intends to punish you," Gracie replied in a sorrowful tone. "But maybe he won't if you say you're sorry and won't do it any more. But hurry, Lulu, or he may punish you for not obeying him promptly."

"Is Mamma Vi there?" asked Lulu, still lingering.

"No, yonder she is. Don't you see?" said Gracie, nodding her head in the direction of the awning under which nearly the whole party were now seated. "There's nobody there but papa. Oh hurry, Lulu, or he will whip you, I'm afraid."

"Don't you ever say that before anybody, Gracie," Lulu said, low and tremulously. Then she turned and walked rapidly toward the stairway that led up the bluff to the cottages.

At a window looking toward the bluff the captain stood, watching for Lulu's coming.

"She is not yielding very prompt obedience to the order," he said to himself. "But what wonder? The poor child doubtless dreads the interview extremely. In fact, I should be only too glad to escape it. 'Tis a disagreeable task to have to deal out justice to one's own child—a child so lovable, in spite of her faults. How much easier to pass the matter over slightly, merely administering a gentle reprimand! But no, I cannot. 'Twould be like healing slightly the festering sore that threatens the citadel of life. I must be faithful to my God-given trust, however trying to my feelings. Ah, there she is!" he said, as a little girl figure appeared at the top of the staircase and hurried across the intervening space to the open doorway.

There she halted, trembling and with downcast eyes. It was a minute or more before she ventured to lift them, and then it was a very timid glance she sent in her father's direction.

He was looking at her with a very grave, rather stern countenance, and her eyes fell again while she shrank from approaching him.

"You are not very glad to see me, I think," he said, holding out his hand, but with no relaxing of the sternness of his expression.

"Oh, papa, yes! Yes, indeed, I am!" she burst out, springing to his side and putting her hand in his. "Even though I suppose you are going to punish me just as you did the last time."

He drew her to his knee, but without offering her the slightest caress.

"Won't you kiss me, papa?" she asked with a stifled little sob.

"I will. But you are not to take it as a token of favor—only of your father's love that is never withdrawn from you, even when he is most severe in the punishment of your faults," he answered, pressing his lips again and again to forehead, cheeks, and lips. "What have you done that you expect so severe a punishment?"

"Papa, you know, don't you?" she said, hiding her blushing face on his chest.

"I choose to have you tell me. I want a full and complete confession of all the wrong-doing you have been guilty of since I left you the other day."

"I disobeyed you last night, papa—about taking a long walk by myself. I forgot to notice how far I was going—at least, I didn't notice," she stammered, remembering that she had willfully refrained from so doing.

"You forgot? Forgot to pay attention to your father's commands? Did you not think them of sufficient importance for you to take the trouble to impress them upon your mind? I cannot accept that excuse as a good and sufficient one.

"And tell me honestly. Are you not, as I strongly suspect, less careful to obey your father's orders when he is away. Do you not feel yourself in a measure more out of his reach, than when he is close at hand?"

"Papa, you ask such hard questions," she replied.

"Hard to my little daughter only because of her wrong-doing. But hard or easy, they must be answered. Tell me the truth. Would you not have been more careful to keep within the prescribed bounds last night if I had been at home, or you had known that you would see me here today?"

"Yes, papa," she answered, in a low, unwilling tone. "I don't think anybody else can have quite so much authority over me as you, and—and so I do, I suppose, act a little more as if I could do as I please when you are away."

"And that after I have explained to you again and again that in my absence you are quite as much under the authority of the kind friends with whom I have placed you as under mine when I am with you. I see there is no effectual way to teach you this lesson but by punishing you for disregarding it."

Then he made her give him a detailed account of her ramble of the night before and its consequences.

When she had gone so far in the narrative as her safe arrival among the alarmed household, he asked whether or not Grandma Elsie inflicted any punishment upon her.

"No, sir," answered Lulu, hanging her head and speaking in a sullen tone. "I told her I didn't feel as if anybody had any right to punish me but you."

"Lulu! Did you dare to talk in that way to her?" exclaimed the captain. "I hope she punished you immediately for your impertinence, for if she did not, I certainly must."

"She lectured me then, and this morning told me my punishment was a prohibition against wandering away from the rest more than just a few yards.

"But, papa, they were all so unkind to me at breakfast—I mean all but Grandma Elsie and Mamma Vi and Gracie. Betty looked sneering, and the others so cold and distant. Rosie said something very insulting about my being a bad, troublesome child and frightening Mamma Vi into a headache."

"Certainly no more than you deserved," her father said. "Did you bear it with patience and humility, as you ought?"

"Do you mean that I must answer you, papa?"

"Most assuredly I do. Tell me at once exactly what you did and said."

"I don't want to, papa," she said, angrily.

"You are never to say that when I give you an order," he returned in a tone of severity. "Never venture to do it again. Tell me, word for word, as nearly as you can remember it, what reply you made to Rosie's taunt."

"Papa, I didn't say anything to her. I just got up and pushed back my chair. I turned to leave the table, but then Grandma Elsie asked me what I wanted. I said I didn't want anything but would rather go without my breakfast than stay there to be insulted. Then she told me to sit down and eat, and Rosie wouldn't make any more unkind speeches."

"And were they all pleasant to you after that?" he asked.

"No, papa. They haven't been pleasant to me at all today. And Uncle Edward has said hateful things about me and to me," she went on, her cheek flushing and her eyes flashing with anger. She had forgotten in the excitement of her passion to whom she was telling her story and showing her want of self-control.

"And I very much fear," he said gravely, "that you were both passionate and impertinent. Tell me just what passed."

"If I do, you'll punish me. I know you will," she burst out. "Papa, don't you think it's a little mean to make me tell on myself and then punish me for what you find out in that way?"

"If my object was merely to give pain, I think it would be mean enough," he said, not unkindly. "But as I am seeking your best interests—your truest happiness—in trying to gain full insight into your character and conduct, meaning to discipline you only for your highest good, I think it is not mean or unkind. From your unwillingness to confess to me, I fear you must have been in a great passion and very impertinent. Is it not so?"

"Papa, I didn't begin it. If I'd been left alone, I shouldn't have got into a passion or said anything at all saucy."

"Possibly not. But what is that virtue worth which cannot stand the least trial? You must learn to rule your own spirit—not only when everything goes smoothly with you, but under provocation. In order to help you to learn that lesson—or rather as a means toward teaching it to you—I shall invariably punish any and every outbreak of yours that comes under my notice when I am at home. Now, tell me exactly what passed between your Uncle Edward and yourself."

Seeing that there was no escape for her, Lulu complied, faithfully repeating every word of the short colloquy at the beach when she went down there directly after breakfast.

Her father listened in astonishment, his face growing sterner every moment.

"Lucilla," he said, "you are certainly the most impertinent, insolent child I ever saw! I don't wonder you were afraid to let me know the whole truth in regard to this affair. I am ashamed of your conduct toward both your Grandma Elsie and your

Uncle Edward. You must apologize to both of them, acknowledging that you have been extremely impertinent and asking for forgiveness for it."

Lulu made no reply. Her eyes were downcast, her face flushed with passion, and she wore quite a stubborn look.

"I won't," the words were on the tip of her tongue. She had almost spoken them but restrained herself just in time. Her father's authority was not to be defied, as she had learned to her cost a year ago.

He saw the struggle that was going on in her heart. "You must do it," he said. "You may write your apologies, though, if you prefer that to speaking them."

He opened a writing desk that stood on a table close at hand, seated her before it with paper, pen, and ink, and bade her write at his dictation.

She did not dare refuse and had really no very strong disinclination to do so in regard to the first, which was addressed to Grandma Elsie—a lady so gentle and kind that even proud Lulu was willing to humble herself to her.

But when it came to Edward's turn, her whole soul rose up in rebellion against it. Yet she dared not say either, "I won't" or, "I don't want to." But pausing, with the pen in her fingers, "Papa," she began timidly, "please, don't make me apologize to him. He really had no real right to talk to me the way he did."

"I am not so sure of that," the captain said. "I don't blame him for trying to uphold his mother's authority. And now I think of it, you are to consider yourself under his control in the absence of your mamma and the older persons to whom I have given authority over you. Begin at once and write what I have told you to."

When the notes were written, signed, and folded he put them in his pocket, turned, and paced the floor to and fro.

"Papa, are you—are you going to punish me?" she asked, tremulously. "I mean as you did the other day?"

"I think I must," he said, pausing beside her. "Though it grieves me to the very heart to do it. Lulu, you have been disobedient, passionate, and very impertinent. It is quite impossible for me to let you slip. But you may take your choice between that and being locked up in the bedroom there for twenty-four hours, on bread and water. Which shall it be?"

"I'd rather take the first, papa," said Lulu promptly. "Because it will be over in a few minutes and nobody but ourselves need know anything about it."

"I was certain you would choose the other," he said in some surprise. "Yet I think your choice is wise. Come!"

"Oh, papa, I'm so frightened," she said, putting her trembling hand in his. "You did hurt me so dreadfully the last time. Must you be so severe today, as well?"

"My poor child, I am afraid I must," he said. "A slight punishment seems to avail nothing in your case, and I must do all in my power to make you a good, gentle, obedient child."

A few minutes later, Captain Raymond joined the others on the beach, but Lulu was not with him. She had been left behind in the bedroom, where she must stay, he told her, until his return.

Everybody seemed glad to see him, and after greeting them all in turn, he drew Violet to a seat a little apart from the others.

Gracie followed, of course, keeping close to her father's side. "Where is Lulu, papa?" she asked with a look of concern.

"Up at the house."

"Won't you let her come down here, papa? She loves so to be close down by the waves."

"She may come after a little, but not just now," he said. Then, taking two tiny notes from his pocket, he said, "Here, Gracie, take this to your Grandma Elsie and this to your Uncle Edward."

"Yes, sir. Must I wait for an answer?"

"Oh, no," he replied with a slight smile. "You may come right back to your place by papa's side."

Elsie read the little missive handed her at a glance, rose up hastily, and went to the captain with it in her hand. She wore a troubled look on her face.

"My dear captain," she said in a tone of gentle remonstrance, "why did you do this? The child's offense against me was not a grave one in my esteem, and I know that to one of her temperament it would be extremely galling to be made to apologize. I wish you had not required it of her."

"I thought it for her good, mother," he answered. "And, I think so still. She is so strongly inclined to impertinence and insubordination that I must do all in my power to train her to proper submission to lawful authority and respect for superiors."

Edward joined them at that moment. He looked disturbed and chagrined.

"Really, captain," he said, "I am not at all sure that Lulu has not as much right to an apology from me as I to this from her. I spoke to her in anger and with an assumption of authority to which I really had no right. There was ample excuse for her not particularly respectful language to me. I am sorry, therefore, she has had the pain of apologizing."

"You are very kind to be so ready to overlook her insolence," the captain said. "But I cannot permit such exhibitions of temper, and I must, at whatever cost, teach her to rule her own spirit."

"Doubtless you are right," Edward said. "But I am concerned and mortified to find that I have got her into such disgrace and trouble. I must own I am quite attracted to Lulu. She has some very noble and lovable traits of character."

"She has indeed," said his mother. "She is so free from the least taint of hypocrisy or deceit, so perfectly honest and truthful, so warm-hearted, too, so diligent and energetic in anything she undertakes to do, so very painstaking and persevering, and so brave and womanly a little thing."

The captain's face brightened very much as he listened to these praises of his child.

"I thank you heartily, mother and brother," he said. "The child is very dear to her father's heart, and praise of her is sweet to my ear. I can see all these lovable traits, but feared that to other eyes than mine they might be entirely obscured by the very grave faults joined with them. But it is just like you both to look at the good rather than the evil.

"And you have done so much for my children! I assure you I often think of it with the feeling that you have laid me under obligations which I can never repay."

"Ah, captain," Elsie said laughingly. "You have a fashion of making a great mountain out of a little mole hill of kindness. Flattery is not good for human nature, you know, so I shall leave you and go back to papa, who has a wholesome way of telling me of my faults and failings."

"I really don't know where he finds them," returned Captain Raymond gallantly, but she was already out of hearing.

"Nor I," said Violet, replying to his last remark. "Mamma seems to me to be so nearly perfect as a human creature can be in this sinful world."

"Now, don't feel troubled about it, Ned," Zoe was saying to her husband who was again at her side. "I think it was just right that she should be made to apologize to you, for she was dreadfully saucy."

"Yes, but I provoked her, and I ought to be and am, greatly ashamed of it. I fear, too, that in so doing I have brought a rather severe punishment upon her."

"Why should you think so?"

"Because I know that such a task could not fail to be exceedingly unpalatable to one of her temperament. Don't you remember how long she stood out against her father's authority last summer when he bade her ask Vi's pardon for her impertinence to her?"

"Yes, it took nearly a week of close confinement to make her do it. But as he showed himself so determined in that instance, she probably saw that it would be useless to attempt opposition to his will in this, and so she obeyed without being compelled by punishment."

"Well, I hope so," he said. "She surely ought to know by this time that the captain is not one to be trifled with."

It seemed to Lulu a long time that she was left alone, shut up in the little bedroom of the cottage, though it was in reality scarcely more than half an hour. She was very glad when at last she heard her father's step in the outer room, then his voice as he opened the door and asked, "Would you like to take a walk with your papa, little girl?"

"Yes, indeed, papa!" was her joyful reply.

"Then put on your hat and come."

She made all haste to obey.

"Is Gracie going too, papa? Or anybody else?" she asked, putting her hand confidingly into his.

"No, you and I are going alone this time. Do you think you will find my company sufficient for once?" he asked, smiling down at her.

"Oh, yes, indeed, papa. I think it will be ever so nice to have you all to myself. It's so seldom I can."

They took the path along the bluffs toward Tom Never's Head.

When they had fairly left the village behind, so that no one could overhear anything they might say to each other, the captain said, "I want to have a talk with you, daughter. We may as well take it out here in the sweet, fresh air as shut up in the house."

"Oh, yes, papa. It is so much more pleasant! I can hardly bear to stay in the house at all down here at the seashore. It seemed a long while that you left me alone there this afternoon."

"Yes, I suppose so. Lulu, I hope I shall not have occasion to do so again. My child, did you ever consider what it is that makes you so rebellious, so unwilling to submit to authority, and so ready to fly into a passion and speak so insolently to your superiors?"

"I don't quite understand you, papa," she said. "I only know that I can't bear to have people try to rule me who have no right."

"Sometimes you are not willing to be ruled even by your father. I hardly suppose you would say he has no right."

"Oh, no, papa, I know better than that," she said, blushing and hanging her head. "I know you have the best right in the world."

"Yet, sometimes you disobey me. At other times you obey in an angry, unwilling way that shows you would rebel if you dared.

"And pride is at the bottom of it all. You think so highly of yourself and your own wisdom that you cannot bear to be controlled or treated as one not capable of guiding herself.

"But the Bible tells us that God hates pride. 'Everyone that is proud in heart is an abomination to the Lord, though hand join in hand, he shall not be unpunished.'

"'Pride goeth before destruction, and a haughty spirit before a fall.'

"'Proud and haughty scorner is his name who dealeth in proud wrath.'

"Ah, my dear daughter, I am sorely troubled when I reflect on how often you deal in that. My great desire for you is that you may learn to rule your own spirit. I pray that you may become meek and lowly in heart, patient and gentle like the Lord Jesus, 'who when He was reviled, reviled not again; when He suffered, He threatened not; but committed Himself to Him that judgeth righteously.' Do you never feel any desire to be like Him?"

"Yes, papa, sometimes, and I determine that I will. But the first thing I know I'm in a passion again. I get so discouraged that I think I'll not try any more to be good, for I just can't."

"It is Satan who puts that thought in your heart," the captain said, giving her a look of grave concern. "He knows that if he can persuade you to cease to fight against the evil that is in your nature, he is sure to get possession of you at last.

"He is a most malignant spirit, and his delight is in destroying souls. The Bible bids us, 'Be sober, be vigilant, because your adversary the devil as a roaring lion walketh about, seeking whom he may devour.'

"We are all sinners by nature, and Satan and many lesser evil spirits under him are constantly seeking our destruction. Therefore, we have a warfare to wage if we would attain eternal life, and no one who refuses or neglects to fight this good fight of faith will ever reach heaven. Nor will anyone who attempts it without asking help from on high.

"So, if you give up trying to be good, you and I will have a sad time because it will be my duty to compel you to try. The Bible tells me, 'Withhold not correction from the child; for if thou beatest him with the rod he shall not die. Thou shalt beat him with the rod, and shalt deliver his soul from hell.'

"I must, if possible, deliver you from going to that awful place, and also from the dreadful calamities indulgence of a furious temper sometimes brings even in this life. Even a woman has been known to commit murder while under the influence of unbridled rage, and I have known of one who lamed her child for life in a fit of passion.

"Sometimes people become deranged simply from the indulgence of their tempers. Do you think I should be a good and kind father if I allowed you to go on in a path that leads to such dreadful ends here and hereafter?"

"No, sir," she said in an awed tone. "I promise I will try to control my temper."

"I am glad to hear that resolve," he replied. "The Bible tells us, 'He that is slow to anger is better than the mighty; and he that ruleth his spirit than he that taketh a city.'"

They were silent for a little while. Hanging her head and blushing, she asked, "Papa, what did you do with those notes you made me write?"

"Sent them to those to whom they were addressed. And they were very kind, Lulu, much kinder than you deserved they should be. Both your Grandma Elsie and your Uncle Edward expressed regret that you had been made to apologize, and spoke of you in very affectionate terms."

"I'm glad," she said with a sigh of relief. "I don't mean ever to be impertinent to them again."

"I trust you will not," he said.

"Papa, I think this is about where I was the other evening when I first noticed how far away I was and that the storm was coming."

"A long way from home for a child of your age, especially alone and at night. You must not indulge your propensity for wandering to a distance from home by yourself. You are too young to understand the danger of it, too young to be a guide to yourself, and must therefore be content to be guided by older and wiser people.

"You said a while ago, 'I just can't be good.' Did you mean to assert that you could not help being disobedient to me that evening?"

She hung her head and her face colored deeply. Then hesitantly, she said, "It was so pleasant to walk along slowly, looking at the beautiful, changing sea, papa, that I couldn't bear to stop and wouldn't let myself think about how very far I was actually going."

"Ah, just as I suspected. Your 'could not' was really 'would not.' The difficulty is all in your will. You must learn to conquer your will when it would take you in the wrong direction.

"We will turn and go back now, as it is not far from tea time."

Lulu shrank from meeting the rest of their party, particularly Grandma Elsie and Edward, but they all treated her so kindly that she was soon at her ease among them again.

CHAPTER TENTH

I am rupt, and cannot
Cover the monstrous bulk of this ingratitude
With any size of words.

— SHAKESPEARE

THE NEXT DAY THEY all set out soon after breakfast for a long drive, taking the direction of the camping ground of the lads where they called and greatly astonished Max with a sight of his father, whom he supposed to be far out on the ocean.

The boy's delight fully equaled his surprise, and he was inclined to return immediately to 'Sconset. However, the captain advised him to stay a little longer where he was. He accordingly decided to do so, though he regretted the loss of even an hour of the society of the father who was to him the best man in the world and the most gallant and capable officer of the navy. In short, Max thought his father the embodiment of all that was good and wise and brave.

The 'Sconset cottages had been engaged only until the first of September. By that time the family was so in love with life upon the island that, learning of some cottages on the cliffs a little northwest of Nantucket Town, which were just vacated and for rent, they engaged two of them and at once moved in.

From their new abodes they had a fine view of the ocean on that side of the island and from their porches could watch the swift sailing yachts and other vessels passing to and fro.

The bathing ground was reached by a succession of stairways built into the face of the cliff. The surf was fine and bathing less dangerous there than at 'Sconset. Those of them who were fond of the sport found it most enjoyable, but the captain took the children into the town almost every day for a lesson in swimming, where the still bathing made it easy for them.

Now they took almost daily sails on the harbor, occasionally venturing out into the ocean itself. There were pleasant drives, also — visiting the old windmill, the old graveyards, the soldiers' monument, and every place of interest in the vicinity.

Besides these, there was a little trip to Martha's Vineyard, and several were taken to various points on the adjacent shores of the mainland.

Much as they had enjoyed the quiet 'Sconset life, it now seemed very pleasant to be again where they could pay frequent visits to libraries and stores, go to church, and now and then attend a concert or lecture.

And there was a good deal of quiet pleasure to be found in rambles about the streets and strange byways and lanes of the quaint old town, looking at its odd houses and gardens and perhaps catching a glimpse of the life going on within.

They gained an entrance to some. One day it was to the home of an old sea captain who had given up his former occupation and now wove baskets of various sizes and shapes — all very neat, strong, and substantial in size.

There was always something pleasant to do. Sometimes it was to take the train on the little three-mile railroad to Surfside and pass an hour or two there. They again visited the Athenaeum and examined its stores for curiosities and treasures, mostly of the sea. They were also known to select a book from its library or to spend an hour among the old china and antique furniture offered for sale to summer visitors.

They were admitted to see the cast of the dauphin and bought photographs of it. They also purchased many of the scenes in and about the town with which to refresh their memories of the delightful old place when far away or to show to friends who had never had the pleasure of a visit to its shores. Violet spent many an enjoyable hour in sketching, finding no lack of subjects worthy of her pencil. Those of the party who liked botany found curious and interesting specimens among the flora of the island.

They had very delightful weather most of the time, but there was an occasional rainy day when their employments and amusements must be such as could be found within doors.

But even these days, with the aid of fancywork and drawing materials, newspapers, magazines and books, conversation and games, were very far from dull and wearisome. Often one read aloud while the others listened.

One day Elsie brought out a story in manuscript.

"I have been thinking," she said, "that this might interest you all as being a tale of actual occurrences during the time of the French Revolution, as we have been thinking and talking so much of that in connection with the story of the little dauphin."

"What is it? Who is the author?" asked her father.

"It is an historical story written by Molly," she answered. "For the benefit of the children I will make a few preparatory remarks," she added lightly and with a pleasant smile.

"While France was torn by those terrible internal convulsions, it was also fighting the combined armies of other nations, particularly Austria and Prussia, who were moved against it in sympathy with the king, a desire to reinstate him on his throne, and a sense of danger to themselves if the disorganizing principles of the revolutionists should spread into their territories.

"Piedmont was involved in this conflict. Perhaps you remember that it is separated from Dauphiny, in France, by the Cottian Alps, and that among the valleys on the Piedmontese side dwell the Waldenses or Vandois-evangelical Christians, who were for twelve hundred years persecuted by the Church of Rome.

"Though their own sovereigns often joined in these persecutions, and the laws of the land were always more oppressive to them than to their popish fellow citizens, the Waldenses were ever more loyal to king and country and were sure to be called upon for their defense in time of war.

"In the spring of 1793—some three months after the beheading of King Louis XVI—and while the poor queen, the dauphin and the princesses, and his sister and aunt still languished in their dreadful prisons—a French army was attempting to enter Piedmont from Dauphiny, which they could do only through the mountain passes. Thus, all the able-bodied Waldenses and even some Swiss troops, under the command of General Godin, a Swiss officer, were engaged in defending these mountain passes.

"It is among the homes of the Waldenses, thus left defenseless against any plot their popish neighbors might hatch for their destruction, that the scene of this story is laid.

"Now, papa, will you be so kind as to read it aloud?" she asked, handing him the manuscript.

"With pleasure," he said, and all having gathered around to listen, he began.

"On a lovely morning in the middle of May, 1793, a young girl and a little lad were climbing the side of a mountain overlooking the beautiful Valley of Lucerne. They were Lucia and Henri Vittoria, children of a brave Waldenses soldier then serving in the army of his king against the French, with whom their country was at war.

"Lucia had a sweet, innocent face, lighted up by a pair of large, soft, dark eyes and was altogether very fair to look upon. Her lithe, slender figure bounded from rock to rock with movements as graceful and almost as swift as those of a young gazelle.

"'Sister,' cried the lad half pantingly, 'how nimble and fleet of foot you are today! I can scarce keep pace with you.'

"'Ah, Henri, it is because my heart is so light and glad!' she returned with a silvery laugh, pausing for an instant that he might overtake her.'

"'Yes,' he said, as he gained her side, 'the good news from our father and also from Pierre and Rudolph Goneto — that they are well and yet unharmed by French sword or bullet — has filled all our hearts with joy. Is it not to carry these glad tidings to Rudolph's mother that we take this early walk?'

"'Yes, a most pleasant errand, Henri,' and the rose deepened on the maiden's cheek, already glowing with health and exercise.

"They were now far above the valley, and another moment brought them to their destination—a broad ledge of rock on which stood a cottage with its grove of chestnut trees and a little patch of carefully cultivated ground.

"Magdalen Goneto, the mother of Rudolph, a matron of placid countenance and sweet and gentle dignity of mien had seen their approach and had come forth to meet them.

"She embraced Lucia with grave tenderness, bestowed a kind caress upon Henri, and leading the way to her neat dwelling, seated them and herself upon its porch. There was a magnificent view of the whole extent of the valley from their vantage point.

"To the left, and close at hand, lay San Giovanni, with its pretty villages, smiling vineyards, cornfields, and verdant meadows sloping gently away to the waters of the Pelice. On the opposite side of the river, situated upon a slight eminence was the Roman Catholic town of Luserna. To the right, almost at their feet, embowered amid beautiful trees—chestnut, walnut, and mulberry—La Tour, the Waldensian capital and home of Lucia and Henri, nestled among its vineyards and orchards.

"Farther up the vale might be seen Bobbi Villar and many smaller villages scattered amid the fields and vineyards or hanging on the slopes of the hills. Hamlets and single cottages clung here and there to the rugged mountainside wherever a terrace, a little basin, or hollow afforded a spot susceptible to cultivation. Beyond all towered the Cottian Alps that form the barrier between Piedmont and Dauphiny, their snowy pinnacles glittering in the rays of the newly risen sun.

"It was thither the able-bodied men of the valley had gone to defend the passes against the French.

"Toward those lofty mountains Lucia's soft eyes turned with wistful, questioning gaze, for there were father, brother, lover, hourly exposed to all the dangers of war.

"Magdalen noted the look and softly murmured, 'God, even the God of our fathers, cover their heads in the day of battle!'

"'He will, I know He will,' said Lucia, turning to her friend with a bright, sweet smile.

"'You bring me tidings, my dear child,' said Magdalen, taking the maiden's hand in hers. 'Good tidings, for your face is full of gladness!'

"'Yes, dear friend, your son is well,' Lucia answered with a modest, ingenuous blush. 'My father also, and Pierre. We had word from them only last night. But, ah, me!' she added with a sigh. 'What fearful scenes of blood and carnage are yet enacted in Paris, the merry French capital! For from thence also, the courier brought news. Blood, he says, flows like water, and not content with having taken the life of the king, they force the queen and the rest of the royal family to languish in prison. And the guillotine is constantly at work dispatching its wretched victims, whose only crime, in many instances, is that of wealth and noble birth.'

"'Alas, poor wretches! Alas, poor king and queen!' cried Magdalen 'And for ourselves, what danger, should such ruffians force an entrance into our valleys! The passes had need be well guarded!'

"Lucia lingered not long with her friend, for home duties claimed her attention.

"Magdalen went with them to the brow of the hill, and again she embraced Lucia and said in tender, joyous accents, 'Though we must now bid adieu, dear child, when the war is over you will come to brighten Rudolph's home and mine with your constant presence.'

"'Yes, such was the pledge he won from me ere we parted,' the maiden answered with modest sincerity, a tender smile hovering about the full red lips and a vivid color suffusing for an instant the delicately rounded cheek.

"Then, with an affectionate good-bye, she tripped away down the rocky path, Henri following.

"A glad flush still lingered on the sweet, girlish face, and a dewy light shone in the soft eyes. Her thoughts were full of Magdalen's parting words, and the picture they had called up of the happy married life awaiting Rudolph and herself when he should return to the pursuits of peace.

"And Rudolph at his post in those more distant mountains, thought of her and his mother—safe, as he fondly trusted, in the homes his strong arm was helping to defend against a foreign foe. The Vaudois, judging others by themselves, were, notwithstanding their many past experiences of the treacherous cruelty of Rome, strangely unsuspicious of their Catholic neighbors.

"The descent was scarcely yet accomplished by Lucia and Henri, when they were startled by the sound of heavy footsteps and gruff voices in their rear. Casting a look behind them, they beheld, rapidly approaching by another path that wound about the base of the mountain, two men of most ruffianly aspect.

"A wild terror seized upon the maiden as for an instant she caught the gaze of mingled malice and sensuality they bent upon her. Seizing Henri's hand, she flew over the ground toward La Tour with the fleetness of a hunted doe.

"For herself what had she not to fear? And for the child — she feared that he might be slain or reserved for a fate esteemed by the Vaudois worse than death, being carried off to Pignerol and brought up in an idolatrous faith.

"The men pursued, calling to her with oaths, curses, obscene words, and jeering laughter.

"These but quickened her speedy flight. She gained the bridge over the Angrogna, sped across it, over the intervening ground, and through the gate into the town the footsteps of her pursuers echoing close behind.

"'Ah, ha! Escaped my embraces for the present, have you, my pretty bird?' cried one of the miscreants, following her with gloating, cruel eyes as she sped onward up the street. She felt only comparatively safe even there. 'Ah, well, it but delays my pleasure a few hours. I know where to find you and shall pay my respects tonight.'

"'And I,' added his companion with a fierce laugh. 'To ye and many another like you. It's work quite to my taste that the Holy Mother Church has laid out for us tonight, Andrea.'

"'Yes, yes, Giuseppe, we'll not quarrel with the work or the wages — all the plunder we can lay hands on, to say naught of the pretty maids such as yon, or the escape from the fires of purgatory.'

"They were wending their way to the convent of the Recollets as they talked. Arriving at its gates, they were immediately admitted to find it filled with cutthroats such as themselves and soon learned that the church also and the house of the bishop were likewise filled.

"'Good!' they cried. 'How many names in all?'

"'Seven hundred,' said one.

"'Eight hundred,' asserted another.

"'Well, well, be it whichever number it may, we're strong enough for the work, as all the able-bodied men are on the frontier,' cried Andrea, exulting. 'We'll make short shrift with the old men, women, and children.'

"'Yes, long live the holy Roman Church! Hurrah for the holy faith! Down with the dogs!' cried a chorus of voices. 'We'll have a second St. Bartholomew in these valleys and rid them of the hated presence of the cursed heretics.'

"'That we will,' responded Giuseppe. 'But what's the order of proceedings?'

"'All the faithful are to meet at Luserna at sunset. The vesper bell of the convent is to give the signal shortly after, and we immediately spread ourselves over the valley on a heretic hunt that from San Giovanni to Bobbi shall leave not a soul alive to tell the tale.'

"While Magdalen and Lucia conversed in the cottage of the former, Monsignor Brianza, bishop of Luserna, seated in the confessional, listened with horror and indignation to a tale of intended wholesale rape, murder, and arson, which his penitent was unfolding.

"'I will have neither part nor lot in this thing,' said the priest to himself, as he left the church a moment later. 'Nay more, I shall warn the intended victims of their danger.'

"Hurrying to his house, he instantly dispatched messengers in all haste to the villages of San Giovanni and La Tour.

"About the same time in the more remote town of Cavour, the fiendish plot was revealed to Captain Odetti, an officer of the Piedmontese militia — then enrolled to act against the French along with a request that he would take part in its execution. Being a rigid Catholic, it was confidently expected that he would willingly do so.

"But as noble and humane a man as Luserna's good bishop, he listened with like horror and detestation. Mounting his horse, he instantly set off for La Tour to warn the helpless folk of the threatened calamity and assist in averting it, if that might yet be possible.

"He traveled quickly, for time pressed. The appointed hour for the attack already drew so near that it was doubtful if even the most prompt action could still avail.

"Pale and breathless with haste and terror, Lucia and Henri gained the shelter of their home, and in reply to the anxious questioning of mother and grandparents, told of the hot pursuit of the evil men who had chased them into town.

"Their story was heard with great concern, not only by the family, but also by a young man who had entered nearly at the same moment with Lucia and Henri.

"His right arm was in a sling. His face, thin and wan with suffering, wore an expression of anxiety and alarm which deepened momentarily as the narrative proceeded.

"'How is Bianca?' he asked, upon its conclusion, the quiet tone telling nothing of the profound solicitude that filled his heart.

"'Much the same,' returned Sara Vittoria, the mother of the house.

"'A little better, I think,' said a weak but cheerful voice from the next room. 'Maurice, how is your poor arm? Come and tell me.'

"He rose and complied with the request.

"Bianca, the elder sister of Lucia, had been for a year or more the betrothed of Maurice Laborie. He found her lying pale and languid upon a couch.

"'What is it, Maurice, dear?' she asked, presently, noticing his troubled look.

"'I wish you were well, Bianca.'

"'Ah, I am more concerned about your wound.'

"His thoughts seemed far away. He rose hastily.

"'I must speak to your grandfather. I will be in again,' and he left the room.

"Marc Rozel, the father of Sara Vittoria, a venerable, white-haired veteran who had seen his fourscore years and ten, sat at the open door of the cottage leaning upon his staff, his eyes fixed thoughtfully upon the towering heights of the Mount Vandelin.

"'"As the mountains are round about Jerusalem, so the Lord is round about His people from henceforth even forever,"' Maurice heard him murmur as he drew near.

"There was comfort in the words, and the cloud of care partially lifted from the brow of the young Vandois. But approaching the aged saint with deep respect and bending down to speak close to his ear, he uttered a few rapid sentences in an undertone.

"'There seems a threatening of danger, Father Rozel. Evil-looking men, such as Lucia and the lad were but now describing, have been seen coming into town for the last two or three days. Now, it is said, the Catholic Church, the convent of Recollets, the house of the bishop, and several other Catholic houses are full of them. What errand think you draws them hither just at this time, when nearly every able-bodied Vandois is absent on the frontier?'

"Rozel's face reflected somewhat the agitation and alarm in that of Maurice, but ere he could open his lips to reply, a neighbor — a young woman with a child in her arms — came rushing across the street and called to them in tones tremulous with excitement and fright. She told of the warning just brought by Brianza's messenger.

"Her face was white with terror, and she clasped her infant to herself with a look of agony as she asked, 'Can it be, oh can it be that we are all to be slain in our helplessness? Something must be done, and that quickly. But what, alas, can we do? Our husbands, brothers, and fathers are all at a distance, and the fatal hour draws near.'

"The tone of her voice and some of her words had reached the ears of those within the cottage, and they now gathered about her in an intensely excited, terrified group. Question and answer followed in rapid succession till each knew all that she had heard.

"'Can it be possible?' cried Sara. 'Can even Catholic cruelty, ingratitude, and treachery go so far? Are not our brave defenders theirs as well, keeping the passes against a common foe?'

"A mournful shake of the head from her aged father was the only reply—save the sobs and cries of the frightened children.

"But at that instant a horseman came dashing up the street, suddenly drew rein before her dwelling, and hastily dismounting, hurrying toward them.

"'Captain Odetti!' exclaimed Rozel in surprise.

"'Yes, Rozel, I come to warn you, though, alas, I fear I am too late to prevent bloodshed,' said the officer, sending a pitying glance from one to another of the terror-stricken group. 'There is a conspiracy against you. The assassins are even now on foot, but if I cannot save, I will perish with, you. The honor of my religion is at stake, and I must justify it by sharing your danger.'

"'Can it possibly be that such designs are really entertained against us?' asked Rozel in trembling tones, glancing from one loved face to another with a look of keenest anguish. 'On what pretext? I know of none.'

"'The late base and cowardly surrender of Fort Mirabouc, Rozel.'

"'There was but one Vaudois present, and his voice was raised against it.'

"'True, but what matters that to foes bent upon your destruction? Some one was to blame, and why not make a scapegoat of the hated Vaudois? But let us not waste time in useless discussion. We must act. We must act now.'

"The fearful tidings flew from house to house, and in the wildest terror the feeble folk began to make what preparations they could for self defense. By Odetti's advice they barricaded the streets and homes, collecting missiles to hurl down from the upper windows upon the heads of the assassins, and at the same time dispatching messenger after messenger to General Godin, the Swiss officer in command of the troops on the frontier, telling of the danger and praying for instant aid.

"But he, alas, unable in the nobility of his soul to credit the existence of a plot so atrocious, turned a deaf ear to their entreaties, declaring his conviction that the alarm was groundless. It had to be a mere panic. His troops could not be spared to go on so useless an errand.

"As one courier after another returned with this same disheartening report, the terror and despair were such as to beggar description.

"Lucia Vittoria, recalling with many a shudder of wild fright the evil looks and fierce words and gestures of her pursuers of the morning, resolved to defend her own, her mother's, and her sister's honor to the last gasp.

"The terrible excitement of the hour seemed to give her unnatural strength for her task of lifting and carrying stones and fragments of rock to be used in repelling the expected assault. Assisted by Henri and every member of the family capable of the exertion, she toiled unceasingly while anything yet remained to be done.

"In the midst of her exertions, Magdalen Goneto suddenly appeared among them.

"'I have heard, and I come to live or die with you, dear friends,' she said and fell to work with the others.

"At length all was completed, and they could only wait in dreadful suspense the coming of event. They had continued to importune the commandant, but with no better success than at first.

"In the closed and barricaded dwellings hearts were going up to God in agonized prayer for help and deliverance.

"In that of the Vittorias few words were spoken save as now and again the voice of the aged Rozel or that of his venerable wife, his daughter, or Magdalen Goneto, broke the awful silence with some promise from the Book of books to those who trust in the Lord.

"Maurice, whose father and brothers were away with the army, torn with anxiety for mother, sisters, and betrothed alike, persuaded the former to follow Magdalen's example in repairing to the house of the Vittorias. This, so that such efforts as he was able to put forth in his crippled condition might be made in their common defense.

"Freely would he shed the last drop of his blood to shield them from harm, but, alas, what could he do? How speedily would he be overpowered? Help must be obtained!

"He stole out through the garden to learn the latest news from the frontier.

"The fourteenth courier had just returned in great sadness. The commandant was still incredulous— still firm in his refusal to render aid.

"'We are then given up to the sword of the assassin!' groaned his hearers.

"'No, no, never! It must not be!' cried Maurice with sudden stern determination, though there was a quiver of pain in his voice. Sending a glance of mingled love and anguish toward the cottage that sheltered those dearer to him than life, he set off at a brisk pace up the valley.

"Love moved him to the task, and in spite of weakness and pain, never before had he trodden those steep and dangerous mountain paths with such celerity.

"Arrived and admitted to Godin's presence, he poured out his petition with the vehemence of one who can take no denial, urging his suit with all the eloquence of intense anxiety and deep conviction of the terrible extremity of the feeble folk in the valley.

"Doubt began to creep into the mind of the brave officer. 'Might there not be some truth in the story after all?' Yet he answered as before. 'A mere panic. I cannot believe in a plot so atrocious. What, murder in cold blood the innocent helpless wives and children of the brave men who are defending theirs from a common foe? No, no, human nature is not so depraved!'

"'So it was thought on the eve of the Sicilian Vespers—on the eve of St. Bartholomew—at the time when Castracaro—when De La Trinite, when Pianeza—'

"'Ah,' interrupted the general with a frown, 'but those were deeds of days long gone by, and men are not now what they then were.'

"'Sir,' returned Maurice earnestly, 'for twelve hundred years the she-wolf of Rome has ravaged our fold, slaying sheep and lambs alike. She has spared neither age nor sex. Sir, it is her boast that she never changes.

"'Nor are men incapable of the grossest injustice and cruelty even in these days. Look at the fearful scenes of blood enacted even now in France! General, the lives of thousands of his majesty's subjects are trembling in the balance. I do most solemnly assure you that unless saved by your speedy intervention or a direct miracle from heaven, they will this night fall victim to a bloody plot.

"'Ah, sir, what more can I say to convince—to move you? The assassins are already assembling, the time wanes fast, and will you stretch forth no hand to save their innocent, helpless victims?'

"The general was evidently moved by the appeal. 'Had I but sufficient proof,' he muttered in an undertone of doubt and perplexity.

"Maurice caught eagerly at the word. 'Proof, general? Would Odetti, or would Brianza, have warned us were the danger not imminent? And do not the annals of your own Switzerland furnish examples of similar plots?'

"'True, too true! Yet—'

"But at this moment the sixteenth courier came panting up to pour out in an agony of haste and fear, the same tale of contemplated wholesale massacre. And, the story having reached the ears of the Vaudois troops, they gathered about the general, imploring, demanding to be sent instantly to the aid of their menaced wives and children.

"General Godin's mind had been filled with conflicting emotions while Maurice spoke. His humanity, his honor as a soldier, and his duty to the government were struggling for the mastery.

"Ought he to march without orders or even the knowledge of his superiors? And that, too, with no more certain proof of the illegal assembling of those who were said to be plotting against the peace and safety of the Vaudois families?

"Yet there was no time to reconnoiter ere the dire mischief might be done. His humanity at last prevailed over more prudent considerations. He commanded the brigade of Waldenses to march instantly, and he followed with another division.

"Bianca Vittoria had been carried to an upper room, where all the family were now gathered about her bed.

"With unutterable anguish the mother looked upon her two lovely daughters in the early bloom of womanhood, the babe sleeping upon her lap, the little ones clinging to her skirts, and her aged and infirm parents—all apparently doomed to a speedy, violent death or fates worse than death. Her own danger was well nigh forgotten in theirs.

"Utter silence reigned in that room and the adjoining one—this time occupied by Magdalen and the mother and sisters of Maurice. Every ear was strained to catch the sound of the approaching footsteps of the assassins or of the longed-for deliverers. A very short season would now decide their fate. Oh, would help never come?

"Lucia, kneeling beside her sister's couch, clasped one thin, white hand in hers, but she suddenly dropped it and sprang to her feet.

"'How fast it grows dark! And what was that?' as a heavy, rolling sound reverberated among the mountains. 'Artillery?' and her tones grew wild with terror.

"'Thunder The heavens are black with clouds,' said Magdalen, coming in and speaking with the calmness of despair.

"A heavy clap nearly drowned her words, then followed crash on crash. The rain came down in torrents, and the wind, which had suddenly risen to almost a hurricane, dashed it with fury against walls and windows. The darkness became intense except as ever and anon the lurid glare of the lightning lit up the scene for an instant, giving to each a momentary glimpse of the pale, terror-stricken faces of the others.

"'Alas, alas, no help can reach us now!' moaned Sara, clasping her babe closer to herself. 'No troops can march over our fearful mountain passes in this terrific storm and thick darkness. We will die!'

"'Oh, God of our fathers, save us! Let us not fall into the hands of those ruffians, who—more to be feared than the wild beasts of the forest—would rob us of honor and of life!' cried Lucia, falling upon her knees again and lifting hands and eyes upward to heaven.

"'Amen!' responded the trembling voice of Rozel. 'Lord, Thine hand is not shortened that it cannot save, neither Thine ear heavy that it cannot hear!'

"The scenes that followed, what pen can portray? The wild anguish of some was expressed in incoherent words, shrieks of terror, and cries for help. They seemed to hear amid the roar of the elements, the hurried footsteps of the assassins and to see in the lightning's flash the glitter of their steel. The mute agony of others was seen in the calmness of despair as they crouched helplessly together awaiting the coming blow.

"Meanwhile the fathers, husbands, sons, and brothers were hastening homeward. Their brave hearts torn with anguish at the thought of the impossibility of arriving before the hour set for the murderers to begin their fiendish work.

"There was no regular order of march, but each rushed onward at his utmost speed, praying aloud to God for help to increase it and calling frantically to his fellows to 'hasten, hasten to the rescue of all they held most dear.'

"Alas, for their hopes! The shades of evening were already falling, and the storm presently came on in terrific violence—the darkness, the blinding momentary glare of the lightning, the crashing thunder peals, the driving, pouring rain, and the fierce wind greatly increasing the difficulties and perils of their advance. God Himself seemed to be against them.

"But urged on by fear and love for their helpless ones and by parties of distracted women and children sent forward from La Tour—some of whom, in their terror and despair, asserted that the work of blood had already begun—they pressed onward without a moment's pause, springing from rock to rock, sliding down precipices, scaling giddy heights, leaping chasms which at another time they would not have dared to attempt, and tearing through the rushing, roaring mountain torrents already greatly swollen by the rain.

"They reached the last of these, and dashing through it, were presently in sight of La Tour when the tolling of the vesper bell of the convent of the Recollets—the prearranged signal for the assassins to sally forth—smote upon their ears.

"'Too late!' cried Rudolph Goneto hoarsely.

"'But if too late to save, we will avenge!' responded a chorus of deep voices, as with frantic haste they flew over the intervening space.

"The next moment the tramp of their feet and the clang of their arms were heard in the streets of the town. Windows and doors flew open, and with cries and tears of joy and thankfulness, wives, children, and aged parents gathered about them—almost smothering them with caresses.

"The storm, which had seemed to seal their doom, had proved their salvation — preventing some of the murderers from reaching the rendezvous in time and so terrifying the others that they dared not attempt the deed alone. Especially as it had already begun to be rumored that troops were on the march to the threatened valley.

"Rudolph soon found himself encircled by his own mother's arms, her kisses and tears warm upon his cheek.

"He held her close, both hearts too full for speech. Then a single word fell from the soldier's lips, 'Lucia?'

"'Safe!'

"Darting into the house, guided by some subtle instinct, he stood the next moment in the upper room where she knelt by her sister's couch. The two mingled their tears and thanksgivings together.

"All was darkness, but at the sound of the well-known step, Lucia sprang up with a cry of joy. 'Saved! Saved!'

"Rudolph's emotions, as he held her to his heart, were too big for utterance.

"Some one entered with a light. It was Magdalen, and behind her came Maurice — pale, haggard, and dripping with rain.

"Bianca's heart gave a joyous bound. Could it be that he too was safe?

"But a tumult of voices from below — some stern, angry, threatening, others sullen, dogged, defiant, or craven with terror — attracted their attention.

"Magdalen set down the light and hurried away in the direction of the sound, Rudolph and Lucia following directly.

"A number of the Waldenses, sword in hand and eyes flashing with righteous indignation, were gathered about two of the would-be assassins, caught by them almost on the threshold of the cottage.

"Their errand who could doubt? Henri had at once recognized them as his and Lucia's pursuers of the morning.

"She, too, knew them instantly and clung pale with fright to Rudolph's arm, while he could scarce restrain himself from rushing upon and running them through with his sword.

"'Spare us, sirs,' entreated Andrea, quaking with fear under the wrathful glance of the father of the maidens. 'Spare us, sir. I beg you. We have not harmed you or yours.'

"'Nor plotted their destruction? Miserable wretch, ask not your life upon the plea that it is not forfeit. Can I doubt what would have been the fate of my wife and daughters had they fallen into your hands?'

"'But your religion teaches you to forgive.'

"'True, yet also to protect all of the helpless ones committed to my care.'

"'We will leave your valleys this hour. We will—never to set foot in them again.'

"'Ah! Yet how far may we trust the word of one whose creed bids him keep no faith with heretics?'

"'"Vengeance is Mine, I will repay."'

"It was the voice of the aged Rozel that broke the momentary silence.

"Vittoria sheathed his sword. It was not his right to usurp the prerogative of Him who had that night given so signal a deliverance to His own 'Israel of the Alps.'"

"Is that all?" asked Lulu, drawing a long breath as Mr. Dinsmore refolded the manuscript and gave it back to his daughter.

"Yes," he replied. "The author has told of the deliverance of the imperiled ones, and that Vittoria refrained from taking vengeance upon their cowardly foes. And so ends the story of that night of terror in the valleys."

"But were all the Waldenses equally forbearing, grandpa?" asked Zoe.

"They were. In all the valleys not a drop of blood was shed. Justly exasperated as the Waldenses were, they contented themselves with sending to the government a list of the names of the baffled conspirators.

"But no notice was taken of it. The would-be murderers were never called to account till they appeared before a greater than an earthly tribunal.

"General Godin was presently superseded in his command and shortly after dismissed from the service — two plain indications that the sympathy of the government was with the assassins and not at all with their intended victims."

"But is it true, sir?" asked Max.

"Yes, it is true that at that time, in those valleys, and under those circumstances, such a plot was hatched and its carrying out prevented in the exact way that this story relates."

"Mean, cowardly, wicked fellows they must have been to want to murder the wives and children and burn and plunder the houses of the men that were defending them and theirs from a common enemy!" exclaimed the boy, his face flushing and eyes flashing with righteous indignation.

"Very true, but such are the lessons that popery teaches and always has taught—'no faith with heretics,' no mercy to any who deny her dogmas, and that anything is right and commendable which is done to destroy those who do not acknowledge her authority and to increase her power. One of her doctrines being that the end sanctifies the means!"

"But what did they mean when they said they were going to have a second St. Bartholomew in the valleys?" asked Gracie.

"Did you never hear of the massacre of St. Bartholomew, my dear daughter?" her father asked, stroking her hair caressingly as she sat upon his knee.

"No, papa, won't you tell me about it?"

"It occurred in France a little more than three hundred years ago. It was a dreadful massacre of the Protestants to the number of from sixty to a hundred thousand. It was begun on the night of the twenty-third of August—which the Catholics call St. Bartholomew's Day.

"The Protestants were shot, stabbed, murdered in various ways—in their beds, in the street, anywhere that they could be found—and for no crime but being Protestants."

"And popery would do the very same now and here, had she the power," commented Mr. Dinsmore. "It is her proudest boast that she never changes. She teaches her own infallibility. What she has done, she will do again if she can."

"What is infallibility, papa?" asked Gracie.

"To be infallible is to be incapable of error or of making mistakes," he answered. "So popery teaching that the Roman church has never done wrong or made a mistake justifies all the horrible cruelties she has practiced in former times. In fact, she occasionally tells us, through some of her bolder or less wary followers, that what she has done she will do again as soon as she attains the power."

"Which she never will do in this free land," exclaimed Edward.

"Never, provided Columbia's sons are faithful to their trust—remembering that 'eternal vigilance is the price of liberty,'" responded his grandfather.

Gracie was clinging tightly to her father, and her little face was pale and wore a look of fright.

"What is it, darling?" he asked.

"Oh, papa, will they come here some time and kill us?" she asked, tremulously.

"Do not be frightened, my dear little one," he said, holding her close. "You are in no danger from them at all."

"I don't believe all Roman Catholics would have Protestants persecuted if they could," remarked Betty. "Do you, uncle?"

"No, I think there are some truly Christian people among them," he answered. "Some who have not yet heard and heeded the call, 'Come out of her, my people, that ye be not partakers of her sins, and that ye receive not of her plagues.' We were talking, not of Catholics, but of Popery. Sincere hatred of the system is not incompatible with sincere love to its followers."

CHAPTER ELEVENTH

My voice shalt thou hear in the morning,
O Lord; in the morning will I direct my prayer
unto thee, and will look up.

— *P*SALM 5:3

IT WAS EARLY MORNING. Captain Raymond was pacing to and fro along the top of the cliffs, sending a glance seaward and now toward the door of the cottage that was his temporary home, as if expecting a companion in his ramble.

Presently the door opened and Lulu stepped out upon the porch. One eager look showed her father, and she bounded with joyful step to meet him.

"Good morning, my dear papa," she cried, holding her face up for a kiss, which he gave with hearty affection.

"Good morning, my dear, little, early bird," he responded. "Come, I will help you down the steps, and we will pace the sands at the water's edge."

This was Lulu's time for having her father to herself, as she phrased it. He was sure to be out at this early hour if the weather would permit, and she was almost equally sure to join him. As the others liked to lie a little longer in bed, there was seldom anyone to share his society with her.

He led her down the long flights of stairs and across the level expanse of sand, close to where the booming waves dashed up their spray.

For some moments the two stood hand in hand silently gazing out upon sea and sky, bright with the morning sunlight. They turned and paced the beach for a time, and then the captain led his little girl to a seat on the porch of a bathing house, from which they could still look far out over the sea.

"Papa," she said, nestling close to his side, "I am very fond of being down here all alone with you."

"Did you do nothing but put on your clothes after leaving your bed?" he asked gravely.

"I washed my hands and face, and I smoothed my hair."

"And was that all?"

She glanced up at him in surprise at the deep gravity of his tone. Then, suddenly comprehending what his questioning meant, she hung her head, while her cheeks flushed hotly. "Yes, papa," she replied in a low, abashed tone.

"I am very, very sorry to hear it," he said. "If my little girl begins the day without a prayer to God for help to do right, without thanking Him for His kind care over her while she slept, she can hardly expect to escape sins and sorrows which will make it anything but a happy day."

"Papa, I do 'most always say my prayers in the morning and at night, but I didn't feel like doing it this time. Do you think people ought to pray when they don't feel like it?"

"Yes, I think that is the very time when they most need to pray. They need to ask God to take away the hardness of their hearts, the evil in them that is hiding His love, and their own needs so that they have no gratitude to express for all His great goodness and mercy to them. Have they no petitions to offer up for strength to resist temptation and to walk steadily in His ways—no desire to confess their sins and plead for pardon for Jesus' sake? Ah! That is certainly the time when we have most urgent need to pray.

"Jesus taught that men—and in the Bible 'men' stands for the whole human race—'ought always to pray and not to faint.' And we are commanded to 'pray without ceasing.'"

"Papa, how can we do that?" she asked. "You know we have to be doing other things sometimes."

"It does not mean that we are to be always on our knees," he said. "But that we are to live so near to God, so loving Him, and so feeling our constant dependence upon Him, that our hearts will be very often going up to His throne in silent petition, praise, or confession.

"And if we live in such union with Him, we will highly prize the privilege of drawing especially near to Him at certain times. We will be glad to be alone with Him often, and we will not forget or neglect to retire to our closets night and morning for a little season of close communion with our best and dearest Friend.

"Lulu, you say you love to be alone with me, your earthly father. I trust the time will come when you will love far better to be alone with your heavenly Father. I must often be far away from you, but He is ever near. I may be powerless to help you, though close at your side, but He is almighty to save, to provide for, and to defend. And He never turns a deaf ear to the cry of His children."

"Yes, papa. But, oh, I wish that you were always near me, too," she said, leaning her cheek affectionately against his arm. "I am very, very sorry that I have ever been a trouble to you and spoiled your enjoyment of your visits home."

"I know you are, daughter, but you have been very good of late. I have rejoiced to see that you were really trying to rule your own spirit. So far as I know, you have been entirely and cheerfully obedient to me and have not indulged in a single fit of passion or sullenness."

"Yes, papa, but I have been nearly in a passion two or three times. But you gave me a look just in time to help me resist it. But when you are gone I shall not have that help."

"Then, my child, you must remember that your heavenly Father is looking at you and that He bids you fight against the evil of your nature. If you seek it of Him, he will give you strength to overcome. Here is a text for you. I want you to remember it constantly—to that end repeat it often to yourself: 'Thou, God, seest me.'

"And do not forget that He sees not only the outward conduct but the innermost thoughts and feelings of the heart."

A boy's glad shout and merry whistle mingled pleasantly with the sound of the dashing of the waves, and Max came bounding over the sands toward their sheltered nook.

"Good morning, papa," he cried. "You, too, Lulu. Ahead of me as usual, I see!"

"Yes," the captain said, reaching out a hand to grasp the lad's and gazing with fatherly affection and pride into the handsome young face glowing with health and happiness. "She is the earliest young bird in the family nest. However, she seeks her roost earlier than her brother does his."

"Yes, and I am not so very late; am I, sir?"

"No, my boy, I do not suppose you have taken any more sleep than you need for your health and growth. And I certainly would not have you do with less."

"I know you wouldn't, papa. Such a good, kind father as you are," responded Max. "I wouldn't swap fathers with any other boy," he added, with a look of mingled fun and affection.

"Nor would I exchange my son for any other — not even a better one," returned the captain laughingly, tightening his clasp of the sturdy, tanned hand he held.

"I haven't heard yet the story of yesterday's success in boating and fishing. Come sit down here by my side and let me have it."

Max obeyed, nothing loath, for he was becoming quite expert in both, and he always found in his father an interested listener to the story of his exploits.

He and the other lads had returned from their camping at the time of the removal of the family party from 'Sconset to Nantucket Town.

On the conclusion of his narrative the captain pronounced it breakfast time, and they returned to the house.

After breakfast, as nearly the whole party were gathered upon the porch, discussing the question of what should be the amusements of the day, a near neighbor with whom they had some acquaintance ran over to ask if they would join a company who were going over to Shimmo to have a clam bake.

"The name of the place is new to me," remarked Mr. Dinsmore. "Is it a town, Mrs. Atwood?"

"Oh, no," replied the lady. "There is only one dwelling—a farmhouse with its barns and other out houses comprises the whole place. It is on the shore of the harbor some miles beyond Nantucket Town. It is a pleasant spot, and I think we shall have an enjoyable time, particularly if I can persuade you all to go."

"A regular New England clam bake!" exclaimed Elsie. "I should really like to attend one and am much obliged for your invitation, Mrs. Atwood. I'm certain we all are."

No one felt disposed to decline the invitation, and it was soon settled that all would go.

The clam bake was to occupy only the afternoon. So they would have time to make all necessary arrangements and for the customary surf bath and swimming.

Mrs. Atwood had risen to take leave. "Ah," she said, "I was near forgetting something I meant to say. We never dress for these expeditions, but, on the contrary, we wear the oldest and shabbiest dresses we have—considering them altogether the most suitable to the occasion. Then we need not be troubled if they should be wet with spray or soiled by contact with seaweed, grass, or anything else."

"A very sensible custom, indeed," Mrs. Dinsmore responded. "One which we shall all probably follow."

Mrs. Atwood had hardly reached the gate when Lulu, turning to her father with a very discontented face, said, "I don't want to wear a shabby old dress! Must I, papa?"

"You will wear whatever your Grandma Elsie or mamma directs," he answered, giving her a warning look. Then motioning her to come close to his side, he whispered in her ear, "I see that you are inclined to be ill-tempered and rebellious again. I feared you would be when I learned that you had begun the day without a prayer for help to do and feel right. Go, now, to your room and ask it."

"You needn't fret, Lu. You don't own a dress that any little girl ought to feel ashamed to wear," remarked Betty, as the child turned to obey.

"And we are all going to wear the very worst we have here with us, I presume," added Zoe. "At least, such is my intention."

"Provided your husband approves," whispered Edward sportively.

"Anyhow," she answered, drawing herself up in pretended offense, "can't a woman do as she pleases even in such trifles?"

"Ah! But it is the privileges of a child-wife which are under discussion now."

"Now, sir, after that remark you shall just have the trouble of telling me what to wear," said Zoe, rising from the couch where they had been sitting side by side. "Come along and choose."

Lulu was in the room where she slept, obeying her father's order so far as outward actions went. But there was little more than lip service in the prayer she offered. Her thoughts were wandering upon the subject of dress and ways and means for obtaining permission to wear what she wished to wear that afternoon.

By the time she had finished "saying her prayers," she had also reached a conclusion as to her best plan for securing the desired privilege.

Grandma Elsie was so very kind and gentle that there seemed more hope of moving her than anyone else. So to her she went, and, delighted to find her comparatively alone with no one being near enough to overhear a low-toned conversation, she began at once. "Grandma Elsie, I would like to wear a white dress to the clambake. I think it would be suitable because the weather is very warm, and white will wash so that it would not matter if I did get it soiled."

"My dear child, it is your father's place to decide what concerns his children, when he is with them," Elsie said, drawing the little girl to her and smoothing her hair with soft, caressing touch.

"Yes, ma'am, but he says you and Mamma Vi are to decide this. So if you will only say I may wear the white dress, he will let me. Won't you, please?"

"If your father is satisfied with your choice, I shall certainly raise no objection nor will your mamma, I am quite sure."

"Oh, thank you, ma'am!" and Lulu ran off gleefully in search of her father.

She found him on the veranda, busied with the morning paper, and to her satisfaction, he too was quite alone.

"What is it, daughter?" he asked, glancing from the paper to her animated, eager face.

"About what I am to wear this afternoon, papa. I would like to wear the white dress I had on yesterday evening. Grandma Elsie does not object, and she says she knows Mamma Vi will not, if you say I may."

"Did she say she thought it a suitable dress?" he asked gravely.

Lulu hung her head. "No, sir, she didn't say that she did or she didn't."

"Go and ask her the question."

Lulu went back and asked it.

"No, my child, I do not," Elsie answered. "It is unlikely that anyone else will be in white or anything at all dressy, and you will look overdressed, which is in very bad taste. Besides, though the weather seems warm enough for such thin material here on shore, it will be a great deal cooler on the water. And should the waves or spray come dashing over us, you would find your dress clinging to you like a wet rag—with neither beauty nor comfort left in it."

"I could wear a waterproof over it while we are sailing," said Lulu.

"Even that might not prove a perfect protection," Elsie replied. "I think, my dear, you would do well to content yourself to wear your traveling dress, which is of a light woolen material. It is neat without being too dressy and of a color that will not show every little soil. It is as good and handsome as the dress I or Rosie shall wear and probably anyone else, for that matter."

"But you can choose for yourself, Grandma Elsie, and I wish I could."

"That is one of the privileges of older years," Elsie answered pleasantly. "I was considerably older than you are now before I was allowed to select my own attire. But I repeat that I shall not raise the slightest objection to your wearing anything your father is willing to see on you."

Lulu's hopes were almost gone, but she would make one more effort.

She went to her father, and putting her arms round his neck, begged in her most coaxing tones for the gratification of her wish.

"What did your Grandma Elsie say?" he asked.

Lulu faithfully, though with no little reluctance, repeated every word Elsie had said to her with regard to the subject.

"I entirely agree with her," said the captain. "So entirely that even had she found no objection to urge against it, I should have forbidden you to wear the dress."

Lulu heard him with a clouded brow. In fact, the expression of her face was decidedly sullen. Her father observed it with sorrow and concern.

"Sit down here till I am ready to talk to you," he said, indicating a chair close at his side.

Lulu obeyed, sitting quietly there while he finished his paper. Throwing it aside at length, he took her hand and drew her in between his knees, putting an arm about her waist.

"My little daughter," he said, in his usual kind tone, "I am afraid you care too much for dress and finery. What I desire for you is that you may 'be clothed with humility,' and have 'the ornament of a meek and quiet spirit, which is, in the sight of God, of great price.'"

"I never can have that, papa, for it isn't a bit like me," she said with a sort of despairing impatience and disgust at herself.

"No, that is too true. It is not like you as you are by nature—the evil nature inherited from me. But God is able to change that and to give you a clean heart and renew within you a right spirit. Jesus is a Savior from sin, and He is able to save to the uttermost and to take away the very last remains of the old corrupt nature with which we were born.

"Oh, my child, seek His help to fight against it and to overcome! It grieves me more than I can express to see you again showing that unlovely, willful temper."

"Oh, papa, don't be grieved," she said, throwing her arms round his neck and pressing her lips to his cheek. "I will be good and wear whatever I'm told. Please look pleasant about it, too, for indeed I do love you too well to want to grieve you and spoil your pleasure."

"Ah, that is my own dear little girl," he answered, returning her caresses.

The sullen expression had vanished from her face and it wore its brightest look. It clouded again the next moment, but with sorrow, not anger, as she sighed, "Oh, if you were always with us, papa, I think I might grow good at last. But I need your help so much, and you are gone more than half the time."

"Your heavenly Father is never gone, daughter, and He will never turn a deaf ear to a cry for strength to resist temptation to sin. He says, 'In Me is thine help.'

"And we are told, 'God is faithful, who will not suffer you to be tempted above that ye are able; but will with the temptation also make a way to escape, that ye may be able to bear it.'"

प्र प्र प्र प्र प्र

In the mean time Mrs. Dinsmore, who from choice took most of the housekeeping cares, was ordering an early dinner and various baskets of provisions for the picnic.

As the family sat down to the table, these last were being conveyed on board a yacht lying at the little pier near the bathing place below the cliffs. Almost immediately upon finishing their meal, all—old and young—trooped down the stairways, across the sandy beach, and were themselves soon aboard the vessel.

Others of the company were already seated in it and the rest followed a few minutes later. The last basket of provisions being safely stowed away in some safe corner of the craft, they set sail, dragging at their stern a dory in which was a large quantity of clams in the shell.

It was a bright day, and a favorable breeze sent the yacht skimming over the water at an exhilarating rate of speed. All hearts seemed light, every face was bright, not excepting Lulu's, though she was attired in the plain-colored dress recommended by Grandma Elsie.

There was no greater display of finery than a knot of bright ribbon on the part of even the happiest young girl present. Betty wore a black bunting— one of her school dresses—with a cardinal ribbon at the throat. Zoe wore the brown woolen that had for her such mingled associations of pain and pleasure, and Edward thought she looked wonderfully sweet and pretty in it.

They sat side by side, and Betty, watching them furtively, said to herself, "They are for all the world just like a pair of lovers yet, though they have been married over a year."

Then, turning her attention first to Violet and Captain Raymond then upon her Aunt and Uncle Dinsmore, she came to the same conclusion in regard to them also.

"And it had been just so with Cousin Elsie and her husband," she mused. "I can remember how devoted they were to each other. But she seems very happy now, and she well may be, with father, sons, and daughters all so devoted to her. And she's so rich, too. She never has to consider how to make one dollar do the work of two—a problem I am so often called upon to solve. In fact, it is to her and uncle that Bob and I owe our education and pretty much everything we have.

"I don't envy her her money, but I do the love that surrounds her all her life. She never knew her own mother, to be sure, but her father adored her as a child. He was father and mother both to her, I've often heard her say. But my father died before I was even born, and mother lost her reason when I was but a little thing."

But Betty was not much given to melancholy musing, or indeed to musing of any kind. Presently, a passing sail attracted her attention and turned her thoughts into a new channel.

And soon, the wind and tide being favorable, the yacht drew near her destination.

There was no wharf, but the passengers were taken to the shore, a few at a time, in the dory It also landed the provision baskets and the clams.

Those ladies and gentlemen to whom clam bakes were a new experience watched with interest the process of cooking the bivalves.

A pit of suitable size for the quantity of clams to be prepared was made in the sand—the bottom covered with stones. It was then heated by a fire kindled in it, the brands removed, seaweed spread over the stones, the clams poured in, an abundance of seaweed piled over and about them, and a piece of an old sail put over that. They were then left to bake or steam while another fire was kindled nearby. A large tin bucket, filled with water, was set on it to boil for making coffee.

While some busied themselves with these culinary operations, others repaired to the dwelling, which stood some little distance back from the beach where the ground sloped gently away from it to the water's edge.

The lady of the house met them at the door and hospitably invited them to come in and rest themselves in her parlor or to sit on the porch. Understanding their errand to the locality, she not only gave ready permission for their table to be spread in the shade of her house, but she also offered to lend anything they might require in the way of utensils.

Accepting her offer, they set to work—the men making a rough sort of impromptu table with some boards, and the ladies spreading upon it the plentiful contents of the provision baskets.

Mrs. Dinsmore, Elsie, and the younger ladies of their party offered to assist in these labors, but they were told that they were considered guests and must be content to look on or wander about and amuse themselves.

There was not much to be seen but grassy slopes destitute of tree or scrub, the harbor, and the open sea beyond.

They seated themselves upon the porch of the house, while Captain Raymond and the younger members of their family party wandered here and there about the place.

There seemed to be some sport going on among the cooks—those engaged in preparing the coffee.

Lulu hurried toward them to see what it was about, then came running back to her father, who stood a little farther up the slope with Gracie clinging to his hand.

"Oh!" she said with a face of disgust. "I don't mean to drink any of that coffee. Why, would you believe they stirred it with a poker?"

"Did they?" laughed the captain. "They might have done worse. I presume that was used for lack of a long enough spoon. We must not be too particular on such occasions as this."

"But you won't drink any of it, will you, papa?"

"I think it altogether likely I shall."

"Why, papa, coffee that was stirred with nothing but a dirty poker?"

"We will suppose the poker was not very dirty," he said with a good-humored smile. "Probably there was nothing worse on it than a little ashes, which, diffused through so large a quantity of liquid, could harm no one."

"Must I drink it if they offer me a cup?"

"No, there need be no compulsion about it. Indeed, I think it better for a child of your age not to take coffee at all."

"But you never said I shouldn't, papa."

"No, because you had formed the habit in my absence, and, as I am not sure that it is a positive injury to you, I have felt loath to deprive you of the pleasure."

"You are so kind, papa," she said, slipping her hand into his and looking up affectionately into his face. "But I will give up coffee if you want me to. I like it, but I can do without it."

"I think milk is far more wholesome for you," he said with a smile of pleased approval. "I should like you to make that your ordinary beverage at meals, but I do not forbid an occasional cup of coffee."

"Thank you, papa," she returned. "Grandma Elsie once told me that when she was a little girl her father wouldn't allow her to drink coffee at all or to eat any kind of hot cakes or rich, sweet cake. Oh, I don't know how many things that she liked that he wouldn't let her have. I don't think he was half as nice a father as ours. Do you, Gracie?"

"'Course I don't, Lu. I just think we've got the very best in the whole world," responded Gracie, laying her cheek affectionately against the hand that held hers in its strong, loving clasp.

"That is only because he is your very own, my darlings," the captain said, smiling down tenderly upon them.

A lady had drawn near and now said, "Supper is ready, Captain Raymond. Will you bring your little girls and come to the table?"

"Thank you, we will do so with pleasure," he said, following her as she led the way.

The table, covered with a snow-white cloth and heaped with tempting viands, presented a very attractive appearance.

The clams were brought on after most of the company was seated, with their coffee and bread and butter before them. They were served hot from the fire and the shell in neat, paper trays and eaten with melted butter. Eaten thus they made a dish fit for a king.

By the time that all appetites were satisfied, the sun was near setting, and it was thought best to return without delay.

On repairing to the beach, they found the tide was so low that even the dory could not come close to dry land, so the ladies and children were carried through the water to the yacht. This gave occasion for some merriment.

"You must carry me, Ned, if I've got to be carried," said Zoe. "I'm not going to let anybody else do it."

"No, nor am I," he returned, laughing as he picked her up and strode forward. "I claim it as my special privilege."

Mr. Dinsmore followed with his wife, then Captain Raymond with his.

"Get in, Mr. Dinsmore," said the captain, as they deposited their burdens. "There is no occasion for further exertion on your part. I'll bring mother."

"No, sir," said Edward, hurrying shoreward. "That's my task. You've your children to take care of."

"Your mother is my child, Ned, and I think I shall take care of her," Mr. Dinsmore said, hastening back to the little crowd still at the water's edge.

"We will have to let her decide which of us shall have the honor," said the captain.

"That I won't," Mr. Dinsmore said laughingly, stepping to his daughter's side and scooping her into his arms.

"Now, you two may take care of the younger ones," he added with a triumphant glance at his two rivals.

"Ah, Ned, I see that we are completely outwitted," laughed the captain.

"Yes, with grandpa about one can't get half a chance to wait upon mother. Betty, shall I have the honor and pleasure of conveying you aboard yonder vessel?"

"Yes, thank you. I see Harold and Herbert are taking Rosie and Walter," she said. "But I warn you that I am a good deal heavier than Zoe."

"Nevertheless, I think my strength will prove equal to the exertion," he returned, as he lifted her from the ground.

Lulu and Gracie stood together, hand in hand, Max on Gracie's other side.

"Take Gracie first, please, papa," said Lulu. "She is frightened, I believe."

"Frightened?" he said, stooping to take her in his arms. "There is nothing to be afraid of, darling. Do you think papa would leave you behind or drop you into the water?"

"No, I know you wouldn't," she said with a little nervous laugh, clinging tightly about his neck.

"Mayn't I wade out, papa?" Max called after him.

"Yes, but stay with your sister till I come for her."

"And where is my baby, Levis?" asked Violet, laughingly, as he set Gracie down by her side.

"The baby! Sure enough, where is she?" he exclaimed, with an anxious glance toward the shore.

"Ah, there stands the nurse with her in her arms. You shall have her in yours in a moment."

"Here's the baby, papa. Please take her first. I don't mind waiting," said Lulu as he stepped ashore.

He gave her a pleased, approving look. "That's right. It will be but a minute or two," he said as he took the babe and turned away with her.

In a few minutes more all the passengers were aboard, and they set sail. But they had not gone far when it became evident that something was amiss. They were making no progress.

"What is the matter?" asked several voices and Violet looked inquiringly at her husband.

"There is no cause for apprehension," he said. "We are aground and may possibly have to wait here for the turn of the tide, that's all."

"It's the lowest tide I ever saw," remarked the captain of the yacht. "We'll have to lighten her. If some of the heaviest of you will get into the dory, it will help."

Quite a number immediately volunteered to do so, among them Edward and Zoe, Bob and Betty, and Harold and Herbert. The dory was speedily filled, and with a little more exertion, the yacht was set afloat.

They moved out into deep water and a gentle breeze wafted them pleasantly on toward their desired haven.

"Look at the sun now, papa," Elsie said, gazing westward. "It has a very peculiar appearance."

"Yes," he said. "It looks a good deal like a red balloon. Its redness is obscured by that leaden-colored cloud. It is very near its setting. We shall not get in till after dark."

"But that will not matter?"

"Oh, no, our captain is so thoroughly acquainted with his vessel, the harbor, and the wharf, that I have no doubt he would land us safely even were it much darker than it will be."

Zoe and Edward, in the dory, were talking with a Nantucket lady, a Mrs. Fry.

"How do you like our island and particularly our town?" she asked.

"Oh, ever so much!" said Zoe. "We have visited a good many watering places and seaside resorts but never one where there was so much to see and to do—so many ways of passing the time. I think I shall vote for Nantucket again next year, when we are considering where to pass the hot months."

"And I echo my wife's sentiments on the subject under discussion," said Edward heartily.

"Your wife?" the lady exclaimed with a look of great surprise.

"I took her to be your sister. You are both so very young in appearance."

"We are not very old," laughed Edward. "Zoe is but sixteen, but we have been married a year."

"You have begun early. It is thought by some that early marriages are apt to be the happiest, and I should think them likely to be, provided the two are willing to conform their tastes and habits each to those of the other. I trust you two have a long life of happiness before you."

"Thank you," they both said. Edward added, "I think we are disposed to accommodate ourselves to each other, and whether our lives be long or short or our trials many or few, I trust we shall always find great happiness in mutual sympathy, love, and confidence."

The lady asked if they had seen all the places of interest on the island, and in reply they named those they had seen.

"Have you been to Mrs. Mack's?" she asked.

"No, madam. We have not so much as heard of her existence," returned Edward, sportively. "May I ask who and what she is?"

"Yes, she is the widow of a sea captain who has a collection of curiosities that she keeps on exhibition, devoting the proceeds, so she says, to benevolent purposes. She is an odd body—herself the greatest curiosity she has to show, I think. You should visit her museum by all means."

"We shall be happy to do so if you will kindly put us in the way of it," said Edward. "How shall we proceed in order to gain admittance?"

"If we can get up a party it will be easy enough. I shall send her word, and she will appoint the hour when she will receive us. She likes to show her independence and will not exhibit unless to a goodly number.

"I know of several visitors on the island who want to go, and if your party will join with them there will be no difficulty."

"I think I can promise that our party will do so," said Edward. "I will let you know positively tomorrow morning."

"That will do nicely. Hark, they are singing aboard the yacht."

They listened in silence till the song was finished. "I recognized most of the voices," Mrs. Fry remarked. "But two lovely sopranos were quite new to me. Do you know the owners?" she inquired turning smilingly to Edward.

"My mother and my sister," he answered with proud satisfaction.

"Naturally fine and very highly cultivated," she said. "You must be very proud of them."

"I am," Edward admitted with a happy laugh.

The sun was down, and twilight had fairly begun. Gracie, seated on her father's knee, was gazing out over the harbor.

"See, papa, how many little lights are close down to the water!" she said.

"Yes, they are lamps on the small boats that are sailing or rowing about. They show them for safety from running into each other."

"And they look so pretty."

"Yes, so they do. And it is a sight one may have every evening from the wharf. Shall I take you down there some evening and let you sit and watch them as they come and go?"

"Oh, yes. Please do, papa! I think it would be so nice. And you would take Max and Lulu, too, wouldn't you?"

"If they should happen to want to go. There are benches on the wharf where we can sit and have a good view. I think we will try it tomorrow evening if nothing happens to prevent us."

"Oh, I'm so glad! You are such a good, kind papa," she said delightedly, giving him a hug.

"The very best you have ever had, I suppose," he responded with a pleased laugh.

"Yes, indeed," she answered, naively, quite missing the point of his jest.

On reaching home, Edward and Zoe reported their conversation with the lady in the dory and asked, "Shall we not go?"

"I think so, by all means, since it is for benevolent objects," said Elsie.

"Or anyhow, since we all feel duty bound to see all that is to be seen on this island," said Captain Raymond.

No dissenting voice was raised. When the next morning, word came that Mrs. Mack would exhibit that afternoon if a party were made up to attend, they all agreed to go.

The distance was too great for ladies and children to walk, so carriages were ordered. Captain Raymond and his family filled one.

"This is the street that the oldest house is on," remarked Lulu, as they turned a corner. "I mean that one we went to see. The one with the big horseshoe on its chimney."

"What do they do that for, papa?" asked Gracie.

"In old times when many people were ignorant and superstitious, it was thought to be a protection from witches."

"Witches, papa? What are they?"

"I don't think there are any," he said with a kindly smile into the eagerly inquiring little face. "But in old times it was a very common belief that there were people—generally some withered-up old women—who had dealings with Satan and were given power by him to torment or bring losses and various calamities upon any one whom they disliked.

"When you are a little older, you shall hear more about it and how that foolish belief led to great crimes and cruelties inflicted upon many innocent, harmless people. But now, while my Gracie is so young and timid, I do not want her to know too much about such horrors."

"Yes, papa," she responded. "I won't try to know till you think I'm quite old enough."

Several vehicles drew up at the same moment in front of Mrs. Mack's door. Greetings and some introductions were exchanged on the sidewalk and doorsteps. Edward introduced his mother and Mrs. Fry to each other, and the latter presented to them a Mrs. Glenn, who, she said, was a native of Nantucket but had only recently returned after an absence of many years.

"Mrs. Mack knew me as a young girl," Mrs. Glenn remarked. "I am quite curious to see whether she will recognize me."

At that instant the door was opened in answer to their ring, and they were invited to enter and walk into the parlor.

They found it comfortably furnished and neat as wax. Seating themselves, they waited patiently for some moments the coming of the lady of the house.

At length she made her appearance. She was a little old lady, neatly attired and with quite a pleasant countenance.

Mrs. Fry saluted her with a good afternoon, adding, "I have brought some friends with me to look at your curiosities. This lady," indicating Mrs. Glenn, "you ought to know, as you were acquainted with her in her girlhood."

"Do you know me, Mrs. Mack?" asked Mrs. Glenn, offering her hand.

"Yes, you look as natural as the pigs," was the rather startling reply—accompanied, however, by a smile and cordial shake of the offered hand.

"Now, we'll take the money first to make sure of it," was the next remark, addressed to the company in general.

"What is your admission fee?" asked Mr. Dinsmore, producing his wallet.

"Fifteen cents apiece."

"By no means exorbitant if your collection is worth seeing," he returned, good-humoredly. "Never mind your purses, Elsie, Raymond, Ned. I'll act as paymaster for the party."

The all-important business of collecting the entrance fee having been duly attended to, Mrs. Mack led the way to an upper room where minerals, shells, sharks' teeth, and various other curiosities and relics were spread out upon tables and shelves—ranged along the sides and in the center of the apartment.

"Now," she said, "the first thing is to register your names. You must all register. You begin," handing the book to Mr. Dinsmore. "You seem to be the oldest."

"I presume I am," he said dryly, taking the book and doing as he was bidden. "Now, you Raymond," passing it on to the captain. "We'll take it for granted that you are next in age or most certainly in importance," he quipped.

"That's right, captain," laughed Betty, as he silently took the book and wrote his name. "It wouldn't be at all polite to seem to think yourself younger than any lady present."

"Of course not, Miss Betty. Will you take your turn next?"

"Of course not, sir. Do you mean to insinuate that I am older than Aunt Rose?" she asked, passing the book on to Mrs. Dinsmore.

"Now, don't be too particular about going according to ages," said Mrs. Mack. "It takes up too much time."

"You may write my name for me, Ned," said Zoe when he took the book.

"Yes, write your sister's name for her. It'll do just as well," said Mrs. Mack.

"But I'm not his sister," said Zoe.

"What then? Is he your lover?"

"No," Edward said laughing. "We're husband and wife."

"You've begun young," she remarked, taking the book and passing it on. "You don't look as if you'd cut your wisdom teeth, either of you. When the ladies have all registered, some of you grown folks had better do it for the children."

Having seen all their names duly inscribed in her register, she said, "Seat yourselves," waving her hand toward some benches and chairs.

Then, with some help of a half-grown girl, she set out a small circular table, placed a box upon it, pushed up chairs and a bench or two, and said, "Now, as many of you as can, come and sit round this tiny table—the others shall have their turn afterward."

When all the places were filled, she opened the box and took from it a number of beautifully carved articles—napkin rings, spoons, and the like.

"Now, all take your turns in looking at this lovely carved work, while I tell you its story," she said. "This is the story of how it came into my possession."

"You see, my husband was a sea captain. Upon one occasion when he was about to set sail for a long voyage, a young man, or lad—he was hardly old enough to be called a man—came and asked to be taken as one of the crew. He gave a name, but it wasn't his true name inherited from his father, as my husband afterward discovered. But not suspecting anything wrong, he engaged the lad and took him with him on the voyage.

"And the lad behaved well aboard the ship and he used to carve wonderfully well, as you may see by looking at these articles. He would carve just with a jack knife, and finally—keeping at it in his leisure moments—he made all these articles, carving them out of sharks' teeth.

"You can see he must have had genius, hadn't he? Yet, he'd run away from home to go to sea, as my husband afterward had good reason to believe."

She made a long story of it, spinning out her yarn until the first set had examined the carved work to their satisfaction.

Then, she said, "Reverse yourselves," indicating by a wave of her hand that they were to give place at the table to the rest of the company.

When all had had an opportunity to examine the specimens of the lad's skill, the young girl was ordered to restore them to the box but first to count them all.

That last clause brought an amused smile to nearly every face in the audience, but Lulu frowned and muttered, "Just as she thought we would steal them!"

Next, Mrs. Mack began the circuit of the room, carrying a long slender stick with which she pointed out those that she considered the most interesting of her specimens or articles of virtue.

One of these last was a very large, old-fashioned backcomb, having a story with a moral attached— the latter recited in doggerel rhyme.

She had other stories in connection with other articles to tell in the same way. In fact, so many and so long were they, that the listeners grew weary and inattentive ere the exhibition was finally brought to a close.

The afternoon was waning when they left the house. As Captain Raymond and his family drove into the heart of town on their way home, their attention was attracted by the loud ringing of a hand bell followed now and again by noisy vociferation in a discordant, man's voice.

"So the evening boat is in," remarked the captain.

"How do you know that, papa?" asked Gracie.

"By hearing the town crier calling his papers, which could not have come in any other way."

"What does he say, papa?" queried Lulu. "I have listened as intently as possible many a time, but I never can make out more than a word or two, sometimes not even that."

"No more can I," he answered with a smile. "It sounds to me like, 'The first news is um mum, and the second news is mum um mum, and the third news is um um mum.'"

The children all laughed.

"Yonder he is, coming this way," said Max, leaning from the carriage window.

"Beckon to him," said the captain. "I should like a paper."

Max obeyed. The carriage stopped, and the crier drew near and handed up the paper asked for.

"How much?" inquired the captain.

"Five cents, sir."

"Why, how is that? You asked me but three for yesterday's edition of this same paper."

"More news in this one."

"Ah, you charge according to the amount of news, do you?" returned the captain, laughing and handing him a nickel.

"Yes, sir, I guess that's about the fair way," said the crier, hastily regaining the sidewalk to renew the clang, clang of his bell and the "um mum mum" of his announcement.

CHAPTER TWELFTH

Wave high your torches on each crag and cliff,
Let many lights blaze on our battlements;
Shout to them in the pauses of the storm,
And tell them there is hope.

— *MATURIN'S BERTRAM*

THE EVENING WAS COOL, and the whole party was gathered in the parlor of the cottage occupied by the Dinsmores and Travillas—games, fancy work, reading, and conversation making the time fly.

Edward and Zoe had drawn a little apart from the others and were conversing together in an undertone.

"Suppose we go out and promenade the veranda for a little while," he said, presently. "I will get you a wrap and that knit affair for your head that I think so pretty and becoming."

"Crocheted," she corrected. "Yes, I'm quite in the mood for a promenade with my husband, and I'm sure the air outside must be delightful. But you won't have to go farther than that stand in the corner for my things."

He brought them, wrapped the shawl carefully about her, and they went out.

Betty, looking after them, remarked aside to her Cousin Elsie, "How loverlike they are still!"

"Yes," Elsie said with a glad smile. "They are very fond of each other and it rejoices my heart to see it."

"And one might say exactly the same of Captain Raymond and Violet," pursued Betty, in a lower tone. Then she glanced toward the couple as they sat side by side on the opposite sofa. Violet had her babe in her arms, and the captain was clucking and whistling to her, while she cooed and laughed in his face. Violet's ever-beautiful face was more beautiful than usual with its expression of exceeding love and happiness as her glance rested first upon her husband and then upon her child.

"Yes," Elsie said again, watching them with a joyous smile still wreathing her lips and shining in her eyes. "It is just so with my dear Elsie and Lester. I am truly blest in seeing my children so well mated and so truly happy."

❀ ❀ ❀ ❀ ❀

"Zoe, little wife," Edward was saying out on the veranda, "can you spare me for a day or two?"

"Spare you, Ned? How do you mean?"

"I should like to join the boys—Bob, Harold, and Herbert—in a little trip on a sailing vessel that leaves here early tomorrow morning and will return on the evening of the next day or the next but one. I should ask my little wife to go with us, but, unfortunately, the vessel has no accommodations for ladies. What do you say, love? I shall not go without your consent."

"Thank you, you dear boy, for saying that," she responded affectionately, squeezing the arm on which she leaned. "Go if you want to. I know I can't help missing the kindest and dearest husband in the world, but I shall try to be happy in looking forward to the joy of reunion on your return."

"That's a dear," he said, bending down to kiss her ruby lips. "It is a great delight to meet after a short separation, and we should miss that entirely if we never parted at all."

"But, oh, Ned, if anything should happen to you!" she said in a quivering voice.

"Hush, hush, love," he answered soothingly. "Don't borrow trouble. Remember we are under the same protection on the sea as on the land, and perhaps we are as safe on one as on the other."

"Yes, but when I am with you I share your danger, if there is any. That is what I wish. Ned, I simply couldn't live without you!"

"I hope you may never have to try it, my darling," he said in tender tones. "Or I be called to endure the trial of having to live without you. Yet we can hardly hope to go together.

"But let us not vex ourselves with useless fears. We have the promise, 'As thy days, so shall thy strength be.' And we know that nothing can befall us without the will of our Heavenly Father, whose love and compassion are infinite. 'We know that all things work together for good to them that love God.'"

"But if one is not at all sure of belonging to Him?" she said, in a voice so low that he barely caught the words.

"Then the way is open to come to Him. He says, 'Come unto me.' 'Him that cometh unto me, I will in no wise cast out.' The invitation is to you, love, as truly as if addressed to you alone—as truly as if you could hear His voice speaking the sweet words and see His kind eyes looking directly at you.

"It is my ardent wish, my most earnest, constant prayer, that my beloved wife may speedily learn to know, love, and trust in Him who is the Way, the Truth, and the Life!"

"You are so good, Ned! I wish I were worthy of such a husband," she murmured, sighing slightly as she spoke.

"Quite a mistake, Zoe," he replied with unaffected humility. "To hear you talk so makes me feel like a hypocrite. I have no righteousness of my own to plead, but, thanks be unto God, I may rejoice in the imputed righteousness of Christ! And that may be yours, too, love, for the asking.

"'Ask, and it shall be given you; seek, and ye shall find; knock, and it shall be opened unto you.'

"They are the Master's own words. And He adds, 'For every one that asketh receiveth; and he that seeketh findeth; and to him that knocketh it shall be opened.'"

Meanwhile, the contemplated trip of the young men was under discussion in the parlor. "Dear me!" said Betty, who had just heard of it. "How much fun men and boys do have. Don't you wish you were one of them, Lulu?"

"No, I don't," returned Lulu promptly. "I'd like to be allowed to do some of the things they do that we mustn't, but I don't want to be a boy."

"That is right," said her father. "There are few things so unpleasant to me as a masculine woman who wishes herself a man and tries to ape the stronger, coarser sex in dress and manners. I hope my girls will always be content, and more than content, to be what God has made them."

"If you meant to hit me that time, captain," remarked Betty in a lively tone, "let me tell you it was a miserable failure. I don't wish I were a man, and never did. Coarse creatures, as you say — present company always excepted. Who would want to be one of them?"

"I'd never have anything to do with one of them if I were in your place, Bet," laughed her brother.

"Perhaps I shouldn't, only that they seem a sort of necessary evil," she retorted. "But why don't you invite some of us ladies to go along?"

"Because you are not necessary evils," returned her brother with a twinkle of fun in his eye.

"You should, one and all, have an invitation if we could make you comfortable," said Harold gallantly. "But the vessel has absolutely no accommodations for ladies."

"Ah, then, you are excused," returned Betty.

The young men left the next morning after an early breakfast. Zoe and Betty drove down to the wharf with them to see them off and watched the departing vessel till she disappeared from sight.

Zoe went home in tears, Betty doing her best to console her.

"Come, now, be a brave little woman. It's for only two or three days at the most. Why, I'd never get married if I thought I shouldn't be able to live so long without the fortunate man I bestowed my hand upon."

"Oh, you don't know anything about it, Betty!" sobbed Zoe. "Ned's all I have in the world, and it's so lonesome without him! And then, how do I know that he'll ever get back? A storm may come up and the vessel be wrecked."

"That's just possible," said Betty. "It's great folly to make ourselves miserable over possibilities — things which may never happen."

"Oh, you are a great deal too wise for me!" said Zoe in disgust.

"Oh," cried Betty, "if it's a pleasure and comfort to you to be miserable—to make yourself so by anticipating the worst—do so by all means. I have heard of people who are never happy but when they are miserable."

"But I am not one of that sort," said Zoe in an aggrieved tone. "I am happy as a lark when Ned is with me. Yes, and I'll show you that I can be cheerful even without him."

She accordingly wiped her eyes, put on a smile, and began talking in a sprightly way about the beauty of the sea as they looked upon it. Her waves were dancing and sparkling in the brilliant light of the morning sun.

"What shall we do today?" queried Betty.

"Take a drive," said Zoe.

"Yes, I wish there was some new route or new place to go to."

"There's a pretty drive to South Shore that maybe you have not tried yet," suggested the hackman.

"South Shore? That's another name for Surfside, isn't it?" asked Betty.

"It's another part of the same side of the island," he answered. "It's a nice drive through the avenue of pines—a road the lovers are fond of. If the south wind is blowing, as it is this morning, you have a fine surf to look at when you get there."

"If a drive is talked of today, let us propose this one, Zoe," said Betty.

"Yes, I dare say it is as pleasant as any we could take," assented Zoe. "I wish Edward were here to go with us."

Elsie, with her usual thoughtfulness for others, had been considering what could be done to prevent Zoe from feeling lonely in Edward's absence. She saw the hack draw up at the door and met the young girls on the threshold with a bright face and pleasant smile. "You have seen the boys off?" she inquired. "The weather is so favorable that I think they can hardly fail to enjoy themselves greatly."

"Yes, mamma. I hope they will, but, ah, a storm may come and wreck them before they can get back," sighed Zoe, furtively wiping away a tear.

"Possibly, but we won't be so foolish as to make ourselves unhappy by anticipating evils that may never come," was the cheery rejoinder. "The *Edna* has a skillful captain, a good crew, and is doubtless entirely seaworthy — at least so Edward assured me. For the rest we must trust in Providence.

"Come in, now, and let me give you each a cup of coffee. Your breakfast with the boys was so early and so slight that you may find appetite for a snack," she added sportively as she led the way into the cozy little dining room of the cottage. There they found a tempting repast spread especially for them, the others having already taken their morning meal.

"How nice of you, Cousin Elsie!" exclaimed Betty. "I wasn't expecting to eat another breakfast, but I find a rapidly coming appetite. These muffins and this coffee are so delicious."

"So they are," said Zoe. "I never knew anybody else quite so kindly thoughtful as mamma."

"I think I know several," Elsie rejoined. "But it is very pleasant to be so highly appreciated. Now, my dear girls, you will confer a favor if you will tell me in what way I can make the day pass most pleasantly for you."

"Thank you, cousin. It is a delightful morning for a drive, I think," said Betty. Then, she went on to repeat what their hackman had said of the drive to South Shore.

"It sounds pleasant, indeed. I think we will make up a party and try it," Elsie said. "You would like it, would you, Zoe?"

"Yes, mamma, better than anything I know of beside. The man says that just there the beach has not been so thoroughly picked over for shells and other curiosities, and we may be able to find some worth having."

No one had made any special plans for the day, so all were ready to fall into this plan proposed by Zoe and Betty. Hacks were ordered—enough to hold all of their party now at hand—and they started.

They found the drive all it had been represented. For some distance their way lay along the bank of a long pond, pretty to look at and interesting as connected with old times and ways of life on the island. Their hackmen told them that formerly large flocks of sheep were raised by the inhabitants and this pond was one of the places where sheep were brought at a certain time of the year to be washed and shorn. On arriving at their destination, they found a long stretch of sandy beach with great thundering waves dashing upon it.

"Oh!" cried Zoe and Betty in delight. "It is like a bit of 'Sconset!"

"Look away yonder," said Lulu. "Isn't that a fisherman's cart?"

"Yes," replied her father. "Suppose we go nearer and see what he is doing."

"Oh, yes, do let us, papa!" cried Lulu, always ready to go everywhere and see everything.

"You may run on with Max and Gracie," he said. "Some of us will follow presently."

He turned and offered his arm to Violet. "It is heavy walking in this deep sand. Let me help you."

"Thank you. It is wearisome, and I am glad to have my husband's strong arm to lean upon," she answered, smiling sweetly up into his eyes as she accepted the offered aid.

The young girls and the children came running back to meet them. "He's catching bluefish," they announced. "He has a good many fish in his cart already."

"Now, watch him, Mamma Vi. You haven't had a chance to see such fishing before," said Max. "See, he's whirling his drail. There! Now he has sent it far out into the water. Now he's hauling it in, and — oh yes, a good big fish with it."

"What is a drail?" Violet asked.

"It is a hook with a long piece of lead above it covered with eel skin," answered her husband.

"There he goes again!" she exclaimed. "It is really an interesting sight, but rather hard work, I should think."

When tired of watching the fisherman, they wandered back and forth along the beach in search of curiosities — picking up bits of sponge, rockweed, seaweed, and a greater variety of shells than they had been able to find on other parts of the shore that they had visited.

It was only when they had barely time enough left to reach home for a late dinner that they were willing to enter the carriages and be driven away from the exceedingly pleasant spot.

As they passed through the streets of the town, the crier was out with his hand bell.

"Oh, yes! Oh, yes! All the windows to be taken out of the Atheneum today, and the Atheneum to be elevated tonight."

After listening intently to several repetitions of the cry, they succeeded in making it out.

"What on earth does he mean?" exclaimed Betty.

"Ventilated, I presume," replied the captain. "There was an exhibition there last night, and complaints were made that the room was close."

ᢋ ᢋ ᢋ ᢋ ᢋ

Toward evening of the next day those in the cliff cottages began to look for the return of the *Edna* with the four young men of their party. But night fell, and they had not yet arrived.

Elsie began to feel anxious, but she tried not to allow her disturbance to be perceived—especially by Zoe, who seemed restless and ill at ease. Often Zoe went out to the edge of the cliff, gazing long and intently toward the quarter of the horizon where she had seen the *Edna* disappear on the morning she sailed out of Nantucket harbor.

She sought her post of observation for the twentieth time just before sunset and remained there until it grew too dark to see much beyond the line of breakers along the shore below.

Turning to reenter the house, she found Captain Raymond standing by her side.

"Oh, captain," she cried, "isn't it time the *Edna* was in?"

"I rather supposed they would be in a little earlier than this, but I am not at all surprised that they are not," he answered in a cheery tone. "Indeed, it is quite possible that they may not get in till tomorrow. When they left, it was uncertain that they would come back today. So, my good sister, I think we have no cause for anxiety."

"Then I shall try not to be anxious," she said. "But it seems like a month since I parted from Ned, and it's sore disappointment not to see him tonight. I don't know how Vi stands your long absences, captain."

"Don't you suppose it's about as hard for me as for her, considering how charming she is?" he asked lightly.

"Perhaps it is, but men don't live in their affections as women do. Love is only half the world to the most loving of them, I verily believe, while it's all the world to us."

"There is some truth in that," he acknowledged. "We men are compelled to give much time and thought to business, yet many of us are ardent lovers or affectionate husbands. I, for one, am extremely fond of wife and children."

"Yes, I am sure of it and quite as sure that Ned is very fond of me."

"There isn't a doubt of it. I think I have never seen a happier couple than you seem to be, or than Leland and his Elsie. However, Violet and I will not yield the palm to either of you."

"Was there ever such a mother in law as mamma?" said Zoe. "I don't remember my own mother very distinctly, but I don't believe I could have loved her much better than I do Edward's mother."

"Words would fail me in an attempt to describe all her excellences," he responded. "Well, Lulu, what is it?" he asked, as the child came running toward them.

"Tea is ready, papa, and Grandma Rose says, 'Please come to it.'"

Shortly after leaving the table, the captain, noticing that Zoe seemed anxious and sad, offered to go into the town and inquire if anything had been seen or heard of the *Edna*.

"Oh, thank you," she said brightening. "But won't you take me along?"

"Certainly, if you think you will not find the walk too long and fatiguing."

"Not a bit," she returned, hastily donning both hat and shawl.

"Have you any objection to my company, Levis?" Violet asked with sportive look and tone.

"My love, I shall be delighted, if you feel equal to the exertion," he answered with a look of pleasure that said more than the words.

"Quite," she said. "Max, I know you like to wait on me. Will you please bring my hat and shawl from the bedroom there?"

"Indeed, with great pleasure, Mamma Vi," the boy answered with alacrity as he hastened to obey.

"Three won't make as agreeable a number for travelling the sidewalks as four, and I ought to be out looking out for Bob," remarked Betty. "So, if anybody will ask me to go along, perhaps I may consent."

"Yes, do come," said Zoe. "I'll take you for my escort Betty."

"And we will walk decorously behind the captain and Vi, feeling no fear under the protection of his wing," added the lively Betty. "But do you think, sir, you have the strength and ability to protect these three helpless females?" she asked, suddenly wheeling round upon him.

"I have no doubt I can render them all the aid and protection they are at all likely to need in this peaceful, law-abiding community," he answered with becoming gravity as he gave his arm to his wife and led the way from the house.

"It is a rather lonely but by no means dangerous walk, Cousin Betty," he added, holding the gate open for her and the others to pass out.

"Lonely enough for me to indulge in a moderate amount of fun and laughter, is it not, sir?" she returned in an inquiring tone.

She seemed full of life and merriment, while Zoe was unusually quiet.

They walked into the town and all the way down to the wharf. The *Ednu* was not there, nor could they hear any news of her. Zoe seemed full of anxiety and distress, though the others tried to convince her there was no occasion for it.

"Come. Come. Cheer up, little woman," the captain said, seeing her eyes fill with tears. "If we do not see or hear from them by this time tomorrow night, we may begin to be anxious, but till then there is really no need."

"There, Zoe, you have an opinion that is worth something, the captain being an experienced sailor," remarked Betty. "So try to be aisy, my dear, and if you can't be aisy, be as aisy as ye can be!"

Zoe laughed faintly at Betty's jest. Then, with heroic effort, put on an air of cheerfulness and contributed her full quota to the sprightly chat on the homeward walk.

She kept up her cheerful manner till she had parted from the rest for the night. But she wet her solitary pillow with tears ere her anxiety and loneliness were forgotten in sleep.

Her spirits revived with the new day, for the sun rose clear and bright, the sea was calm, and she said to herself, "Oh, surely the *Edna* will come in before night and Ned and I will be together again!"

Many times that day both she and his mother scanned intently the wide waters and watched with eager eyes the approach of some distant sail, hoping it may prove the one they looked for.

"Mamma, what can be keeping them?" sighed Zoe as the two stood together on the brow of the hill, still engaged in their fruitless search.

"Remember that when they went it was quite uncertain whether they would return earlier than tonight, so let us not suffer ourselves to be uneasy because they are not yet here," Elsie replied.

"I am ashamed," Zoe said. "I wish I could learn to be as patient and cheerful as you are, mamma."

"I trust you will be more so by the time you are my age," Elsie said, putting an arm about Zoe's waist. "I still at times feel the risings of impatience. I have not fully learned to 'let patience have her perfect work.'

"There is an old proverb, 'A watched pot never boils,'" she added with sportive look and tone. "Suppose we seat ourselves in the veranda and try to forget the *Edna* for awhile. I have a new book that looks interesting and has been highly commended. We will get papa to read it aloud to us while we busy ourselves with our fancywork. Shall we not?"

Zoe assented, though with rather an indifferent air, and they returned to the house.

Mr. and Mrs. Dinsmore, the only ones there—the others being all down on the beach—fell readily into the plan. The book and the work were brought out and the reading began.

It was a good, well told story, and even Zoe presently became thoroughly interested.

Violet and the captain sat together in the sand on the beach, he searching sea and sky with a spyglass.

She noticed a look of anxiety creeping over his face.

"What is it, Levis?" she asked.

"I fear there is a heavy storm coming," he said. "I wish with all my heart the *Edna* was in. But I trust they have been wise enough not to put out to sea and are safe in harbor somewhere."

"I hope so, indeed," she responded fervently. "But the sky does not look very threatening to me, Levis."

"Does it not? I wish I could say the same," he asked laughingly.

"Not wise in any way except as I may lay claim to the wisdom of my other half," she returned, adopting his sportive tone.

"Ah, I, too, begin to see some indications of a storm. It is growing very dark yonder in the northeast!"

Betty came hurrying up, panting and frightened. "Oh, captain, be a dear, good man and say you don't think we are to have a storm directly—before Bob and the rest get safe to shore!"

"I should be glad to oblige you Betty," he said. "But I cannot say that. And what would it avail if I did? Could my opinion stay the storm?"

"Zoe will be frightened to death about Edward," she said, turning her face seaward again as she spoke, gazing at the black and threatening clouds that were fast spreading from horizon to zenith. "And I—oh, Bob is nearer to me than any other creature on earth!"

"Let us hope for the best, Betty," the captain said kindly. "It is quite possible, perhaps I might say probable, that the *Edna* is now lying at anchor in some safe harbor and will stay there till this storm is over."

"Oh, thank you for telling me that!" she cried. "I'll just try to believe it is so and not fret. It will do no good to fret."

"Prayer would do far more," said Violet softly— "prayer to Him whom even the winds and the sea obey. But isn't it time to go in, Levis? The storm seems to be coming up so very fast."

"Yes," he said, rising and helping her to get to her feet. "Where are the children?"

"Yonder," said Betty, nodding her head in their direction. "I'll tell them—shall I?"

"No, thank you. You and Violet hurry on to the house as fast as you can. I will call the children, follow with them, and probably overtake you in time to help you up the stairs."

Before they were all safely housed, the wind had come down upon them and was blowing almost a gale. It was with considerable difficulty the captain succeeded in getting them all up the long steep flights of stairs to the top of the cliff.

About the time they started for the house, the party on the veranda became aware that a storm was rising.

Zoe saw it first and dropped her work in her lap with a cry. "Oh, I knew it would be so! A dreadful storm is coming. The *Edna* will be wrecked, and Edward will drown. I shall never see him again!"

The others were too much startled and alarmed to notice her wild words or to make any reply. They all rose and hurried into the house, and Mr. Dinsmore began closing windows and doors.

"The children, papa!" cried Elsie. "They must be down on the beach and—"

"The captain is with them, and I will go to their aid," he replied before she could finish her sentence.

He rushed, to return the next moment with Walter in his arms and the rest closely following.

"These are all safe and for the others I must trust the Lord," Elsie said softly to herself as her father set Walter down and she drew the child to her side.

But her cheek was very pale, and her lips trembled as she pressed them to the little fellow's forehead.

He looked up wonderingly. "Mamma, what is the matter? You're not afraid of wind and thunder?"

"No, dear, but I fear for your brothers out on this stormy sea," she whispered in his ear. "Pray for them, darling, that if God will, they may reach home in safety."

"Yes, mamma, I will. I believe He'll bring them. Is it 'cause Ned's in the ship that Zoe's crying so?"

"Yes, I must try to comfort her." Elsie went to her young daughter-in-law who had thrown herself upon a couch and was weeping and sobbing as if her heart would break.

"Zoe, love," Elsie said, kneeling at her side and putting her arms about her, "do not despair. 'Behold the Lord's hand is not shortened that it cannot save; neither His ear heavy that it cannot hear.'"

"No, but—He does let people drown. Oh, I can never live without my husband!"

"Child, there is no need to consider that question till it is forced upon you. Try, dear one, to rest in the promise, 'As thy days, so shall thy strength be.'"

The captain had drawn near and was standing close beside them.

"Mother has given you the best of advice, my little sister," he said in his kind, cheery way. "For your further comfort, let me say that it is altogether likely the

Edna is safe in harbor somewhere. I think they probably perceived the approach of the storm in time to be warned not to put out to sea till it was over."

"Do you really think so, captain?" she asked, lifting her head to wipe away her tears.

He assured her that he did, and thinking him a competent judge of what seamen would be likely to do in such an emergency, she grew calm for a time, though her face was still sad.

"If not in harbor, they must be in great peril?" Mr. Dinsmore remarked aside to the captain.

"Yes, sir. Yes, indeed. I am far more anxious than I should like to own to their mother, Zoe, or Violet."

It was near the tea hour when the storm burst. They gathered about the table as usual, but there was little eating done except by the children. The meal was not enlivened, as was customary with them, though efforts in that direction were not wanting on the part of several of their number.

The storm raged on with unabated fury and Zoe, as she listened to the howling of the wind and the deafening thunder peals, grew wild with terror for her husband. She could not be persuaded to go to bed, even when her accustomed hour for retiring was long past. She would sit in her chair moaning. Then, she would spring up and pace the floor — sobbing, wringing her hands, and as a fierce blast shook the cottage or a deafening thunder peal crashed overhead, even shrieking out in terror.

In vain Elsie tried to soothe her with reassuring, comforting words or caresses and endearments.

"Oh, I can't bear it!" she cried again and again. "Ned is all I have, and it will kill me to lose him. Nobody can know how I suffer at the very thought of it."

"My dear," Elsie said with a voice trembling with emotion, "you forget that Edward is my dearly loved son, and that I have two others who are no less dear to their mother's heart on board that vessel."

"Forgive me, mamma," Zoe sobbed. "I did forget, and it was very shameful, for you are so kind, putting aside your own grief and anxiety to help me in bearing mine. But how is it you can be so calm?"

"Because, dear, I am enabled to stay my heart on God, my Almighty Friend, my kind, wise, Heavenly Father. Listen, love, to these sweet words: 'O Lord God of hosts, who is a strong Lord like unto Thee? Or to thy faithfulness round about Thee? Thou rulest the raging of the sea; when the waves thereof arise, Thou stillest them.'"

"They are beautiful," said Betty, who sat near in a despondent attitude. "Oh, Cousin Elsie, I would give all the world for your faith and to be able to find the comfort and support in Bible promises and teaching that you do!"

The outer door opened, and Mr. Dinsmore and Captain Raymond came in, their waterproof coats dripping with rain.

They had been out on the edge of the cliff taking an observation, though it was little they could see through the darkness. But occasionally the lightning's lurid flash lit up the scene for a moment and afforded a glimpse of the storm-tossed deep.

"Be comforted, ladies," the captain said. There are no signs of any vessel in distress. I think we may hope my conjecture that our boys are safe in harbor somewhere is correct."

"And the storm is passing over now," said Mr. Dinsmore. "The thunder and the lightning have almost ceased."

"But the wind has not fallen and that is what makes the great danger, grandpa, isn't it?" asked Zoe. "Oh, hark, what was that? I heard a step and voice!" Rushing to the outer door, she threw it open and found herself in her husband's arms.

"Oh, Ned!" she cried in a transport of joy. "Is it really you? I thought I should never see you again!"

She clung round his neck, and he held her close with many a caress and endearing word. His brothers stepped past them and embraced the tender mother who wept for joy as she received them, as if restored to her from the very gates of death.

"There, love, I must let you go while I take off this dripping coat," Edward said, releasing Zoe. "How wet I have made you! I fear your dress is quite spoiled," he added with a tender, regretful smile.

"That's nothing," she answered with a happy laugh. "You'll only have to buy me another, and you've plenty of money."

"Plenty to supply all the wants of my wife, I hope."

"Ah, mother," as he took her in his arms, "were you alarmed for the safety of your three sons?"

"Indeed I was," she said, returning his kisses. "I feel that I have great cause for thankfulness in that you are all brought back to me unharmed. 'Oh, that men would praise the Lord for His goodness and for His wonderful works to the children of men!'"

Betty started up on the entrance of her cousins, glancing eagerly from one dripping figure to another, then staggered back and leaned against the wall. In the excitement no one had noticed her, but now she exclaimed in tremulous accents, "Bob — my brother. Where is he?"

"Oh, Betty," Harold answered, turning hastily at the sound of her voice. "Forgive our thoughtlessness in not explaining that at once! Bob went to a hotel. He said we could bring the news of his safety and our own, and it wasn't worthwhile for him to travel all the way up here through the storm."

"No, of course not. I wouldn't have had him do so," she returned with a sigh of relief, her face resuming its usual happy expression. "But I'm mighty glad he's safe on *terra firma.*"

"Your story, boys. Let's have it," said Mr. Dinsmore.

"Yes, we have a story, grandpa," said Edward with emphasis and excitement. "But Harold should tell it. He could do it better than I."

"No, no," Harold said. "You are as good a story teller as I."

"There!" laughed Herbert. "I believe I'll have to do it myself, or with your extreme politeness to each other you'll keep the audience waiting all night.

"The storm came suddenly upon us when we were about half way home, or maybe something more. It presently became evident that we were in imminent danger of wreck. The captain soon concluded our only chance was in letting the *Edna* drive right before the wind, which would take us in exactly the direction we wished to pursue, but with rather startling celerity—and that was what he did.

"She flew over the water like a wild, winged bird and into the harbor with great velocity. Safely enough, till we were almost at the wharf, when we struck against another vessel anchored near and actually cut her in two, spilling the crew into the water."

"Don't look so horrified, mother dear," said Harold, as Herbert paused for breath. "No one was drowned, no one even hurt."

"Barring the wetting and the fright, as the Irish say," added Edward.

"But the latter was a real hurt," said Harold. "The cry they sent up as they made the sudden, involuntary plunge from their berths, where they were probably asleep at the moment of collision, into the cold, deep water of the harbor, was something terrible to hear."

"Enough to curdle one's blood," added Herbert.

"And you are quite sure all were picked up without incident?" asked Elsie, her sweet face full of pity for the poor sufferers.

"Yes, mother, quite sure," answered Edward. "The captain of the other will probably have pretty heavy damages to pay," remarked Mr. Dinsmore.

"I presume so," said Edward. "But that would be far better than the loss of his vessel with all the lives of those on board."

"Money could not pay for the last," Elsie said, low and tremulously, as she looked at her three tall sons through a mist of unshed tears. "And I will gladly help the *Edna's* captain to meet the damages incurred in his effort to save them."

"Just like you, mother," Edward said giving her a look of proud, fond affection.

"I entirely approve and shall also be ready to contribute my share," said her father. "But it is very late, or rather early—long past midnight—and we should be getting to bed. But let us first unite in a prayer of thanksgiving to our God for all His mercies, especially this—that our dear boys are restored to us unharmed."

They knelt, and led by him all hearts united in a fervent outpouring of gratitude and praise to the Giver of all good.

CHAPTER THIRTEENTH

Hitherto hath the Lord helped us.

—1 Samuel 7:12

It was a lovely Sunday afternoon, still and bright. Elsie sat alone on the veranda, enjoying the beauty of the sea and the delicious breeze coming in from it. She had been reading, and the book lay on her lap, one hand resting upon the open page. She was deep in meditation, her eyes following the restless movements of the waves that, with the rising tide, dashed higher and higher upon the beach below.

For the last hour she had been the solitary tenant of the veranda, while the others enjoyed their siesta or lounge upon the beach.

Presently a noiseless step drew near, and someone bent down over her and softly kissed her cheek.

"Papa," she said, looking up into his face with smiling eyes, "you have come to sit with me? Let me give you this chair," and she would have risen to do so. But he laid his hand on her shoulder, saying, "No, sit still. I will take this one," drawing up another and seating himself close to her side.

"Do you know that I have been watching you from the doorway there for the last five minutes?" he asked.

"No, sir, I deemed myself quite alone," she said. "Why did you not let me know that my dear father, whose company I prize so highly, was so near?"

"Because you seemed so deep in thought, and evidently such happy thought, that I was loath to disturb it."

"Yes," she said, "they were happy thoughts. I have seemed to myself for the last few days to be in the very land of Beulah, so delightful has been the sure hope — I may say certainty — that Jesus is mine and I am His. I am His servant forever, for time and for eternity, as truly and entirely His as words can express. Is it not a sweet thought, papa? Is it not untold bliss to know that we may — that we shall — serve Him forever and that nothing can ever separate us from the love of Christ?"

"It is, indeed — Christ who is our life. He says, 'Because I live, ye shall live also.' Thus, He is our life. Is He not our life also because He is the dearest of all friends to us — His own people?"

"Yes, and how the thought of His love, His perfect sympathy, His infinite power to help and to save, gives strength and courage to face the unknown future. 'The Lord is my light and my salvation; whom shall I fear? The Lord is the strength of my life, of whom shall I be afraid?' 'Surely, goodness and mercy shall follow me all the days of my life.'

"In view of the many dangers that lie around our every path, the many terrible trials that may be sent to any one of us, I often wonder how those who do not trust in this almighty Friend can have the least real, true happiness. Were it my case, I should be devoured with anxiety and fears for myself and my dear ones."

"But as it is," her father said, gazing tenderly upon her, "you are able to leave the future for them and for yourself in His kind, wise, all-powerful hands, knowing that nothing can befall you without His will. And that He will send no trial that shall not be for your good, and none that He will not give you strength to endure?"

"Yes, that is it, papa. And oh, what rest it is! One feels so safe and happy—so free from fear and care—like a little child whose kind and loving earthly father is holding her by the hand or in his strong, kind arms."

"You have loved and trusted Him since you were a very little child," he remarked, half musingly.

"Yes, papa. I cannot remember when I did not. Could there be a greater cause for gratitude?"

"No, such love and trust are worth more to the happy possessor than the wealth of the universe. But there was a time when, though my little girl had it, I was altogether ignorant of it, and I marveled greatly at her love for God's word and her joy and peace in believing. I shall never cease to bless God for giving me such a child."

"Or I to thank Him for my dear father," she responded, putting her hand into his with the very same loving, confiding gesture she had been wont to use in childhood days.

His fingers closed over his hand and he held hers fast in a warm, loving grasp, while they continued their talk concerning the things that lay nearest their hearts—the love of the Master, His infinite perfection, the interests of His kingdom, the many great and precious promises of His word—thus renewing their strength and provoking one another to love and to good works.

"Then they that feared the Lord spake often one to another; and the Lord hearkened and heard it; and a book of remembrance was written before Him for them that feared the Lord, and that thought upon His name.

"And they shall be mine, saith the Lord of hosts, in that day when I make up my jewels; and I will spare them, as a man spareth his own son that serveth him."

Ere another week had rolled round, events had occurred which tested the sustaining power of their faith in God, and the joy of the Lord proved to be indeed their strength, keeping their hearts from failing in an hour of sore anxiety and distress.

※ ※ ※ ※ ※

The evening was bright with the radiance of a full moon and unusually warm for the season. So pleasant was it out of doors that most of the family preferred the veranda to the cottage parlors and some of the younger ones were strolling about town or the beach.

Betty had gone down to the beach and with the captain's permission had taken Lulu with her, both promising not to go out of sight of home.

"Oh, how lovely the sea is tonight with the moon shining so brightly on all the little dancing waves!" exclaimed Lulu as they stood side by side close to the water's edge.

"Yes," said Betty. "Doesn't it make you feel like going in?"

"Do people ever swim at night?" asked Lulu.

"I don't know why they shouldn't," returned her seaside companion.

"It might be more dangerous than in the day, perhaps," suggested Lulu.

"Why should it?" said Betty. "It's almost as light as day. Oh, Bob," perceiving her brother close at hand, "don't you want to go in? I will if you will go with me."

"I don't care if I do," he answered after a moment's reflection. "A moonlight swim in the sea might be something out of the common, and there seems to be just surf enough to make it enjoyable."

"Yes, and my bathing suit is in the bathhouse yonder. I can be ready in five minutes."

"Can you? So can I. We'll go in if only for a few minutes. Won't you go with us, Lulu?"

"I'd like to," she said. "But I can't without Papa's permission. I know papa wouldn't give it because I had a swim this morning, and he says one a day is quite enough."

"I was in this morning," said Bob. "Betty, too, I think, and—I say, Bet, it strikes me I've heard that it's a little risky to go in at night."

"Not such a night as this, I'm sure, Bob. Why it's as light as day. If there is danger it can be only about enough to give spice to the undertaking."

With the last words she started for the bathhouse, and Bob, not to be outdone in courage, hurried toward another appropriate to his use.

Lulu stood waiting for their return, not at all afraid to be left alone with not another creature in sight on the beach. Yet, the solitude disturbed her as the thought arose that Bob and Betty might be about to put themselves in danger while no help was at hand for their rescue. The nearest she knew of was at the cottages on the bluff, and for her to climb those long flights of stairs and give the alarm in case anything went wrong with the venturesome swimmers would be a work of time.

"I'd better not wait for them to get into danger, for they would surely drown before help could reach them," she said to herself after a moment's thought. "I'll only wait till I see them really in and then hurry home to see if somebody can't come down and be ready to help if they should begin to drown."

But as they passed her on their way to the water, Bob said, "We're trusting you to keep our secret, Lulu. Don't tell tales on us."

She made no reply, but thought within herself, "That shows he doesn't think he's doing exactly right. I'm afraid it must be quite dangerous."

But while his remark and injunction increased her apprehensions for them, it also made her hesitate to carry to their friends the news of their escapade till she should see that it brought them into actual danger and need of assistance.

She watched them trembling as they waded slowly out beyond the surf into the smooth, swelling waves where they began to swim.

For a few moments all seemed to be well. Then came a sudden shrill cry from Betty, followed by a hoarser one from Bob, which could mean nothing else than fright and danger.

For an instant Lulu was nearly paralyzed with terror, but rousing herself by a determined effort, she shouted at the top of her voice, "Don't give up. I'll go for help as fast as ever I can," and instantly shot off for home at her utmost speed.

"Help, help! They'll drown, oh, they'll drown!" she screamed as she ran.

Harold, who was in the act of descending the last flight of stairs, saw her running toward him and heard her cry. The noise of the surf prevented his catching all the words, though.

"What's the matter?" he shouted, clearing the remainder of the flight at a bound.

"Betty, Bob—drowning!" she cried without slackening her speed. "I'm going for help."

He waited to hear no more but sped on toward the water. Only pausing to divest himself of his outer clothing, he plunged in and, buffeting with the waves, made his way as rapidly as possible toward the struggling forms. By the light of the moon, he could dimly discern their shapes at some distance from the shore.

Faint cries for help and the gleam of Betty's white arm, as for an instant she raised it above the wave, guided him to the spot.

Harold was an excellent swimmer, strong and courageous. But he had undertaken a task beyond his strength, and his young life was very near falling a sacrifice to the folly of his cousins and his own generous impulse to fly to their aid.

Both Bob and Betty were already so nearly exhausted as to be scarcely capable of doing anything to help themselves. In their mad struggle for life, they caught hold of him and so impeded his movements that he was like to perish with them.

Meanwhile Lulu had reached the top of the cliff, then the veranda where the older members of the family party were seated. All out of breath with fight and the exertion of climbing and running, she stammered out, "Bob and Betty—they'll drown if they don't get help quickly."

"What? Are they in the water?" cried Mr. Dinsmore and Captain Raymond simultaneously, springing to their feet. Captain Raymond added, "I fear they'll drown before we can possibly get help to them."

"Oh, yes, they're drowning now," sobbed Lulu. "But Harold's gone in to help them."

"Harold? He's lost if he tries it alone!" "The boy's mad to think of such a thing!" exclaimed Mr. Dinsmore and Edward in a breath, while Elsie's cheek turned deathly pale. Her heart went up in an agonized cry that her boy's life might be spared — the others also.

The gentlemen held a hasty consultation, then scattered. Mr. Dinsmore hastened in search of other aid, while Captain Raymond and Edward hurried to the beach, the ladies following with entreaties to them to be careful.

But fortunately for the endangered ones, other aid had already reached them — a boat had come out from Nantucket for a moonlit sail and from the shore a noble Newfoundland dog belonging to a retired sea captain. Strolling along the beach with his master, the dog heard the cries for help, saw the struggling forms, and instantly plunging in among the waves, swam to the rescue.

Seizing Betty by the hair, he held her head above the water till the sailboat drew near and strong arms caught hold of her and dragged her in — pale, dripping, and seemingly lifeless.

They then picked up the young men, both entirely unconscious, and made for the shore with all possible haste.

It was doubtful if the last spark of life had not been extinguished in every one of the three. But the most prompt, wise, and vigorous measures were instantly taken and continued for hours—hours of agonizing suspense to those who loved them.

At length Bob gave unmistakable signs of life, and shortly after Betty sighed, opened her eyes, and asked feebly, "Where am I? What has happened?"

But Harold still lay as one dead and would have been given up as such had not his mother clung to hope and insisted that the efforts at restoration should be continued.

Through the whole trying scene she had maintained an unbroken calmness of demeanor, staying herself upon her God and lifting her heart to His throne in never-ceasing petitions. In the midst of her bitter grief and anxiety she rejoiced that if her boy were taken from her for a time, it would be but to exchange the trials and cares of earth for the joys of heaven. The parting from him here would soon be followed by a blissful reunion with father and others gone before in that blessed land where sin and sorrow and suffering can never enter.

But at length, when their efforts were rewarded so that he breathed and spoke, and she knew he had been restored to her, the reaction came.

She had given him a gentle, tender kiss and had seen him fall into a natural, refreshing sleep. As she was passing from his bedside into an adjoining room, she fainted in her father's arms.

"My darling. My dear, brave, darling!" he softly murmured, as he laid her down upon a couch and bent over her in tenderest solicitude, while Mrs. Dinsmore hastened to apply restoratives.

It was not a long faint. She presently opened her eyes and lifted them with a bewildered look up into her father's face.

"What is it, papa?" she murmured. "Was I ill?"

"Only a short faint," he answered. "But you must be quite worn out."

"Oh, I remember! Harold, my dear son—" she cried.

"Is doing well, love. And now I want you to go to your bed and try to get some rest. See, day is breaking, and you have had no sleep, no rest."

"Nor have you, papa. Do go and lie down, but I must watch over my poor boy," she said, trying to rise from the couch.

"Lie still," he said, gently detaining her. "Lie here if you are not willing to go to your bed. I am better able to sit up than you are, and I will see to Harold."

"His brothers are with him, mamma," said Zoe, standing by. "Edward says they will stay beside him as long as they are needed."

"Then you and I will both retire and try to rest some, shall we not?" Mr. Dinsmore asked, bending over Elsie and softly smoothing her hair.

"Yes, papa, but I must first take one peek at the dear son so nearly lost to me."

He helped her to rise. Then she perceived that Captain Raymond and Violet were in the room.

"Dearest mamma," said Violet, coming forward to embrace her, "how glad I am that you are better, and our dear Harold is spared to us!" She broke down in sobs and tears.

"Yes, my child. Oh, let us thank the Lord for His great goodness! But this night has been quite too much for us all. Do go at once and try to get some rest."

"I shall see that she obeys, mother," the captain said in a tenderly sportive tone, taking Elsie's hand and lifting it to his lips.

"I think I may trust you," she returned with a faint smile. "You were with Bob. How is he now?"

"Doing as well as possible under the present circumstances, as is Betty also. You need trouble your kind heart with no fear or care for them."

It had been a terrible night to all the family—the children the only ones who had taken any rest or sleep. Days of nursing followed before the three who had so narrowly escaped death were restored to their usual health and strength.

Mr. and Mrs. Dinsmore, Elsie, and the Raymonds devoted themselves to that work and were often assisted in it by Zoe, Edward, and Herbert.

Harold was quite a hero with these last and with Max and Lulu. In fact, he was a hero with all who knew or heard of his brave deed. He modestly disclaimed any right to the praises heaped upon him, asserting that he had done no more than anyone with common courage and humanity would have done in his place.

Bob and Betty were heartily ashamed of their escapade and were much sobered at the thought of their narrow escape from sudden death. Both dreaded the severe reproof they had reason to expect from their uncle, but he was very forbearing. Thinking the fright and suffering entailed by their folly sufficient to deter them from a repetition of it, he kindly refrained from lecturing them on the subject. Though, when a suitable opportunity offered, he did talk seriously and tenderly, with now one and now the other, on the guilt and danger of putting off repentance toward God and faith toward the Lord Jesus Christ. He reminded them that they had had a very solemn warning of the shortness and uncertainty of life. He asked them to consider the question whether they were ready for a sudden call into the immediate presence of their Judge.

"Really now, uncle," remarked Bob on one of these occasions, "there are worse fellows in the world than I am—much worse."

"I am willing to admit that, my boy," returned Mr. Dinsmore. "But many of these fellows have not enjoyed the privileges and teachings that you have, and responsibility is largely in proportion to one's light and opportunities.

"Jesus said, 'That servant, who knew his Lord's will, and prepared not himself, neither did according to His will, shall be beaten with many stripes. But he that knew not, and did commit things worthy of stripes, shall be beaten with few stripes.'"

"Yes, and you think I'm one of the first class, uncle, I suppose?"

"I do, my boy, for you have been well instructed, both in the church and in the family. Also, you have a Bible and may study it for yourself as often and carefully as you will."

"But I have never done anything very bad, uncle."

"How can you say that, Robert, when you know that you have lived all your life in utter neglect of God's appointed way of salvation? You have heard the gracious invitation of Him who died that you might live, when he said, 'Come unto me.' Are you refusing to accept it?

"Bob, 'God so loved the world that He gave His only begotten Son, that whosoever believeth in Him should not perish, but have everlasting life.' You have for years refused to believe. How can you assert that you have done nothing very bad? 'How shall we escape, if we neglect so great salvation?'"

Bob made no reply but looked thoughtful, and his uncle went quietly from the room, thinking it well to leave the lad to his own reflections.

Passing the door of the room where Harold lay, he was about to enter, but perceiving that the boy and his mother were in earnest conversation, he moved on, leaving them undisturbed.

"Mamma," Harold was saying, "I have been thinking much of sudden death since my very narrow escape from it. You know it comes sometimes without a moment's warning. As we all sin continually in thought and feeling, if not in word and deed, and as our very best deeds and services are so stained with sin that they need to be repented of and forgiven, how is it that even a true Christian can get to heaven if called away so suddenly?"

"Because when one comes to Jesus Christ and accepts His offered salvation, all his sins, future as well as past and present, are forgiven. 'The blood of Jesus Christ, His Son, cleanseth us from all sin.'

"Jesus said, 'He that believeth on the Son hath everlasting life.' 'I give unto them eternal life; and they shall never perish, neither shall any man pluck them out of my hand.'"

"But, mamma, I find myself so weak and sinful, so ready to yield to temptation, that I sometimes fear I shall never be able to hold out to the end!"

"My dear boy, let that fear lead you to cling all the closer to the Master, who is able to save unto the uttermost. If our holding out depended upon ourselves or our own weak wills, we might well be in despair. But 'He will keep the feet of His saints.'

"'Blessed be the God and Father of our Lord Jesus Christ, who, according to His abundant mercy, hath begotten us again unto a lively hope by the resurrection of Jesus Christ from the dead, to an inheritance incorruptible and undefiled, and that fadeth not away, reserved in heaven for you, who are kept by the power of God through faith unto salvation.' Son, can they be in danger who are kept by the power of God?"

CHAPTER
FOURTEENTH

My Father's house on high,
Home of my soul, how near
At times to Faith's discerning eye
Thy pearly gates appear.

HAROLD AND HIS COUSINS had scarcely more than fully recovered from the effects of their near drowning when Captain Raymond again received orders to join his ship. It was decided that the time had come for all to leave the island.

Bob and Betty received letters from their brother and sister in Louisiana, giving them a cordial invitation to their homes. Dick proposed that Bob should study medicine with him in view of becoming his partner, and Molly gave Betty a cordial invitation from herself and husband to take up residence at Magnolia Hall.

With the approval of their uncle and other close relatives, these kind offers were promptly accepted.

Letters came about the same time from Lansdale, Ohio, inviting the Dinsmores, Travillas, and Raymonds to attend the celebration of Miss Stanhope's one-hundredth birthday, which was now near at hand.

Mr. Harry Duncan wrote for her, saying that she had a great longing to see her nephews and nieces once more, and that she would like very much to make the acquaintance of Violet's husband and their children.

The captain could not go, but it was decided that all the others should. The necessary arrangements were quickly made, and the whole party left the island together. They left, but not without some regret and a resolution to return at some future day to enjoy its refreshing breezes and other delights during the hot season.

On reaching New York, they sadly parted with the captain, whose vessel lay in that harbor.

Bob and Betty left them farther on in the journey, and the remainder of the little company traveled on to Lansdale, arriving the day before the important occasion that had called them there.

Mrs. Dinsmore's brother, Richard Allison, who had married Elsie's old friend Lottie King shortly after the close of the war, had taken up his abode in Lansdale years ago.

Both he and his sister May's husband, Harry Duncan, had prospered greatly. Each had a large, handsome dwelling adjacent to Miss Stanhope's cottage, in which she still kept house. She could not bring herself to give up the comfort of living in a home of her own.

She had attached and capable servants. And amid her multitude of nieces and grandnieces, there was almost always one or more who was willing—nay, glad—to relieve her of the care and labor of house-keeping. They took great pleasure in making life's pathway smooth and easy to the aged feet and her last days bright and happy.

She still had possession of all of her faculties, was very active for one of her age, and felt unabated interest in the welfare of kindred and friends. She had by no means outlived her usefulness or grown querulous with age. She was ever the same bright, cheerful, happy Christian that she had been in earlier years.

The birthday party was to be held under her own roof, and a numerous company of near and dear relatives were gathering there and at the houses of the Duncans and Allisons.

Richard and Lottie, Harry and May were at the depot to meet the train on which our travelers arrived.

It was an altogether joyous meeting after long years of separation.

The whole party repaired at once to Miss Stanhope's cottage to greet and chat a little with her and others who had come before to the gathering — prominent among them Mr. and Mrs. Keith from Pleasant Plains, Indiana, with their daughters, Mrs. Landreth, Mrs. Ormsby, and Annis who was still unmarried.

Very glad indeed were Mrs. Keith and Mrs. Dinsmore, Mildred and Rose, Elsie and Annis to meet and renew the old intimacies of former days.

Time had wrought many changes since they were first together more than thirty years ago. Mr. and Mrs. Keith were now old and infirm, yet bright and cheery, looking hopefully forward to that better place — that Celestial City, toward which they were fast hastening with no unwilling steps. Dr. and Mrs. Landreth and Mr. and Mrs. Dinsmore had changed from youthful married couples into elderly people. Annis and Elsie had left childhood far behind and were now — the one a cheery, happy maiden lady whom aged parents leaned upon as their stay and staff, brothers and sisters dearly loved, and nieces and nephews doted upon and the other a mother whom her children blessed for her faithful love and care and delighted to honor.

This renewal of these dear friendships and the reminiscences of early days that it called up were very delightful to all.

The gathering of relatives and friends of course formed too large a company for all to lodge in one house. But the three — Aunt Wealthy's and those of the Duncans and Allisons — accommodated them comfortably for the few days of their stay or rather the nights — for during the day they were very apt to assemble in the parlors and porches of the cottage.

It was there Elsie and her younger children and Violet and hers took up their quarters by invitation for the time of the visit.

"But where is the captain, your husband?" inquired Aunt Wealthy of Violet on giving her a welcoming embrace. "I wanted particularly to see him, and he should not have neglected the kind invitation of a woman one hundred years old."

"Dear auntie, I assure you he did so only by compulsion. He would have come gladly if Uncle Sam had not ordered him off in another direction," Violet answered with pretty playfulness of look and tone.

"Ah, then, we must excuse him. But you brought the children, I hope. I want to see them."

"Yes, this is his son," Violet said, motioning Max to approach. "And here are the little girls," she added, drawing Lulu and Gracie forward.

The old lady shook hands with and kissed them, saying, "It will be something for you to remember, dears, that you have seen a woman who has lived a hundred years in this world and can testify that goodness and mercy have followed her all the days of her life. Trust in the Lord, my children, and you, even if you should live as long as I have, will be able to bear the same testimony that He is faithful to His promises.

"I say the same to you, too, Rosie and Walter, my Elsie's children," she added, turning to them with a tenderly affectionate look and smile.

They gazed upon her with awe for a moment. Then Rosie said, "You don't look so very old, Aunt Wealthy—not older than some ladies of eighty that I have seen."

"Perhaps not older than I did when I was only eighty, my dear, but I am glad to know that I am a good deal nearer home now than I was then," Miss Stanhope responded, her face growing bright with joyous anticipation.

"Are you really glad to know you must die before very long?" asked Max, in wonder and surprise.

"Wouldn't it be strange if I were not?" she asked. "Heaven is my home."

"'There my best friends, my kindred dwell. There God my Saviour reigns.' I live in daily, hourly, longing expectation of the call."

"And yet you are not weary of life? You are happy here, are you not, dear Aunt Wealthy?" asked Mrs. Keith.

"Yes, dear Marcia, I am happy among my kind relatives and friends, and I am entirely willing to stay till the Master sees fit to call me home—for I know that His will is always best. Oh, the sweet peace and joy of trusting Him and leaving all to His care and direction! Who that has experienced that assurance could ever again want to choose for him or herself?"

"And you have been long in His service, Aunt Wealthy?" Mr. Dinsmore said, half in assertion, half in query.

"Since I was ten years old, Horace, and that is ninety years. And let me bear testimony now, before you all, that I have ever found Him faithful to His promises and His service is growing constantly sweeter and sweeter. And so it shall be to all eternity. 'My soul doth magnify the Lord, and my spirit hath rejoiced in God my Savior.'"

Then, turning to Mrs. Keith, "How is it with you, Marcia?" she asked. "You have attained to your four score years, and you also have been in the service since early childhood. What have you to say for your Master now?"

"Just what you have said, dear aunt. Never have I had cause to repent of choosing His service. It has been a blessed service to me, full of joy and consolation. A joy that ever abounds more and more as I draw nearer and nearer to my journey's end.

"I know it is the same with my husband," she added, giving him a look of wifely affection. "And I doubt not with my cousins — Horace, Rose, Elsie — with all here present who have had experience as soldiers and servants of Jesus Christ."

"In that you are entirely right, Marcia," responded Mr. Dinsmore. "I can speak for myself, my wife, and my daughter."

Both ladies gave an unqualified confirmation of his words, while their happy countenances testified to the truth of the assertion.

"And, Milly dear, you and your husband, your brothers and sisters, can all say the same," remarked Miss Stanhope, laying a withered hand affectionately upon Mrs. Landreth's arm as she sat in a low seat by her side.

"We can, indeed," Mildred said with feeling. "What blessed people we are! We all know and love the dear Master and look forward to an eternity of bliss together at His right hand."

The interview between the aged saint and her long-absent relatives was continued for a few moments more. Then, she dismissed them with the remark that doubtless they would all like to retire to their rooms for a little, and she must take a short rest in order to be fresh for the evening, when she hoped they would all gather about her again.

"I want you all to feel perfectly at home and to enjoy yourselves as much as you can," she said in conclusion. "Play about the grounds, children, whenever you like."

Her cottage stood between the houses of the Duncans and Allisons. The grounds of all three were extensive, highly cultivated, and adorned with beautiful trees, shrubbery, and flowers. There were no separating fences or hedges so that they seemed to form one large park or garden.

Rosie and Walter Travilla and the young Raymonds were delighted with the permission to roam at will about these lovely grounds, and they hastened to avail themselves of that permission as soon as the removal of dust from travel and a change of attire rendered them fit.

They found a tall Dutch gardener busied here and there. Presently, the children opened up a conversation with him, quite winning his heart by their unstinted praises of the beauty of his plants and flowers.

"It must be a great deal of hard work to keep those large gardens in such perfect order," remarked Rosie.

"Dat it ish, miss," he said. "But I vorks pretty hard mineself, and my son Shakey, he gifs me von leetle lift ven he don't mees too much in school."

"Do you live here?' asked little Gracie.

"Here in dis garden? No, miss, I lifs oud boud t'ree mile in de country."

"That's a long walk for you, isn't it?" asked Lulu.

"Nein, I don't valks, miss. Ven I ish god dings to pring—abbles or botatoes or some dings else—I say Shakey, 'Just hitch de harness on de horse and hang him to de stable door.' Or if I god nodings to pring I tells de poy, 'Hitch him up a horseback.' Den I comes in to mine vork and I tash! I don't hafs to valk—nod a shtep."

"How funny he talks," whispered Gracie to Lulu. "I can hardly understand him."

"It's because he's Dutch," returned Lulu in the same low tone. "But I can tell almost all he says. His son's name is Jakey—the short for Jacob."

"What is your name?' asked Max.

"Hencle—Shou Hencle. I dinks you all come to see Miss Stanhope pe von huntred years olt, isn't you all?"

"Yes," said Rosie. "It seems very wonderful to think that she has lived so long."

The children, weary with their journey, were sent to bed early that night. Lulu and Gracie found they were to sleep together in a small room opening into a larger one, where two beds had been placed for the time to meet the unusual demand for sleeping quarters. These were to be occupied by Grandma Elsie, Violet, Rosie, and Walter.

Timid little Gracie heard with great satisfaction that all these were to be so near, and Lulu, though not at all cowardly, was well pleased with the arrangement. She little thought how severely her courage was to be tested that night.

She and Gracie had scarcely laid their heads upon their pillows ere they fell into profound slumber. Lulu did not know how long she had slept, and all was darkness and silence within and without the house when something, she could not have told what, suddenly roused her completely.

She lay still, trying to recall the events of the past day and remember where she was. And just as she had succeeded in doing so, a strange sound, as of restless movements and the clanking of chains, came from beneath the bed.

Her heart seemed to stand still with fear. She had never before in all her short life felt so terrified, helpless, and alone.

"What can it be?" she asked herself. "An escaped criminal — a murderer — or a maniac from an insane asylum, I suppose. Who else would wear a clanking chain? And what can he want here but to kill Gracie and me? I suppose he got in the house before they shut the doors for the night and hid under the bed till everybody should be fast asleep, meaning to begin then to murder and rob. Oh, I do wish I'd looked under the bed while all the gentlemen were about to catch him and keep him from hurting us! But now what shall I do? If I try to get out of bed, he'll catch hold of my foot and kill me before anybody can come. And if I scream for help, he'll do the same. The best plan is to lie as quiet as I can so he'll think I'm still asleep. Maybe he only means to rob and not murder if nobody wakes up to see what he's about and tell on him. Oh, I do hope Gracie won't wake! She could never help screaming, and then he'd jump out and kill both of us."

So with heroic courage she lay there, perfectly quiet and hardly moving a muscle for what seemed to her an age of suffering. Every moment she expected the creature under the bed to spring out upon her, and she was in constant fear that Gracie would awake and precipitate the calamity by a scream of fright.

All was quiet again for some time as she lay there, straining her ears for a repetition of the dreaded sounds. Then, as they came again louder than before, she had great difficulty in restraining herself from springing from the bed and shrieking aloud in a paroxysm of panic and terror.

But she did control herself, lay perfectly still, and allowed not the slightest sound to escape her lips.

That last clanking noise had awakened Elsie, and she too now lay wide-awake, silent and still, while intently listening for a repetition of it. She hardly knew whence the sound had come, or what it was. When repeated, as it was in a moment or two, she was satisfied that it issued from the room where Lulu and Gracie were, and her conjectures in regard to its origin coincided with Lulu's.

She, too, was greatly alarmed, but did not lose her presence of mind. Hoping the little girls were still asleep and judging from the silence that they were, she lay for a few minutes without moving — indeed scarcely breathing, while she tried to decide upon the wisest course to pursue. She asked guidance and help from on high, as she always did in every emergency.

Her resolution was quickly taken. Slipping softly out of bed, she stole noiselessly from the room and into another on the opposite side of the hall, occupied by Edward and Zoe.

"Edward," she said, speaking in a whisper close to his ear. "Wake, my son. I am in need of help."

"What is it, mother?" he asked, starting up.

"Softly," she whispered. "Make no noise but come with me. Somebody or something is in the room where Lulu and Gracie sleep. I distinctly heard the clanking of a chain."

"Mother!" he cried, but hardly above his breath "An escaped lunatic, probably! Stay here, and let me encounter him alone. I have loaded pistols—"

"Oh, don't use them if you can help it!" she cried.

"I shall not," he assured her. "Unless it is absolutely necessary."

He snatched the weapons from beneath his pillow as he spoke, and went from the room. She followed closely.

At the instant that they entered hers, a low growl came from the inner room, and simultaneously they exclaimed, "A dog!"

"Somewhat less to be feared than a lunatic, unless the dog should be mad, which is not likely," added Edward, striking a light.

Lulu sprang up with a low cry of intense relief. "Oh, Grandma Elsie, it's only a dog. I thought it a crazy man or a wicked murderer!"

As she spoke the animal emerged from his hiding place and walked into the outer room, dragging his chain after him.

Edward at once recognized him as a large mastiff Harry Duncan had shown him the previous day.

"It's Mr. Duncan's dog," he said. "He must have broken his chain and come in unobserved before the house was closed for the night. Here, Nero, good fellow, this way! You've done mischief enough for one night. We'll send you home."

He led the way to the outer door, the dog following quite peaceably. Elsie, hearing sobs coming from the other room, hastened in to comfort and relieve the frightened children.

Gracie still slept on in blessed unconsciousness, but she found Lulu crying hysterically, quite unable to continue her efforts at self-control now that the necessity for it was past.

"Poor child!" Elsie said, folding her in her kind arms. "You have had a terrible fright, haven't you?"

"Yes, Grandma Elsie. Oh, I've been lying here so long, so long. I thought a murderer or crazy man was under the bed, just ready to jump out and kill Gracie and me!" she sobbed, clinging convulsively about Elsie's neck.

"And did not scream for help? What a brave little girl you are!"

"I wanted to, and, oh, I could hardly keep from it! But I thought if I did it would wake Gracie and scare her to death, and the man would be sure to jump out and kill us at once."

"Dear child," Elsie said, "you have shown yourself thoughtful, brave, and unselfish. How proud your father will be of his eldest daughter when he hears all about it!"

"Oh, Grandma Elsie, do you think he will? How glad that would make me! It would pay for all the dreadful fright I have had," Lulu said. Her tone was tremulous with joy, while, but a moment ago, it had been full of nervousness and fright.

"I am quite sure of it," Elsie answered, smoothing the little girl's hair with a caressing hand. "Quite sure, because I know he loves you very dearly, and that he admires such courage, unselfishness, and presence of mind as you have shown tonight."

These kind words did much to turn Lulu's thoughts into a new channel and thus relieve the bad effects of her fright. But Elsie continued for some time longer her efforts to soothe her into calmness and forgetfulness, using tender, caressing words and endearments. Then, she left her with an injunction to try to go immediately to sleep.

Lulu promised compliance, and, attempting it, succeeded far sooner than she had thought possible.

The whole occurrence seemed like a troubled dream when she awoke the next morning. It was a delicious day in early October, and as soon as she was dressed she went into the garden where she found John Hencle already at work, industriously weeding and watering his plants and flowers.

"Goot morning, mine leetle mees," he said, catching sight of her. "Was it so goot a night mit you?"

"No," she said and went on to tell the entire story of her fright.

"Dot ish lige me," he remarked phlegmatically at the conclusion of her tale. "Von night I hears somedings what make me scare. I know notings what he ish. I shust hears a noise, an' I shumpt de bed out and ran de shtairs down and looked de window out, and it wasn't notings but a leetle tog going 'Bow wow.'"

"I don't think it was very much like my fright," remarked Lulu. "It couldn't have been half so bad."

"Vell, maybe not, but dat Nero ish a goot, kind tog. He bide dramps but nefer dose nice leetle girl.

Dis ish de great day when dose nice old lady pees von huntred years old. What you dinks? Dat's a fery long dime to live?"

"Yes, very long," returned Lulu emphatically. "I wish I knew papa would live to be that old, for then he'd be at home with us almost forty years after he retires from the navy."

"Somebody ish call you, I dinks," said John, and at the same moment Gracie's clear, birdlike voice came floating on the morning breeze, "Lulu, Lulu!" as her dainty, little figure danced merrily down the garden path in search of her missing sister.

"Oh, there you are!" she exclaimed catching sight of Lulu. "Come into Aunt Wealthy's house and see the pretty presents everybody has given her for her hundredth birthday. She hasn't seen them yet, but she is going to when she comes down to eat her breakfast."

"Oh, I'd like to see them!" exclaimed Lulu. She and Gracie tripped back to the house together and on into the sitting room where, on a large table, the gifts were displayed.

They were many and some of them costly, for the old lady was very dear to the hearts of these relatives. They were able as well as willing to show their affection in this substantial way.

There were fine paintings and engravings to adorn her walls, fine china and glittering cut glass, silver and gold ware for her tables, vases for her mantels, richly bound and illustrated books whose literary contents were worthy of the costly adornment, and various other things calculated to give her pleasure or add to her ease and comfort.

She was not anticipating any such material demonstration of affection—not expecting such substantial evidences of the love and esteem in which she was held — and when brought face to face with them was almost overcome, so that tears of joy and gratitude streamed from her aged eyes.

They were soon wiped away, however, and she was again her own bright, cheery self — full of thought and care for others and the kindest and most genial of hostesses.

She took the head of the breakfast table herself and poured coffee for her guests with her own hands, entertaining them the while with the old time tripping of her tongue — a laugh in which she always joined with hearty relish.

"There is too much salt in this butter," she remarked. "It is some John Hencle brought this morning. I must see him after breakfast and bid him caution his wife to use less."

But as they rose from the table, John came in unsummoned, carrying a fine, large goose under each arm.

Bowing low, "I ish come to pring two gooses to de von hundredth birthday," he announced. "Dey pees goot, peaceable pirds. I ish know dem for twenty years and dey nefer makes no droubles."

A smile went round the little circle but Miss Stanhope said with a very pleased look, "Thank you, John. They shall be well fed and I hope they will like their new quarters. How is Jake doing? I haven't seen him for some time."

"No, Shakey is go to school most days. I vants Shakey to knows somedings."

"Yes, indeed. I, too, hope Jakey is going to have a very good education, John. But what do you mean to do with him after he is finished going to school?"

"Vy, I dinks I prings mine Shakey to town and hang him on to Sheneral Scmidt and makes a brinting office out of him."

"A printer, John? Well, that might be a very good thing if you don't need him to help you about the farm or our grounds. I should think you would, though."

"Nein, nein," said John shaking his head. "'Tis not so long as I vants Shakey to makes mit me a fence. Put I tash, Miss Stanhope, he says he ton't can know how to do it. And I say, 'I tash, Shakey, you peen goin' to school all your life, and you don't know de vay to makes a fence yet.'"

"Not so very strange," remarked Edward with unmoved countenance. "They don't teach fence making in ordinary schools."

"Vell, den, de more's de bity," returned John, taking his departure. But turning back at the door, he says to Miss Stanhope, "I vill put dose gooses in von safe place."

"Any place where they can do no mischief, John," she answered good-humoredly.

"Now, Aunt Wealthy," said Annis, "what can we do to make this wonderful day pass most happily to you?"

"Whatever will be most enjoyable to my guests," was the smiling reply. "An old body like me can ask nothing better than to sit and look on and listen."

"Ah, but we would have you talk, too, auntie, when you don't find it wearisome."

"Please tell us, what are you going to do with all your new treasures, Aunt Wealthy?" asked Edward. "Wouldn't you like your pictures hung and a place found for each vase and other new household ornament?"

"Certainly," she said with a pleased look. "And this is the very time, while I have you all here to give your opinions and advice."

"And help," added Edward. "If you will accept it. As I am tall and strong, I volunteer to hang the pictures after the place for each has been duly considered and decided upon."

His offer was promptly accepted, and the work entered upon in a spirit of fun and frolic, which made it enjoyable to all.

Whatever the others decided upon met with Miss Stanhope's approval. She watched their proceedings with keen interest and was greatly delighted with the effect of their labors.

"My dears," she said, "you have made my house so beautiful! Whenever I look at these lovely things my thoughts will be full of the dear givers. I shall not be here long, but while I stay my happiness will be the greater because of your kindness."

"And the remembrance of these words of yours, dear aunt, will add to ours," said Mr. Keith with great feeling.

"But old as you are, Aunt Wealthy," remarked Mr. Dinsmore, "it is quite possible that some of us may reach home before you. It matters little, however, as we are all traveling the same road to the same happy country. We are all children of one Father — servants of the same blessed Master."

"And He shall choose all our changes for us," she said. "Calling each one home at such time as He sees best. Ah, it is sweet to leave all our interests in His dear hands and have Him choose our inheritance for us!"

There was a pause in the conversation while Miss Stanhope seemed lost in thought. Then, Mrs. Keith remarked, "You look weary, dear Aunt Wealthy. Will you not lie down and rest for a little?"

"Yes," she said. "I shall take it as the privilege of age, leaving you all to entertain yourselves and each other for a time."

At that Mr. Dinsmore hastened to give her his arm and support her to her bedroom—his wife and Mrs. Keith following to see her comfortably established upon a couch, where they left her to take her rest.

The others scattered in various directions as their inclinations dictated.

Elsie and Annis sought the grounds and, taking possession of a rustic seat beneath a spreading tree, had a long, quiet talk, recalling incidents of other days and exchanging mutual confidences.

"What changes we have passed through since our first acquaintance!" exclaimed Annis. "Ah, what carefree, happy children we were then!"

"And what happy women we are now!" added Elsie with a joyous smile.

"Yes, and you a grandmother! I hardly know how to believe it! You seem wonderfully young for that, my dear."

"Do I?" laughed Elsie. "I acknowledge that I feel young—that I have never yet been able to reason myself into feeling old."

"Don't try. Keep young as long as ever you can," was Annis's advice.

"It is what you seem to be doing," replied Elsie sportively with an admiring look at her cousin. "Dear Annis, may I ask why it is you have never married? It must certainly have been your own fault."

"Really, I hardly know what reply to make to that last remark," returned Annis in her sprightly way.

"But I have not the slightest objection to answering your question. I will tell 'the truth, the whole truth, and nothing but the truth.' I have had friends and admirers among the members of the other sex, but I have never yet seen the man for love of whom I could for a moment think of leaving my father and my mother."

"How fortunate for them!" Elsie said with earnest sincerity. "I know they must esteem it a great blessing that they have been able to keep one dear daughter in the old home."

"And I esteem myself blest indeed in having had my dear father and mother spared to me all these years," Annis said with feeling. "What a privilege it is, Elsie, to be permitted to smooth some of the roughness from their pathway now in their declining years and to make life even a trifle easier and happier than it might otherwise be for them. Why, they are the dear parents who so tenderly watched over me in infancy and youth! I know you can appreciate it — you who love your father so devotedly.

"But Cousin Horace is still a comparatively young man — hale and hearty — and to all appearances likely to live many years, while my parents are aged and infirm. I cannot hope to keep them much longer." Her voice was husky with emotion as she concluded.

"My dear Annis," Elsie said, pressing tenderly the hand she held in hers, "you are never to lose them. They certainly may be called home before you are, but the separation will be short and the reunion for all eternity — an eternity of unspeakable joy, unclouded bliss at the right hand of Him whom you all love better than you love each other."

"That is true," Annis responded, struggling with her tears. "And there is very great comfort in the thought. Yet, one cannot help dreading the parting and feeling that death is a thing to be feared for one's dear ones and for one's self. Death is a terrible thing, Elsie."

"Not half so much to me as it once was, dear cousin," Elsie said in a tenderly sympathizing tone. "I have thought much lately on that sweet text, 'Precious in the sight of the Lord is the death of His saints,' and that other, 'He shall see of the travail of his soul, and shall be satisfied.' The contemplation has shown me so much of the love of Jesus for the souls He has bought with his own precious blood and the joyful reception He gives them as one by one they are gathered home. It seems to me that the death of a Christian should hardly bring sorrow to any heart. Oh, it has comforted me much in my separation from the dear husband of my youth and made me at times look almost eagerly forward to the day when my dear Lord shall call me home and I shall see His face!"

"Oh, Elsie," cried Annis, "I trust that day may be far distant. Many hearts would be likely to break at parting with you! But there is consolation for the bereaved in the thoughts you suggest. I shall try to cherish them and forget the gloom and the dread for myself and for those I love."

They were silent for a moment. Then Elsie said, as if struck by a sudden thought, "Annis, why should not you and your father and mother come home with us and spend both the fall and winter at Ion and Viamede?"

"I cannot think of anything more delightful!" exclaimed Annis. Her face lit up with pleasure.

"And I believe it would be good for their health to escape the winter in our more severe climate—for they are both subject to colds and rheumatism at that season."

"Then you will persuade them?"

"If I can, Elsie. How kind of you for the invitation!"

"Not at all, Annis, for in so doing I seek my own gratification as well as theirs and yours," Elsie answered with earnest sincerity. "We purpose going from here to Ion, and from there to Viamede, perhaps two months later, to spend the remainder of the winter. And you and your father and mother will find plenty of room and a warm welcome in both places."

"I know it, Elsie," Annis said. "I know you would not say so if it were not entirely true, and I feel certain of a great deal of enjoyment in your loved society—if father and mother accept your kind invitation."

While these two conversed together thus on the grounds, a grand banquet was being prepared in Miss Stanhope's house under the supervision of old friends, May and Lottie. To it Elsie and Annis were presently summoned, in common with the other guests.

When the feasting was concluded, and all were again gathered in the parlors, Elsie renewed her invitation already made to Annis—this time addressing herself to Mr. and Mrs. Keith.

They heard it with evident pleasure, and after some conversation accepted.

Edward and Zoe returned to Ion the following day, and Herbert and Harold left at the same time for college. The rest of the Travillas, the Dinsmores, and the Raymonds lingered a week or two longer with Miss Stanhope, who was very loath to part with them, especially Elsie. Then, they bade their hostess a fond farewell, scarcely expecting to see her again on earth. With pleasure, they turned their faces homeward, rejoicing in the promise of Mr. and Mrs. Keith that they and Annis would soon follow, should nothing happen to prevent it.

The End